MURDER
AT
MOOT
POINT

Also by Marlys Millhiser

MURDER AT MOOT POINT

Marlys Millhiser

A PERFECT CRIME BOOK
DOUBLEDAY
NEW YORK   LONDON   TORONTO   SYDNEY   AUCKLAND

A PERFECT CRIME BOOK

PUBLISHED BY DOUBLEDAY
a division of Bantam Doubleday Dell Publishing Group, Inc.
666 Fifth Avenue, New York, New York 10103

DOUBLEDAY is a trademark of Doubleday, a division
of Bantam Doubleday Dell Publishing Group, Inc.

All of the characters in this book are fictitious,
and any resemblance to actual persons, living or
dead, is purely coincidental.

Book design by Tasha Hall

Library of Congress Cataloging-in-Publication Data

Millhiser, Marlys.
Murder at Moot Point / by Marlys Millhiser.
p.   cm.
"A Perfect Crime book."
I. Title.
PS3563.I4225M87   1992
813'.54—dc20   92-12439
                                CIP

ISBN 0-385-42295-4

1   3   5   7   9   10   8   6   4   2

FIRST EDITION

For Deborah Schneider

Murder
at
Moot
Point

Chapter 1

Outside, Charlie Greene pressed her nose against the cold glass of the window. Inside, a man dressed in black meditated next to a bronze Buddha, legs folded in the classic lotus, back straight, thumbs and forefingers pressed together.

Outside, surf exploded against rock somewhere near and somewhere distant a buoy croaked warning. The sounds carried on air so clogged with fog Charlie could barely make out the shape of the car she'd left at the bottom of the steps. A fog so dense it held flavors—sea salt and raw wood, exhalations of wet plant life.

Inside was a clutter of oddities—antiques, books, signs, shelves of things, and things hanging from the rafters. Outside, a rustling of leaves and the ragged howling of a house cat—all vowels, no consonants.

Charlie rapped at the window again, moved back to the door to rap there again too. Finally she heard movement and the man clearing his throat. When he opened the door he stood blinking rapidly to transfer his mind from his meditations. Then he squinted and mumbled something about a dog.

"Are you Jack Monroe?"

"I'm closed." His voice was still thick but perception leaked steadily into his eyes. His body seemed to gather energy.

"I'm Charlie Greene . . . your agent?"

He backed up just enough for her to slip out of the fog into murky light drugged with incense, his sigh more depressing than the warning buoy. He closed the door. An embroidered sign above it read, *To the blind all things are sudden.*

"I'm sorry to barge in this late but I've been driving all day. I'm not even sure where my motel is and the fog's so thick I was lucky to find Moot Point." Which wasn't what Charlie had planned to say but nothing about this trip was going as she had planned.

Jack Monroe was a short stocky man, his dark hair laced with gray, the sleeves of his turtleneck pushed up to show hairy fore-arms. ONE was printed in large white letters on the shirt's front. His eyes were an electric blue that appeared to take on a charge as she watched. He was all wrong. Nothing like she'd expected after meeting his son or reading his stuff. Keegan was colored fair, built light, his temperament gentle, whimsical. Charlie remembered the father's writing as ebullient, almost fey in tone. There was nothing ebullient about the dark muscular man standing before her.

"I would have called first but—why did you stop answering your phone and your mail, Jack? Keegan's worried, too."

He reached out a hand to give hers a choppy shake but there was little welcome in his expression. "Have you had dinner, Charlie Greene?"

He turned before she could answer and she followed him to a curtain at the rear of the store. NESS was printed on the back of his shirt. Behind the curtain a miniature kitchen with two stools for seating at a U-shaped counter shared space with an unmade bed. Another embroidered sign above the bed read, *"Toto, I've a feeling we're not in Kansas anymore."*

Charlie crawled up on one of the stools while he savaged things with a knife the size of a machete. She'd always thought of "New Agers" as being more mellowed out, smug in their know-it-allness. Maybe his meditation hadn't taken.

"This is it?" She gestured to the room.

"There's a bathroom there." He pointed the knife at a side door.

"Where do you write?"

"I write in here." He pointed the knife at his head.

"Keegan says hello and please contact him." She hoped he wouldn't point the knife at her. Keegan Monroe was also a client of Charlie's. But he was a screenwriter and him she could deal with. Screenwriters were used to having their work hacked, razed, and reconstituted beyond recognition by story committees and soon lost any prima donna illusions.

Keegan had said, "My dad's writing this book. Could you show it around for him? I mean as a favor to me? It's harder to . get an agent than a publisher these days."

The air in the tiny kitchen filled with frying garlic and olive oil and peppers and spices as Jack Monroe threw chopped thingies at a pan while making soft growling noises in his throat.

Charlie had recently moved from a literary agency in New York to Congdon and Morse Representation, a talent agency in Beverly Hills. She'd brought some of her book clients with her but now she mainly handled screenwriters like Keegan.

Once the son had described the type of book it was, Charlie turned it down with relief. "I don't think I have the right contacts for your dad. He'd probably be better off shooting it to a smaller publisher here on the West Coast on his own. And don't forget you've got a treatment due day after tomorrow yourself."

Charlie forgot about Keegan's dad until several days later. She was on a trip to New York and having lunch with Shelly Hummer, an editor friend at McMullins, when Shelly expressed interest in New Age nonfiction. "California's always been the hotbed of New Age thinking. Can you scout out some possibilities for our list, Charlie?"

"I don't know about California, and you won't believe this, but there's this guy on the coast of Oregon who may be writing just the book you have in mind."

Charlie knew little about New Age thinking except what had crept into the mainstream and she didn't really understand that. She knew and understood even less after reading Jack Monroe's sample chapters and outline but sent them on to New York where they were met with great excitement. The proposal must be turned into a completed manuscript last week. A contract specifying a nice but modest advance and a letter specifying editorial suggestions and changes would be rushed through the mill the soonest. There hadn't been another word for six months.

Keegan's dad sliced the sautéed meal down the middle of the frying pan and ladled each half onto a separate plate. He sliced crusty bread, poured a deep red wine, and came to sit beside her on the other stool. The wine was a smooth rich merlot and the sauté was light and crunchy, hot and satisfying.

"Like it?" Jack Monroe asked after a while.

"Love it," Charlie answered. "But I don't want to know what it is, okay?"

"Okay." He poured more wine, sliced more bread.

"Probably scrambled tofu with seaweed or something else awful."

"You have very discriminating taste buds." His voice dripped condescension.

Charlie pushed her plate away. "No, really I did love it, but I always only eat half of what's on my plate. Weight control. Fat women aren't highly regarded in our culture."

"Why don't you take half to begin with and not waste food?"

"That doesn't work. I tried it. Gained ten pounds."

"You people living in the old world get very peculiar." He emptied his plate and then finished off hers.

His movements may have been slightly slowed because of his interrupted meditation when he answered the door but his eyes sparked energy now and his movements had grown increasingly

6

fidgety. He slammed their plates into soapy water with a vengeance and then jammed coffee beans into the grinder. Charlie hoped she hadn't made a mistake coming here alone. Keegan was such a lamb, she couldn't believe his father was dangerous.

"You know why I didn't answer my mail, Charlie Greene?" Jack Monroe exploded finally. "Because I didn't go to the post office to pick it up. You know why I didn't answer my phone? Because I ripped it out of the wall."

"Listen, if you're going to get violent I'm going back out into the fog."

"You know why I tore out the phone? Do you? Because I don't give a fucking nose hair what those silly-assed, prissy, snot-nosed little editors in New York City think of my book. Isn't one of them old enough to know her behind from her left kneecap anyway." He grabbed the screaming teakettle from the stove and poured water over the grounds in the filter. He was lucky he didn't scald himself the way he jerked the kettle around.

"And even if this Shelly, whatever her name is, did want to buy the damn thing, she'd have to get it through the little lard-assed Fauntleroys in marketing who don't read books anyway. All they can read is charts and the charts don't mean a damn thing because the pimply adolescents who make the charts don't know shit about what they're doing but that doesn't matter because they're just stopping over in publishing on their way up the corporate ladder to something meaningful like chemicals and bombers and old world trivia."

"You been reading *Writer's Digest*, Jack?"

He grabbed the coffee pot and the wine bottle and slammed through the curtain. Even the *NESS* on the back of his shirt appeared to pulsate with rage.

"Welcome to Oregon," Charlie told herself and slid off her stool.

Out in the store Jack Monroe pulled floor cushions up to the bronze Buddha, who dwarfed them both, and grabbed mugs off a nearby shelf.

They sipped coffee deeper, richer even than the merlot. The warning buoy croaked so far away, now that Charlie was inside some walls, it sounded almost comforting. Buddha smiled indulgently, his metal gaze locked on some distant Nirvana. The inscription on Charlie's plastic mug read WHOLENESS. Its price tape read $19.95.

Just as she felt the energy about to erupt from the man on the other side of the Buddha, she said, "Morton and Fish wants to buy your book, Jack. They're offering a far better deal than McMullins. Keegan would have come up himself but—"

"Morton and Fish?" Jack Monroe asked the Buddha.

"And all the Fauntleroys and at least one of the prissy-assed editors who doesn't know her behind from her hubcap."

"Kneecap." Jack's eyes followed Buddha's nose down to Charlie's eyes.

"Can I have some more coffee?"

"The Morton and Fish?" He poured wine into her WHOLENESS mug, but his energy rage had dropped by half.

"You'll have to travel. This kind of book needs author promotion."

"Promotion."

"I think you'd be good at it if you didn't swear too much."

"They want my book? They want me to promote it?"

"I've been here over an hour, Jack. Didn't you once ask yourself why I came all this way? Where is it you live? I can almost understand how you write books in your head instead of on a computer, but is that where you live too?"

"You drove all the way up here from Los Angeles to deliver a book contract, Charlie Greene the agent?"

"I don't have the contract, I had to talk to you first. But the terms sound great to me for an author with no track record. Keegan would have come but he's in a cast. He broke his leg jogging on a bike path. I mean some bikes broke his . . . this all happened about the time this offer came from Morton and Fish. And I have some vacation time and my mother arrived to take care of my daughter while I was away and I always want to get away from my mother and . . . you see, Jack, Shelly Hummer didn't forget your book. She loved it. It's just she got an offer for a better job at—"

"Morton and Fish."

"No. *Field and Stream*. They don't do books. But she passed the word along to a friend at Morton and Fish—Susan Talbot. And Susan asked me for a copy of the proposal and we got a deal if I can get you to okay it. But I couldn't get in touch because you ripped out your phone." Charlie took a gulp of merlot from her coffee mug and wondered why reasonable, dependable, ordinary, workable people didn't write books she could sell.

"Morton and Fish."

"*Writer's Digest* doesn't have all the answers, Jack, trust me. And your agent's got mostly questions. Like, I've got reservations for a cabin at a place called Hide-a-bye. Is it near here, I hope? And can I have some more wine?"

Jack Monroe was staring off into nirvana with the Buddha and pouring Charlie more coffee when the door burst in with a gust of fog and heightened warning from the buoy and a man in a beard and yellow slicker over knobby knees and hiking boots.

"Jack," he shouted and swept the slicker into swirls of plastic crackling mayhem, "who is it drove that Toyota to your doorstep?"

"Frank?" Jack Monroe, the best-selling author, came back from the Oprah Winfrey Show.

"My Georgette, she's under that Toyota. She's dead, damnit." He spied Charlie peering out from under Buddha's nose. "You're the one. Run her over in the fog. And then have the nerve to stay around and visit. Why'd you do it for? She never hurt no one. Her bike's a mess too."

"I couldn't have," Charlie said helplessly as the fury in the yellow slicker advanced on her.

Chapter 2

Not even the emergency lights on the sheriff's car and the ambulance could penetrate more than a few feet of the fog that night.

"Don't know why they sent an ambulance," Frank of the yellow slicker confided to Charlie. "Told them she was dead."

Charlie had heard rumors about the Oregon coast. Those in the know would wink as though it were the best-kept secret in tourism. Charlie had yet to see the Oregon coast. All she knew of it was the violent sound of the Pacific against its shore and the haunting groan of a warning buoy. And now the body of a dead woman.

Georgette had worn a shocked gape when Jack Monroe first shone a flashlight on her face. Broken wire-rimmed eyeglasses hung by one earpiece in thin gray hair.

"Not that she was worth looking at anymore, but what'd you want to kill her for?" the poor woman's husband asked. "Rode her bicycle to keep from getting porky, raised the children till they was fine on their own. Not like she'd never done a thing."

Charlie was about to explain that although the road into Moot Point had been bumpy she'd had no idea she'd run over anyone in the thick fog, when two things happened almost simultaneously to still her tongue. The twisted bike swung through the beam of a headlight on an emergency vehicle as the investigators moved it—somehow more poignant than the broken body of the dead woman herself. And Frank cupped a hand around one of Charlie's buns.

Charlie sat curled up in a comfortably sprung chair and considered the possibility of losing the scrambled tofu and merlot. Between the ambiguous sickness and flashbacks of the mangled bike trailing fog webs as it was handed across headlight beams, a voice in her mind kept repeating—like the lyrics to a television commercial you want to forget but can't—"Toto, I've a feeling we're not in Kansas anymore."

Perhaps it was because Frank and Georgette's living room was heavily accented with embroidered signs similar to those in Jack's store. A calico cat lounged on top of a darkened television set, staring hatred at Charlie.

"Ms. Greene, I'll admit this fog is heavy even for us, but I can't believe you didn't see a thing in front of your headlights when you struck Mrs. Glick and her bike. Particularly since you were pulling to a stop at the Earth Spirit at the time. I can't believe you didn't feel a bump or hear any sound of impact."

"I can't either," Charlie told Sheriff Bennett, trying to avoid the accusation in the cat's stare. She'd read that cats won't look you directly in the eye for long but this cat hadn't heard about that.

Sheriff Bennett sat on a coffee table facing her. Jack Monroe and Frank Glick perched on the edge of a leather couch peering around him to watch Charlie. Frank wore a safari outfit—shirt and shorts and hiking boots. His stick legs had no shape except bulges for knees. A neighbor stood behind the couch fussing around him. Another offered coffee and some kind of sliced nutty/fruity bread on a tray, setting her lips in grim disapproval when nobody took any.

This was one of those double trailer homes you'd never want to move, set on a concrete foundation with a patio and porch. It sat next to Jack's store.

"Wes," Jack touched the sheriff's shoulder, "could Georgette have ridden by Charlie's car when it was parked and slid underneath it?"

"Hard to see how that would crimp up her bike that way and how it would kill her." The sheriff shifted slightly and Charlie waited for the coffee table's legs to buckle. "We'll have to wait for the coroner's report."

One of the women bent over to whisper in Frank's ear and he brushed her away like a mosquito. "Don't want no doctor, no hot milk, no sedatives. I do want to hear what it is this young lady has to say for herself. Now you old bats just get on home and leave me alone. My wife that was killed."

The women retreated toward the door, but didn't leave. The one with the refreshment tray asked, "Shouldn't you call the family, Frank?"

He sat up and rubbed at his beard. Without the slicker he was skeletal. "Hadn't thought of that yet. Would you do that for me, Martha?"

"Mary."

"Mary. Oh, and tell them to make reservations someplace else cause I can't house 'em all here, that's for sure."

Sheriff Wes of Moot County drove Charlie to her cabin at the Hide-a-bye instead of to the jail because her car was impounded for the investigation and because it seemed clear that she hadn't run over Georgette Glick on purpose, nor had she fled the scene of the accident. They stopped at the main lodge on the road to pick up the key and allow the sleepy girl at the desk to imprint Charlie's American Express card, and then parked at one of a series of cottages presumably overlooking the ocean. That's what the brochure had said, that's what the sound on the fog sounded like.

Sheriff Wes followed Charlie into the cottage carrying her suitcase, briefcase, and garment bag. First door to the right opened to the bedroom—old knotty pine furniture and paneling that reminded her of Frank's knees. To the left was the bathroom. A short hall opened to one room divided into carpeted living room and tiled kitchen areas.

Two recliner-rockers in the middle of the carpet could swivel between the TV and the stone fireplace built into the inner wall shared with the bedroom. A couch sat against a side wall. A Formica table with plastic chairs graced the kitchen end. The place smelled of moldy carpet and sour drains. Sliding doors and picture windows formed the outside wall.

"The agency paid all that for this?"

A chuckle rumbled behind her. "Just wait till the fog lifts and you won't believe the view. People come clear from foreign countries for *this*."

Even though they were pulled open, sections of the drapes on the Pacific wall pouched loose from their hooks. Only a blanket of dark showed through from outside. The sheriff lit one of those pressed logs in the grate and they sat in the recliners to watch it burn as if they'd never seen fire.

He was built like a tank. All square edges. Massive, but solid. Not a soft-looking place on him except where he smiled. "We keep having to go to all these consciousness-raising seminars," he said finally. "When you're trying to help little kids through some of life's shit it's teddy bears. But for tough agents from LA, I'm not sure what's best."

Charlie managed a grin to thank him for not leaving her alone just yet. None of the people she'd met tonight fit her expectations. This man was no exception. She leaned toward the welcome warmth of the fire. "What I can't help thinking of is how unsad her husband was about the whole thing."

"Probably hasn't hit him yet. Men of that generation grieve different, but they grieve."

"He felt up my ass while you were hauling hers out from under my car. That's grief?"

Now he grinned. Even his teeth were big. "You one of those feminist types?"

Charlie stared down the challenge in his drawl and sat a little straighter. She heard the hardness in her voice that her mother hated. "I was not speeding down the road, Sheriff. I was pulling to a stop in front of the Earth Spirit. I can almost rationalize not seeing Mrs. Glick on her bike because I was so relieved to have finally found Moot Point and my client. I'd been nervous driving for nearly an hour on a strange road, unable to see . . . but I'll be damned if I can believe Mrs. Glick and her Schwinn wouldn't have felt like more than a bump in the road."

There was still a sympathetic twinge to his grin but he rose and yawned. "Get some sleep. It'll all shake down when the investigation gets in gear. Complimentary packets of coffee over by the sink, teakettle and cups in the cupboard. Since you don't have a car I'll pick you up for breakfast in the morning."

"Do all suspected killers get such thoughtful treatment in Moot County?"

"Just tough little agents named Charlie, with gravelly voices and brassy coils." He gave her a fatherly wink and moved down the hall to the door with the stealthy tread of a cat burglar. Which didn't seem possible for a man who must weigh over two-fifty.

It was too late to call her mother and she didn't know if she needed a lawyer yet. Charlie fell into the oversoft bed, so exhausted from a day of driving and its inexplicable aftermath she was sure she wouldn't be able to sleep, not sure she hadn't left reality behind her when she crossed the Moot County line.

The next she knew she was coming straight up out of the bed, yelling *no* silently in her head as loud as she could, heart pumping panic to the tips of her toes and the ends of her hair, and daylight seeping around the curtain at the small window. By the time Charlie stood in the shower washing away the terror, she'd forgotten the dream that had caused it. By the time

14

Sheriff Wes arrived she was dressed in loose forest green pants with a leather jacket dyed to match and had her "brassy coils" tied back with a scarf. All this dampness gave them a life of their own.

"You were right about the view." She handed him a mug of instant motel coffee and took hers to the deck outside that had been a blank wall of darkness and fog the night before. What greeted them now was endless sky filled with sun and puffy clouds, and rollers eight deep washing onto a nearly white beach about fifty feet below the railing.

Charlie took a closer look at the law. "Did you get to sleep at all last night?"

He studied her face for a drawn-out moment and turned to stare at the sea. Last night he'd worn a sport coat and tie while his deputies were in uniform. This morning he wore jeans and sneakers and dark patches under his eyes. Finally he drained the mug, which in his hand looked like a Chinese teacup. "Tell you one thing. I need breakfast. Let's head for Rose's."

Rose's was in the village of Moot Point, which was on the other side of the headland from the Hide-a-bye. The road took them up along the mountainside and Charlie could see the Moot Point lighthouse at the end of the promontory sitting white in a sea of dripping jade vegetation. Its light still circled in the old way but modern antennas poked into the sky around it.

They turned off the highway onto the road Charlie had followed, but could barely see, the night before. It swooped down through trees and thick underbrush, then broke out into a dramatic view of the bay. The village stair-stepped by street up the hillside. Rose's was on the lowest step just above the beach, a building of sea-weathered gray wood with old-fashioned oilcloth on the tables, candles in miniature ships' lanterns, a black wood stove taking the chill off the morning, padded cushions on ancient hardwood chairs, and the odor of careful cooking.

Sheriff Bennett sat with his head between the tremendous breasts of a woman adorning a fake ship's figurehead that sprouted from the wall behind him. Rose herself came to fuss over him.

"She the one?" Rose stared openly at Charlie. She was short and heavy, wore a saggy cardigan over a shapeless dress and floppy terry-cloth bedroom slippers. The other waitpersons wore tailored black pants, white shirts, black string ties, and straight spines.

"See you haven't translated the menu into Japanese yet, Rose," he said instead of answering her, and ordered pancakes and bacon.

"You got yourself a lot bigger worries right now than the Japanese, Sheriff." She patted the top of his big head and took Charlie's order. Her slippers clapped measured applause as she shuffled off.

"When can I have my car back?" Charlie asked him, his change of mood from last night making her uneasy. Maybe that was part of law enforcement these days like teddy bears. Or maybe it was just that he didn't care for sunshine.

"Do you own a weapon, Charlie?" he said instead of answering her and leaned back into the painted bosom, part of his face shadowed from the light coming into the window next to them. Even the twinge of sympathy for her seemed to have been drowned in waves of exhaustion.

Charlie sipped at her coffee and stared out to sea. She could see the lighthouse from here too. It looked too good to be true, like a calendar picture. "There're knives in our kitchen but I don't own a gun. Guess my Toyota was a weapon last night, wasn't it?"

They sat in outward silence until their food arrived. Inwardly Charlie was talking over the possibilities with him. "Listen, I'm in some kind of serious shit here, right? Should I call my lawyer or what?" And he'd say, "You got one?" And she'd say, "A lawyer? Doesn't everyone?"

Charlie knew people who had lawyers. She wasn't one of them. Her egg came, over easy, and she chopped it up so the yolk ran and mixed it in with half the home fries and glanced up at Sheriff Wes. He was watching her plate, looking a little sick. Charlie had always done this to eggs. Was it a pathological sign?

She tried to peer between the wooden boobs into his eyes. "Listen, Sheriff Bennett, I'll say it again. I had been driving all day, hit bad weather. I'd had some trouble at home and I know I wasn't in great shape. But I still don't see how I could have hit and killed a grown woman on a bicycle and not known it, even in heavy fog. It just doesn't work. Now can I have my car back or what?"

"Your car is still under investigation. There are no signs of impact in the bodywork or paint immediately identifiable as being related to the death of Mrs. Glick or the destruction of her Schwinn. But we'll let the experts confirm that before we return your car."

He would say no more until they'd eaten. Finally when the dishes were cleared he came out with it. "Charlie, Georgette Glick died of a bullet to the head. But her bike appears to have been struck and run over by a heavy object such as a motor vehicle."

"You mean she was shot and dead before I ran over her?"

"She wasn't run over. Just the Schwinn."

Chapter 3

The area in front of the Earth Spirit where the Toyota, Georgette Glick, and her bicycle had mysteriously come together in the fog was still cordoned off. A uniformed sheriff's deputy stood guard. He was talking to a tall lanky man in acid-washed jeans whose black hair was tied back with a ribbon but still reached halfway down his back. Oddly shingled bangs and side wisps curled and fluffed about his face as if he'd taken a blow dryer and a curling iron to it.

"Might know it was a California license plate," the deputy muttered and then looked sheepish when he saw Charlie and the sheriff approach.

Wes Bennett gave him a stony look and introduced the other man to Charlie as "Brother Dennis."

Brother Dennis was fifty if he was a day. He had arrow-straight posture and no paunch but the grooves and lines in his face were accentuated by the improbable flat black of his hair. He nodded at Charlie, studying her closely, as Rose had.

She looked away to the graveled area supposedly protected by bands of bright tape strung between street repair posts weighted with sandbags. It seemed everyone had tracked through the blood and stains on the ground, including a small animal. Probably the house cat she'd heard.

"How could you not have known about the gunshot wound last night?" she asked the law.

"Too much dark and fog and hair. Not enough blood." Sheriff Wes jingled change deep in his pockets. "Seemed so obvious she'd been run over—dumbest fuck-up I've ever pulled on a crime scene. Can't wait to read all about it in the papers."

"Election's not for a year yet, Wes," Brother Dennis said. "Maybe by that time people will have forgotten this for something bigger you saved the day on. Are you going to arrest Miss Greene here? Going to have to do something."

Frank Glick stepped out onto the porch of his immobile home with a cup in his hand, still in his safari outfit. It looked like he'd slept in it, and he would have looked less ridiculous if he'd had a tan. But like everybody here he was as white as baby powder. He stared morosely at Charlie, forcing her eyes back to the blood and footprints. She noticed a couple of gray hairs stuck in the stain and swallowed a throat lump so big it made her eyes tear. Was she really about to be arrested for the murder of a woman she'd never seen alive?

"Charlie, I've plugged the phone back in. You can call New York now." Jack Monroe literally bounced across the porch of his shop and down the steps. "Must be halfway through the business day back there. See you've met my agent, Brother Dennis."

"Your agent." Brother Dennis nearly choked on his scoff.

"She's got me a deal with Morton and Fish. Must be a good agent, Brother."

They dueled with their eyes, the tall man and the short, until Brother Dennis broke into a slow smile that threatened to join his ears. His teeth were spotted with stained plastic fillings. "For that pretense of a book you're working on, Jack? You don't know a chakra from a hole in a bucket. What's Bad Dog have to say about this?"

"What's he know about books? Can't even read." But Jack had lost the eye duel.

"Who's Bad Dog?" Charlie asked her client when the communication with New York had ended.

"My spirit guide." They sat on the unmade bed, under the prophetic sign, the telephone between them. "He was a member of the Modoc tribe. His father was Running Dog and his mother, Lame Deer."

"I would have thought Mad Dog, for some reason," Charlie said, really trying to get into this. Ten percent, after all, was ten percent. "But Bad Dog—"

"Mad Dog was his sister."

"Right." Charlie was clearly out of her element here. "Look, Jack, I have to call home. May I use your phone? I have my card."

"It never ends, does it?" her mother laid into her right away. "You've got your own daughter to raise now. How do you expect her to turn out normal if you can't stay out of trouble yourself?"

"I told you it's all a mistake, Edwina. Can't you ever take my side on anything? Where is Libby?"

"She's going to need braces on those teeth and soon, got a mouth just like you did. You can't put this off any longer."

"Is she there?"

"I knew I shouldn't have come out here. If I hadn't, you wouldn't have gone traipsing off up there and this whole business wouldn't have happened." Edwina lived in Colorado where Charlie had grown up and where Libby was born. A biology professor at the university in Boulder, Edwina had dropped in on her only daughter and grandchild before a planned field trip to the desert. Charlie's work called for a good bit of travel and finding someone to baby-sit a fourteen-year-old, who was a baby-sitter herself, was something of a nightmare. "What if you can't get back before I have to leave?"

"I'll get back, Edwina. I've left her before. Maggie in the condo next door keeps track of her for me sometimes. Can I talk to Libby?"

"I'm here alone except for the cat."

"We don't have a cat."

"Remember when you brought that smelly schnauzer home one day? Followed you from school? Well—"

"Edwina, we can't afford a cat."

"I couldn't afford Bowzer either, as I remember."

"You tell her to take that animal to the shelter the minute she gets back. Do you hear me?" Edwina could never get enough revenge on her daughter by way of her granddaughter.

"Cute little thing, black and white. Name's Tuxedo."

"Edwina, I'm going to hang up now, but you have my daughter by the phone tonight so I can talk to her from the motel or the jail or wherever I am. And that kitty damn well better be outta there when the phone rings. Edwina?" Her mother of course had gotten in the last word by hanging up first.

The lowest terrace of the village of Moot Point sat on a ledge about fifteen feet above the beach. A wooden stairway, complete with handrails, continued on down to the sand from all four of the streets that ended there. The horizontal street on that first terrace held what commercial district the town possessed—a craft shop, Rose's, tourist cabins, an art gallery, an antique store, a community center, several boarded-up buildings and a few falling down, an occasional vacant lot.

Charlie Greene pulled at a can of diet Pepsi and wandered up to the next terrace, still seething. Tuxedo, Jesus. Vet bills, kitty shots, stinking litter boxes, torn curtains, chewed houseplants. On top of the national debt to straighten Libby's teeth. *"Every child needs a pet, Charlie, it's part of having a home."*

"Libby doesn't need a pet. She's got a boyfriend who follows her around like a faithful dog."

"Wouldn't you rather she became involved with a harmless little animal than become too involved with droopy old Doug?"

"A cat isn't going to ward off that danger. Ask Edwina. She thought Bowzer the schnauzer would take some of the pressure off my teen-raging hormones and was she wrong."

"You're about to be arrested for the murder of a woman you never heard of until last night and you can still waste energy ranting on about how wrong your mother was?"

"Oh, piss off."

On this street, and the other two above, the houses were built to face the ocean and attached to the hillside so you looked at the roof of the buildings on the downside and the stairs leading to the front doors of those on the upside. This way the neighbor across the street didn't block your view. It made for some tortuous driveways though. Most of the homes were modest. There were no sidewalks and little lawn grass, but the yards dripped flowers. Charlie thought she'd seen roses in southern California, but there were some here the size of cabbages. She couldn't imagine how the bushes and spindly stalks held them up.

Charlie climbed to the top street and decided the whole village wasn't the size of a reasonable subdivision. The bay was formed by a long spit to the south and the promontory with the lighthouse to the north. Jack's store and the Glick's house, along with two more of the permanent mobile homes, faced the bay from the north side along the road that came into town from the highway and continued on out and up to the lighthouse.

The belated crime scene crew (which hadn't been called in until this morning when it was light and the news had spread of the bullet hole in Mrs. Glick's head) piled their samples or whatever and their cameras into the van. The deputy was hosing down what little remained of the gore when a battalion of cyclists swooped down from the highway and nearly collided with the official traffic headed the other way. The stream of bicycles managed to swerve in formation and eventually pull to a bunched-up stop in front of Rose's. They dismounted like cowboys and left their wheeled steeds lying flat in the vacant lot next to the restaurant with a delegated watchman.

"You going to toss that empty pop can or let me recycle the sucker?" Brother Dennis said behind her and laughed at her surprised yelp. He took the Pepsi can and mashed it flat between the heels of each hand. "Waste not, want not."

"Were you following me?"

"I live here." He jerked a thumb over his shoulder to an oddly shaped building that appeared to be mostly roof. "I thought you were following me." He and the can disappeared into the forest next to his house and Charlie was left with the impression of a scrawny wood nymph of exaggerated height.

By the time Charlie got down to the main street, Rose herself stood on the sidewalk in front of her eatery supervising the removal of the cleated footwear from the last of the cyclists. Pairs of such shoes lined the wooden sidewalk in rows stretching from one end of the building to the other. It made Charlie think of the old West and of sheriffs collecting sidearms when the cowboys came to town.

Speaking of sheriffs, Wes Bennett moved away from the small gathering on the steps of the Earth Spirit and sauntered down the street toward her. Charlie stopped and waited for him, trying on a hopeful smile that felt more like a wince. "So, am I under arrest or what?"

"Let's take a walk on the beach and have a talk."

"I think Brother Dennis is scandalized that I'm not in handcuffs already," she said as they descended the steep stairs to the sand. "Why *Brother* Dennis? Because of some kind of religion or just flaky stuff like Jack's store?"

"God knows," Wes said heavily but again she was struck by the graceful almost stealthy way he moved across the sand. "This town's full of Grape-Nuts. But other than an improper mushroom or two they haven't given me much trouble."

He went on to explain that, although there was some overlap, the village was made up of four basic subcultures. The true natives were mostly retired fishermen or lumbermen or their widows who lived on pensions and social security in the smaller wooden bungalows on the terraces. The second group were retired citizens from other places, like Frank, who'd come from California to Oregon where a piece of Pacific view was still affordable.

"They tend to live in those double trailer homes off minor investments and pensions and social security, but they aren't rich by any means. Then there's the merchant class trying to lure the tourist to these shores. They have the nicer homes on the hill as a rule. And last, the New Wavers or Agers or whatever they are. I still can't get a handle on these guys. Warlocks and witches is what they seem to me, Grape-Nuts one and all. But I'm just a country boy who wouldn't understand. Aren't many in any of the groups who'll see forty again."

The country boy had a few gray hairs himself, but his curls were cut short and tight to his head. His eyes weren't brown or hazel so they must have been blue. Nothing startling like Jack Monroe's but with a lot of savvy lurking behind a weary front.

"So where do those young waitpersons at Rose's live?"

"Mostly in Chinook, where there's apartment-type housing and a small college. Hardly fifteen miles from here."

"So why are we walking the beach and why are you filling me in on the history of Moot Point if I'm a suspect in a murder in your county, Sheriff Bennett?"

They had come to the beginning of the headland that held the lighthouse and he sat on one of the black rocks at its base. Swallows dived and swooped from the cliff above and noisy sea birds filled the air around three huge rocks in the sea in front of them. "Because, Charlie Greene, I like your company. Because I'm thoroughly stumped as to why anyone would want to harm so harmless a person as Georgette Glick—Frank maybe—but Georgette? And mostly because, Charlie Greene, I'm waiting for the computer in the courthouse to cough up your entire life history."

Chapter 4

"So Libby doesn't have a father, never did?" Wes asked around a bite of his banana split with nuts and whipped cream and chocolate sprinkles and maraschino cherries over three flavors of yogurt.

They sat in a booth in The Witch's Tit, a frozen yogurt shop in Chinook that had one menu for the fat and one for the lean. Charlie worked on a small cone with less enthusiasm. This was supposed to be lunch but every time she brought the yogurt to her mouth she noticed again the ink smudges left on her hands from when he'd had her fingerprinted at the courthouse.

"I suppose the computer told you my bank balance and my bra size too."

"You didn't answer my question." The thing was, he wasn't fat, just big enough to eat like he was.

"Obviously there was a man involved, boy really—it would have been stupid to marry him. I'm just one of the statistics you read about."

"Looks like you landed on your feet. Lots of kids don't. Col-

lege degree. Car and condo payments in LA. Good job. No
police record. Your daughter either. Must have been a hard
pull."

"I had a lot of help from my mother," Charlie admitted with
that familiar twinge of guilt. "Can a computer really tell you
everything about a person? Aren't there privacy laws or anything?"

"Tells us a lot more than we need to know. Have to hire
somebody just to sort through all the sludge."

"You didn't answer my question either. About the laws."

"Nothing modern technology can't get around." He was still
doing that low rumble in his chest that was supposed to be a
laugh and his tongue was still working cashew bits from between his teeth when they stepped out onto the sidewalk.

"Well, even without a computer I'll bet I can come up with a
few facts about you, too," Charlie told the sheriff of Moot
County. "You had some experience with football and the Ma-
rines before you got into law enforcement. Am I right?"

"Something like that."

"You don't seem pigheaded, rednecked, or mean enough."

"You'd be surprised how life can rub some of the rough edges
off even us rednecks."

They strolled companionably down a block to the wharf, the
sheriff and his suspect in a murder that didn't make sense. The
sun was warm and the harbor smelled of dead fish and deader
sewage. The sea gulls appeared to be enjoying both. Here the
bars and restaurants had names like the Harbor Master and
Pilot House and the Broken Ore. The dockworkers were beefy
and pale skinned, lots of red and blond hair and names like
Bjorg and Olaf and Sandy. Wes greeted them all and they all
called him Wes and they all gave Charlie a curious once-over.

"Most murders make a lot of sense," the sheriff said as though
reading her mind, "even the accidental ones." He took off his
jacket for her to sit on and sprawled beside her on the wooden
planking.

"Maybe someone intended to shoot somebody else and Mrs.

Glick got in the way in the fog," she said, "and then he stuffed her body under my car to make it look like an accident long enough for him to get away. I can see somebody wanting to shoot Frank."

"Maybe we don't know all there is to know about the Glicks. Or Charlie Greene for that matter. Maybe there's something the computer and I haven't turned up yet." He leaned on an elbow to stare at a humongous black-and-red cargo ship sitting high in the water and empty.

"I suppose it delivered Hondas," Charlie said lazily. "Wonder what it will take back?"

"Part of the national forest probably. Their own population explosion took care of theirs long ago. Now because people like you buy their cars they can afford to buy up our dwindling forests. Along with most everything else."

"I have no use for a gargantuan gas guzzler I can't find parking space for," Charlie said defensively. "Old macho Detroit refused to build a reliable, energy-efficient, well-made, affordable compact so I had to go foreign. They didn't want my business for so long I got tired of waiting."

"What do all those limos on Rodeo Drive do for parking?"

"They don't have to park. Their chauffeurs just keep driving around the block."

He grunted and laid his head back on his hands to gaze up at scudding cloud puffs. He had to be the most unsherifflike sheriff in the country.

"Don't you have work to do in your office or anything?"

"I do my best work outside. And I'm working right now. I'm thinking."

"Must be a great confidence builder for your voters." Charlie was thinking she should call her own office, let them know what happened. "How long before I can go home?"

"Couple days, probably. Unless we find the gun that killed Mrs. Glick and your fingerprints are on it. Or we find out you have some connection with the lady. Or you could go home sooner if the murderer steps forward. Which doesn't happen often. Relax and enjoy the scenery. We don't get sun like this on a regular basis."

Charlie's head was too busy looking for a way out of this mess. "Tell me more about Moot Point and these New Ager people. What exactly is it that they do?"

"Christ, what don't they do? They go out to communicate with the whales when the poor critters are trying to migrate. They sell crystals and tarot cards . . . hell, broomsticks for all I know. They make a living on mail order tapes and video cassettes telling people how to wrap their bodies into knots and communicate with the universe. They compose music that sounds like wind chimes in a San-O-Let. They hold seminars and retreats on how to see auras and go back to talk to the people you were in previous lives. Grape-Nuts. But nothing you can't find worse in Southern California. And nothing that would lead anyone to want to kill a little old lady on a Schwinn. You read Jack Monroe's book, you tell me."

"Just the proposal. It's about how to raise your 'level of consciousness' so you can always be serene and successful through meditation, yoga exercises, diet, and training your mind to leave your body or something. Maybe Jack's mind left his body while he was meditating while I was watching him through the window, and he shot Georgette, stuffed her under my car, and crawled back into his body to answer the door. Tell me about the murders you've worked on that do make sense."

Problems with family and/or sexual relationships came first to his mind, and drug-related crime was next. "Comes under the heading of greed. There's so much loose cash around before it can be laundered. Ripping off dealers is a growing industry and often leads to murder, given the sums and personalities involved."

"What about accidental murder? Someone's target shooting and Georgette rides by and—"

"At night? In the fog? On a public road?" He came back up onto an elbow and squinted at her suspiciously. "What was a seventy-eight-year-old woman doing riding her bicycle at night in the fog? This case is all questions and no answers. There's no place to start putting the puzzle together from." He stood and lifted her off his jacket. "I'm taking you back to the Hide-a-bye. Tough little agents from LA are too distracting."

"But I'm hungry and there's no food there."

"You just had lunch."

"You just had lunch. I had worries."

"You don't now?"

They stopped at a bakery for French bread and sticky buns, screeched up to a supermarket for smoked salmon, butter, coffee, milk, cold cereal, Tillimook cheese, coleslaw, ripe Bing and Royal Ann cherries, juicy plums, and a bottle of Knudsen Erath Cabernet. As he broke the speed law on their way to the Hide-a-bye he pointed out that everything but the cereal was made not only in the U.S. but in Oregon. He didn't offer to help her carry the food into her cabin, but shooshed her out of the Bronco and took off for the village of Moot Point to talk to Frank Glick.

Sitting on the built-in bench out on the deck, her Keds propped on the railing, Charlie ate bread and fruit and watched the Pacific roll in and roll in and roll in and a jogger go by in the direction of the point. She finished the last tasty crunch of bread crust and waited. The jogger didn't come back. Now that she thought about it, the jogger had been a dead ringer for her client. Charlie sat forward and stared at the southern end of the beach. She could see the lighthouse on the cliff above and part of one of the huge rocks out in front of the point with birds all over it.

She stared until her contacts started scratching. Jack still hadn't come back. Why should he? He lived over there. There must be a way to walk over there and back for a poor suspect bereft of her car. Perhaps to talk to her client. Perhaps to snoop around the town, since nobody was going to fess up to Wes Bennett. He was the law for godsake. But why would anyone fess up to the logical suspect who was also a perfect stranger to everyone in town and therefore the last priority on anyone's conscience? Except Jack's. Then again Jack could decide he didn't need her now that the deal was all but done with Morton and Fish.

Charlie found a path leading to the beach on the other side of the first cabin. It was longer than it looked to the black rocks that cluttered the shore at the end of the point. They were foamy with approaching tide but she could see the path leading up the cliff. Surely Jack Monroe could drive her back to her cabin.

One of the rocks moved and startled Charlie into a sudden stop. A sea lion sunning on the rock had been rolled by a rogue wave. It flapped a flipper at her as if waving hello and made a sound he intended to be a roar suggesting she buzz off.

This was the closest Charlie had ever come to one of these creatures and she wished she hadn't left her little camera in her luggage. She could remember how taken Libby had been with the sea lions that hung around the wharf in Santa Cruz because local vendors sold bait fish to the tourists for feeding them. Libby had begged for every last buck in Charlie's billfold to buy fish.

But this one was young and slim and unscarred and wild. He was beautiful. Even with his fangs showing and his whiskers laid back there was something sweet and innocent about him that Charlie wished she could share with her daughter. Another wave forced Charlie to run up the beach to keep her Keds dry, and when she turned he was gone. She was almost to the path when the obvious struck her. What was a seventy-eight-year-old woman doing on a bicycle, period? Never mind that it was at night, that it was in the fog.

Charlie didn't realize she'd stopped again to stare at the sea birds screeching around the black behemoths offshore and clinging to the grassy areas on top until sea foam slithered up over her shoes to her ankles. It receded, slipping the sand out from under her heels and tugging at her to come with it.

She swore and squelched on up to dry land, following the footpath around the point until it met the road that led up to the lighthouse. Charlie followed this road down instead to the Earth Spirit. The Moot County sheriff's patrol Bronco still sat in front of the Glicks'.

Charlie slipped quickly into the Earth Spirit. Jack Monroe perched behind the cash register with a pencil and a yellow legal pad. He still wore his jogging sweats.

"Aha, caught you. You don't either write in your head." Before a tourist could wander in or her author could conjure up one of his diatribes, she asked him about Georgette Glick. "Was she really strong enough to ride that bike at her age?"

"Every day the weather permitted. That's why they retired here. Frank wanted to live in Chinook where there were young high school and college girls walking around to gape at, but Georgette wanted to study under Brother Dennis. Cycling is one of his methods of achieving cosmic consciousness. Now Frank just walks. Good days, he walks the beach clear into Chinook to watch the girls go by. I believe he's a year older than Georgette. But he wouldn't give Brother Dennis the time of day. So who's to say why they were so chipper a couple?"

"He walks fifteen miles—that would be thirty both ways—and he's seventy-nine? Come on, Jack."

"When the tide's out you can walk the beach and it's not even five miles. There's a rush hour bus to bring him home." He checked his watch. "I've got to shower and get to the celebration. Could you watch the store for me? I was going to close but I probably won't be more than an hour. It's being a slow day."

"What celebration?"

"Georgette's. I'd invite you to come along but you're in kind of a strange position around here. Not that I believe for a moment you shot her."

"You're celebrating a woman's murder?"

"She has finally attained the highest consciousness possible."

Chapter 5

LIFE FORCE VITAMINS!, Charlie read on the label, were not only organically grown, but naturally grown too. They were *FULLY ABSORBABLE!* They were unrefined whole food vitamin and mineral concentrates that were grown by nature and not laboratory chemicals and they were 1000 *TIMES MORE POTENT!* They were also extremely expensive. But then they provided the buyer with shinier hair, stronger nails, fewer colds, nicer complexion, an end to PMS, and more energy. Not to mention a *REJUVENATED SEX LIFE!*

Although everything was pretty dusty there was something homey about the clutter. Bumper stickers, T-shirts, coffee mugs, pot holders, outdoor cooking aprons, trivets with messages ranging from one word to crowded paragraphs. *WHOLENESS* or *HOLNESS* or *HOLENESS*—three different spellings on three different mugs. *MIND, BODY, SPIRIT* instead of God, Son, and Holy Ghost, *ALTERNATIVE REALITIES* instead of Jesus loves you—still the place did remind Charlie of a religious novelty shop.

There were tapes and books and videos. If you just wanted a lazy browse you could read the quotes on the sample T-shirts stapled to corkboard high on one wall—

"It is necessary; therefore it is possible."—Borgese.

"We are living at a time when history is holding its breath." —Arthur Clarke.

"What we are looking for is what is looking."—Saint Francis of Assisi.

"We have to move into the unknown; the known has failed us too completely."—Marilyn Ferguson.

"Marilyn Ferguson?" Charlie was asking the air when footsteps sounded on the wooden porch outside.

A woman entered the Earth Spirit, smiling dimples into plump cheeks when she saw Charlie. She tucked waist-length hair behind her ears and introduced herself as Paige Magill. "Jack told me he'd left his agent in charge of the store and asked me to stop by to see how things were going."

"I haven't had any customers. Jack said he'd be back an hour ago."

"The celebration for Georgie's getting out of hand. I think you and I better close up shop. I doubt Jack'll be back any time soon." Paige's cheeks were plump because of youth, her thighs plump in tight jeans because of just plain plump. Still, she was the type Frank Glick would cop a feel on every chance he got. Charlie couldn't fit her into the guideline of resident types set down by Sheriff Wes.

Paige produced a key from behind the *To the blind all things are sudden* sign above the door and locked it as they stepped out onto the porch. She hid it in a carved slot under the top stair. All signs of Georgette Glick had been rinsed from the road. But her calico cat sat on the hood of the station wagon that had replaced Wes's Bronco. It had suitcases strapped to its top. Two boys of late grade school age sat morosely on a bench swing on the patio. Georgette's family was arriving.

"I just came up here to see Jack and get away from home and now I feel guilty about some tragic crime that happened to somebody I'd never heard of yesterday at this time," Charlie confided. "Pretty soon that guilt will convince me I did have something to do with it. It's depressing." But having said that, she felt better for it and could almost see the empathy radiating from the warm features of the girl beside her.

"Come on up to my place for a cup of tea. Must be awful having no one to talk to." Paige reached for an expensive mountain bike leaning against the porch and wheeled it along as they walked. "I can imagine how you must feel, but don't be too hard on us. It's easier to suspect a stranger. And it's scary to think it might have been one of us. We'll all get ourselves sorted out once we get over the shock."

Paige Magill lived on the second terrace. Her little flower shop and greenhouse was called the Dream Emporium and was really more of a glass-wrap addition built around three sides of a small house. She lived in three gloomy rooms and a bath at the back. But a deck had been jerry-built onto one end of the greenhouse and it was here they brought their tea.

"Dream Emporium is a funny name for a florist shop," Charlie thought aloud and then hoped she hadn't been rude. She wanted more than sympathy from this woman, she wanted information.

"I do dream counseling too." Paige shrugged, rolled her eyes, grimaced. "And I keep Jack's books for the Earth Spirit." She pulled her knees up to hug them, setting her heels into the metal mesh of her rusting deck chair. "And I help Brother Dennis with his seminars and workshops. And I get a small monthly allotment from my grandmother's estate." She offered up her financial status without embarrassment. "Anything to survive and be able to stay here at the point."

Under an endless expanse of clean sky the Pacific broke in four or five hypnotic foam lines before rolling up onto the beach. Sea gulls skipped in and out harvesting what the waves left behind.

"It is a beautiful place to live," Charlie agreed.

"And I believe in the work going on here."

"What exactly is the work going on here?"

"Defining reality. The reality of the spirit as well as the mind. Learning to experience the whole world instead of just the narrow slice allowed us by science and the tunnel vision of society and religion. Freeing the spirit to learn . . . awareness . . . becoming . . ." Paige shook her head helplessly. "It's impossible to define it to someone who's . . . not awake yet."

Charlie could come up with no reasonable comment on all that, so they sat in companionable silence, sipping tea, squinting in the sunlight at the verdant greens and creamy blues of land and sea and sky, the whitewashed lighthouse and its several buildings with their red roofs looking "storybook" out on the point. The tea had a smoky, earthy flavor that melded with the odors of the greenhouse. A chicken clucked contentment somewhere behind the house and the warning buoy still warned ships off the rocks out to sea.

Charlie turned to find her hostess's smile so beguiling and unaffected she didn't hesitate to speak her thoughts. "Did Georgette embroider those signs with the New Age messages for Jack's store?"

Paige nodded. "She was wonderful with a needle and thread, did sewing and mending for everyone."

"She was apparently quite an old lady otherwise too—able to ride a bike at her age."

Paige explained that Georgette Glick and her husband had moved to the point about fourteen years ago after Georgette had come to a weekend seminar on transcendence.

"Isn't that a pretty big topic for one weekend?"

"It was just an introductory course, but it took hold of Georgie and she's . . . she was studying with Brother Dennis ever since. He put her on a diet, exercise, and meditation program."

Charlie could see Jack's store and the short line of retirement trailer homes along the road below. Another car pulled into the spot in front of the station wagon. A teenage girl slid out from behind the wheel and an older man got out from the passenger side.

"Georgie had four children, nine grandchildren, and some great grandchildren," Paige said, following Charlie's look. "And she'd been married only once and to Frank Glick all that time. Can you believe it?"

"I suppose everyone loved her. Everyone in Moot Point. I mean in the New Age community."

"I'm not sure it's a community—more a bunch of unorganizable individuals—but we are all striving to love everyone. Ourselves included. Because we are all inherently one. Even you. It's just that our biocomputers were programmed wrong at an early age."

"So not everyone found it that easy to love Georgette?"

"Well, she was sort of a busybody and that got on some people's nerves a lot."

"How about you? Did she get on your nerves a lot?"

Paige smiled that serene smile again and the dimples made her appear younger than she was. A cute little giggle went with it. "You're beginning to sound like Sheriff Bennett. How about some more tea?" When Paige Magill returned with the teapot, the conversation changed purposefully to dreams. "Almost everybody dreamed more than usual last night. Fog does that—and then hearing about Georgie. I'll bet you had a few after all you went through."

"I had one at least," Charlie obliged her. "And it must have been something. Woke me up screaming this morning—well, not out loud."

Paige sat forward. "What happened to you in your dream?"

"Can't remember a thing," Charlie answered and watched relief and something else Charlie couldn't identify reshape the contours of the dream counselor's face.

As Charlie left the Dream Emporium a man in a lumberjack shirt pirouetted through the intricate balances and momentums of t'ai chi on the vacant lot next door. On the next property an old woman in a housedress and head scarf, tied under her chin peasant fashion, bent to her garden ignoring him. But she looked up to give Charlie a sharp scrutiny.

So Georgette Glick wasn't necessarily the beloved and harmless little old lady Charlie had assumed. She was a busybody who got on people's nerves. Maybe the busybody saw something that got her shot.

What could she see in Moot Point in the fog? How could she even see to ride her bike in Moot Point in the fog? How could a seventy-eight year old woman ride a bike at all? Why didn't this seem to surprise anyone but Charlie?

Charlie dawdled along the tiny shopping district on the first terrace, unsure what to do next. She had so much to do back in the office and at home she resented having to misuse an afternoon this way. It was too early for dinner at Rose's. It didn't look like Jack would be available to drive her back to the Hide-a-bye. Perhaps she should start now in case the tide was coming in and would trap her here. But there was nothing to do there either. God, she wished she'd never come to Oregon.

She glanced in the window of the Scandia Art Gallery. There was, of course, a seascape. Charlie stepped inside to find more of the same with a few renditions of the lighthouse for balance. Unlike the greenhouse, the gallery was strangely sterile of odors. The carpeting was thick and dark and deadened any sound but the quiet ticking of an old-fashioned wall clock. The rest of the colors were neutral to heighten the contrast of the paintings.

Only one oil really drew Charlie in. It depicted the skeleton of a ship wrecked long ago sitting on the shore with fog fingers threading through naked ribs. It was titled "Wreck of the *Peter Iredale*," was priced at two thousand dollars, and was signed simply, "Michael."

Charlie had studied it for several seconds before she identified discomfort as the source of her fascination. She imagined she could feel her pulse speed up in her ears. It was as she turned away from it that she saw several of the fog fingers take the shape of human bodies, one hanging over a railing of fog somewhere in the bowels of the ship and another on the floor of a fog cabin no longer there. When she turned back they were gone.

"I see you found them," a woman said, slipping through an interesting slit in the wall formed by panels tilted out to display each painting in its own attention space. "Most people don't. Isn't Michael something? Almost like a hologram the way he does that."

"Found what?"

"The dead sailors." She was a comfortably middle-aged woman with bleached hair, and a magenta jumpsuit to match her fingernails. Charlie counted three gold chains, five gold rings, and an unbelievable number of bracelets. The woman clanked like machinery when she moved. "There are supposed to be five. How many did you pick out?"

"Just two. Is this a real shipwreck?"

"Well, yes, but I don't believe there were any men lost. It just went aground. Michael has to add his little touches, macabre sense of humor. Is there anything in particular you're looking for today?"

"Does he live here in Moot Point?"

"Oh, yes, he has a studio up on the hill." She gestured vaguely behind them and all the bracelets tried to clank down to her elbow.

"He's probably at Georgie's celebration this afternoon," Charlie led.

"Not Michael. He hated her—" the woman followed and then blinked. "Did you know Georgie Glick? Isn't it awful what's happened? Oh, goodness, you're not one of the family?"

"No, I just—why did Michael hate Georgie?"

The bracelets all clanked back to her wrist. "I'm Gladys Bergkvist. I don't believe I caught your name."

"Greene. Charlie Greene. I'm visiting Jack Monroe."

Gladys Bergkvist's pallor paled. "You're the one who murdered Georgie Glick."

"No, haven't you heard? She wasn't run over. I didn't run over her in my car."

"What is this world coming to that you can just be walking around like this, free to do it again to anyone?"

"I didn't do anything to her. Please let me explain." But Charlie backed toward the door as the woman's outrage turned to visible fear.

"Everyone's saying you shot the poor woman."

Chapter 6

Charlie's face stung as if she'd been slapped. She stomped down the street, afraid to look in any of the other shops. If the word was out she was the murderer, no one was going to answer her questions about Georgette Glick. The last time Charlie had felt quite this way she'd just learned the rabbit died. Then she'd stomped through Crossroads Mall in Boulder sure that every stranger there had heard the news before she had, sure that every detached smile she met was a personal leer. She'd trudged for hours considering abortion and suicide and running away to some fantasy world that welcomed imperfect teenagers. Some-place they didn't have to admit they'd screwed up.

A third car had parked in front of Frank's trailer and the porch and patio were crowded with people, plastic glasses in hand. It looked like yet another celebration. Charlie turned abruptly before anyone noticed her and headed up the road toward the lighthouse. If there was no way off the point to the Hide-a-bye, if the tide was up and she couldn't follow the route she'd come, she'd slip back to Jack's store after dark. If he wasn't home she knew where the key was.

Tides were still a mystery to Charlie, despite having lived on both coasts. They were always coming in or going out and the time changed by night and day and by day of the month and by month of the year and by flip of the coin for all she knew. Charlie stayed away from places she was likely to get caught in at high tide. The beach below the lighthouse looked to be just such a place.

Sea wind tore her hair out of the rolled scarf she'd subdued it with and teased her face with blasts of fresh salt air. Sea birds shrieked derision.

"All the desperate people in this world and you're feeling sorry for Charlie Greene. You're not that desperate teenager of fifteen years ago."

"Fuck off."

"The minute they find you have no gun, no motive, and have never had contact with the late Georgie, you'll no longer be a suspect. The worst that can happen is you'll have to come back up here to testify in a murder trial. Probably Brother Dennis's or even Jack's. You don't know when she was shot."

"I know she was still bleeding."

"Then there's Gladys Bergkvist. And the dimpled, luscious Paige."

"If you like drumsticks."

"There's also Rose, at the restaurant."

"What about the obvious suspect—the husband—old randy, handy Frank?"

"And don't forget Sheriff Wes. At least we know he has a gun to shoot someone with. Or this Michael who hated Georgie. Or someone we haven't met. Which is almost everyone in Moot Point."

"It could have been anyone within shooting distance of Moot Point last night. Someone on the highway."

"Someone with a motive and a secret and a gun."

Charlie realized she'd missed the path down to the beach when she rounded a curve in the road and came out into the full brunt of the wind. The road continued on up to the lighthouse above her and she could look over at the tops of the massive rocks off the point. She gave up on the scarf and held it in her hand, let it snap in the wind that slapped her hair across her face. This might be June and the sun might be out but it was cold here. A heartier soul would have called it brisk. She could see nesting birds on the rock rookeries and occasional battles when a nest seemed threatened. Had Georgette Glick threatened something that basic to someone in the village?

Someone's home, business, livelihood, relationship? Surely not someone's life.

Charlie wanted to look over the cliff edge to see if the tide threatened her pathway to the Hide-a-bye but knew she could handle high places only if she didn't look down.

Instead of walking back to the path to find out she started up the road to the lighthouse. The path ended in a paved parking lot with plenty of room for visitors who liked lighthouses. But they still had to climb what looked like a hundred and fifty stairs to get to the lighthouse itself. A big rusting Ford, a small red Ferrari, and a pickup were parked in the lot.

Though there was no fog today the light at the top of the tower still rotated and the buoy out at sea still warned ships off the rocky shoreline. Charlie had been hearing that sound for so long she'd forgotten to listen for it.

A lady in a windbreaker and stretch jeans stepped out of the old Ford and waved at Charlie. "Have you come to see the birds? Did you park along the road?"

"I walked up from the village."

She smiled and all her back teeth appeared to be made of gold. "I should have too, I know. Such a waste of fuel. But there's no shelter from the wind here and after a while it forces the chill right into your bone marrow. You won't welcome that either when you get to be my age."

"I don't welcome it now." Charlie hunched her shoulders in her light jacket.

"Would you like a cup of hot coffee? I have a thermos in the car and we can get out of the wind." She'd let her hair mature to a lovely gray with silver highlights. It would have settled into short smooth waves if not for the wind. "We can see the birds through the windshield and I can explain them to you in comfort." She turned to the car and then turned back before taking a second step and said, "Oh, I'm sorry. I'm Clara Peterson. I live in Moot Point."

Charlie had no idea why this woman wanted to explain birds to her, but it was a chance to talk with another citizen of the village before her own identity was discovered. The bird lady soon had her ensconced in the passenger seat with a paper cup of coffee, a pair of binoculars, and a leaflet describing tufted puffins, common murres, storm petrels, cormorants, and sea gulls.

"Are you with the Audubon Society?"

"Oh no, I'm just with the Senior Volunteer Corps. We take turns explaining things to visitors. We help the Forest Service and the state parks people with whatever natural wonders are near our homes. It's something to do and fun to meet people. Although it seems all too often to rain on my shift and make the visitors leave and the birds hard to see."

"All the more reason to bring your car."

"I'm so glad you understand. I thought you might be one of those young fitness people opposed to automobiles and packaged foods and homemade jam and refined sugars and every good thing that makes getting older at all comfortable. Oh, look, there on the rock closest to us, just to the right of that thumb-like outcrop near the end away from us and down about three feet? All the movement and color there? It's a nest of puffins the gulls have been after and the parents are afraid to leave, even though all the eggs I can see have hatched."

Charlie obediently wedged her cup between her legs and raised the binoculars. She pretended to find the puffins and their endangered nest but managed to adjust the focus in time to catch the lesson in cormorants and their diving and fishing skills and the common murres who were supposed to look like penguins.

"My husband wanted to retire near the ocean." Clara Peterson's husband had died two years later and she stayed on for the last fifteen alone. "Had I known I wouldn't have left Milwaukee and near and dear friends. But Ralph loved oceans and mountains and there's both here in very close proximity. Still, I've always enjoyed birds. I've made a life for myself. Moving home would be so expensive by now and most everyone's passed away."

"I heard a woman passed away in some mysterious way last night."

"A neighbor of mine." Clara sat silent staring out the windshield but not at birds. "I still can't believe it. One of the reasons I'm delighted my shift is sunny and I have an excuse to come up here." She didn't look delighted. She looked half sick.

"I thought I heard someone say she was riding a bicycle at seventy-eight? In the fog? At night?" Charlie took another slug of coffee and raised the binoculars again. "Obviously I heard wrong."

"Georgie was an amazing woman. So is Frank for that matter. That's her husband. She scorned my driving up here, Georgie, and my using sugar in my baking. She wouldn't let Frank eat meat or come to the senior citizen dinners at the community center. So he would walk into Chinook, mind you at his age, along the beach, and eat hot beef sandwiches with mashed potatoes and gravy and wash them down with chocolate malteds. Sometimes, when she was at a group meditation or whatever, he'd sneak over to my place for a piece of pie."

"Are you telling me that old a woman could still ride a bicycle because she didn't eat meat or sugar and that her husband could walk clear to Chinook because of that?"

"Oh, no, they obviously must have extraordinary health to begin with. But she used medicinal herbs and positive thinking and made her husband do it too. They never doctored that I know of, even when the county nurse would come around and check blood pressure, cholesterol, vision, and hearing free for seniors. They even took their cat to this holistic veterinarian we have in Moot Point. Georgie said it was all a different way of living and thinking and perceiving."

"Well, the results were certainly impressive. Did she often ride her bike at night?"

The bird lady stared owllike through the magnification of thick trifocals. "That is odd, isn't it? I don't remember that it even had a light on it. But then I've thought recently she's been getting a little strange. Old people often do, you know."

Charlie could see suspicion forming in three different sizes behind the trifocals so she changed the subject. "That artist, Michael, who has so many paintings at the Scandia down in the village, has he done any of the rookeries or the birds, do you know?"

Clara's dawning suspicion switched to disapproval in a blink and a distinct straightening of the spine. "I wouldn't know. His 'art' is far too expensive for me to bother with. He's up at the lighthouse right now. You can ask him." The lighthouse, she explained, her manner less friendly, was manned by the National Guard and visitors were rarely allowed inside. But the view was *stunning*.

Charlie thanked her and headed for the wooden stairs, knowing she should be heading for the Hide-a-bye instead. Stunning views, she'd found, often meant yawning areas of nothing where next you step. Besides, she'd have to come down them again. A dangerous thing if you're afraid to watch your feet.

Charlie stopped at the top of the stairs to catch her breath and tried not to stare. Michael was what was stunning. Michael brought to mind a combination of Heathcliff and Nureyev, and his bored glance carried the wallop of Mitch Hilsten, the superstar. He sat on a folding canvas stool, a sketch pad crimped between his knees, a camera hanging by a strap down his chest, a palette and brush in hand. His easel was hammered into the soil, the canvas lashed to it with an intricate arrangement of wires that kept it from being blown off the point.

Dark, jagged-cut, shoulder-length hair whipped out behind him as did a white scarf tied about his neck above a Navy pea jacket. He was beautiful and looked completely mad.

Charlie stepped quickly out of his line of vision.

"Glance at my work, madam, and you are dead," he said between his teeth. He sounded like Peter O'Toole but more arty than British.

"I was just looking for a pathway down the north side of the headland to get to the Hide-a-bye. Is there one?"

"Behind the lighthouse and assorted buildings and then behind the latrines, you will find a macadam pathway leading down off this precipice, across a small meadow, and to your destination. Please do make haste so that you will not be late."

Charlie copped a glance at the canvas and took off for the lighthouse. This was obviously not the time to ask him why he hated Georgette Glick, but she could certainly see how she might have come to hate him.

The lighthouse was solid and uninformative, but a one-story building nestled up against it was half window on three sides. A woman in a uniform and a ponytail dangling from under a baseball cap, worn backwards, talked into a microphone hanging from the ceiling and chewed gum at the same time. There were several sheds behind the lighthouse with the same whitewash and red roofs and then two Porta Potties. Next to them a black-topped trail had been cut between bushes.

The path was certainly preferable to a flight of stairs. But as Charlie followed it, it grew darker, more claustrophobic. The bushes wanted to grow together across the path. They'd been sliced off smooth on either side but rebellious twig fingers poked through a restraining fence of wire mesh and caught at her hair, prodded her shoulders as if to get her attention. Charlie was highly aware of unknown bird calls and rustlings in the impenetrable underbrush to either side.

Chapter 7

Charlie's breath came in labored gasps as she climbed the path up from the beach to the Hide-a-bye. She'd been alone for what seemed hours with the sounds of Mother Nature menacing her every step. She'd seen not one other soul since the lighthouse and had ended up walking so fast she was soon running in a body highly unaccustomed to such things.

She was half ashamed for letting herself get so spooked, but her kidneys were in full agony because of the tea and coffee she'd consumed while being nosy. So when she saw the lights in the windows of her cabin and the official county Bronco parked at the door behind, she stormed inside. "Just what the hell do you think you're doing?"

Which was a stupid question. The sheriff obviously was sitting at her table stuffing his face again and watching the tube at the same time. Before he could answer her, she raced back to the john.

"And where the hell have you been?" he countered when she returned. "You knew you were supposed to stay put."

"How did you get in here?"

"Through the door. You left it unlocked."

"I did not."

He lifted her room key, unmistakable on the end of its plastic sea urchin, and waved it at her. "There's been murder done around here and you don't even lock your door. Unless you're the murderer, that's pretty stupid."

"You know perfectly well I'm not the murderer."

He poured Oregon cabernet into a thick wine glass, Hide-a-bye scrolled in white letters across it, and handed it to her, his brow heavy with menace. "So what have you been up to?"

She took a sip and glared back at him. This guy was getting to her. "This wine's sour."

"Oregon wine has structure." His glance kept shifting back and forth from her face to the television screen behind her. "So what have you been up to? Or have I already asked that?"

"I tended the Earth Spirit for Jack while he went to the celebration for Georgette."

"Where? What's to celebrate?"

"I don't know where. But Georgette is to be congratulated because she has now entered the highest consciousness possible."

"She'd dead."

"Right." The second sip wasn't so sour. The third began to feel good. "Then I had tea and sympathy with Paige Magill, the greenhouse dream counselor. She left the celebration early."

"*. . . the Soviet foreign minister said today while on a tour of day-care centers.*"

"What's a dream counselor do?"

"Beats me. You're the sheriff, you find out. Then I sat still for a full lecture on sea birds off the point from the bird lady, you know—puffins and murres and cormorants. Then I met Michael-Nureyev-Heathcliff-Hilsten, probably the rudest artist in the world. He does the seascapes in the Scandia. Oh, I forgot, in between the bird lady and the tea and sympathy I met Gladys Bergkvist at the Scandia Art Gallery."

"Just out visiting, or doing a little detecting on the side? I don't need anymore screwups on this case. My own are enough."

"Why would I be out detecting, Sheriff? Why not just sit around and wait for somebody to drop the answers in my lap, give me back my car, and let me go home? Wait maybe three, four years? I have nothing better to do. Except a daughter, a job, a mortgage, car payments, assorted bills, and if I'm not careful— a cat. Your problem is, you watch too much television."

"My second wife reads nothing but mysteries, not even newspapers. Won't read anything where the woman doesn't solve the crime on her own and show up the law. What comes from having been married to a cop."

"The Dow Jones was down again today but trading on the world markets remained steady."

"What do women cops read?" Charlie asked him.

"Famed film star, Mitch Hilsten, broke ground for a hospital for sea and shore birds and mammals in Anchorage today. He says the new two-million dollar installation will help save the lives of hundreds of thousands of creatures caught in the deadly mire of oil spills in one of the last inhabited pristine areas left on earth."

"I do not understand what you women see in that guy," the sheriff said when Charlie turned back from the television screen that had finally caught her attention. "He can't even be six foot."

"So what have *you* been up to?" she asked.

"Talked to some of the same people you did. But nobody mentioned a bird lady or a Michael Heathcliff."

"Clara Peterson. She lives next to the Glicks, explains sea birds to tourists for some senior volunteer organization. Did you ask Frank why his wife was out riding her bike in the fog at night? His seventy-eight-year-old wife? Clara didn't think the bike even had a headlight."

Sheriff Bennett took a small notebook from his shirt pocket and flipped through a few pages. "Clara Peterson, sixty-eight, widow. Lives in the house just behind the Glicks'. Wasn't home when I called. What else did you find out about her?"

"She used to slip desserts to Frank when Georgette was away.

Georgette wouldn't let him have refined sugar or meat. Bird lady Clara thinks Frank walked the beach clear to Chinook to eat hot beef sandwiches with mashed potatoes and gravy. Jack thinks he did it to ogle sweet young things. Clara doesn't like Michael. His pictures are strange. He's definitely a Grape-Nut. Georgette hated him."

"Wait a minute." His full attention returned to her from the sports news. "Who told you this?"

"Gladys from the Scandia. But she didn't tell me why. But Paige said that Georgie was a busybody and got on some people's nerves. Maybe Michael's. Maybe Paige's."

"Hold it right there." He came around to her side of the table and switched off the TV. Standing behind her chair, he rocked on his feet so hard the floor shook. "Paige Magill didn't tell me that about Mrs. Glick. And Gladys Bergkvist didn't even mention this Michael. Not to me."

"Nobody's going to offer up information to you, you're the law. You're the sheriff investigating a murder in their tiny village. They're confused and scared. Don't know what they might say that could incriminate them even if they're innocent."

"I've known most of them for years. Most of them voted for me."

"That was before a little old lady was shot to death practically in their front yards. Get real."

"You're talking to me. And you're a stranger."

"Did you wine them and dine them and console them? You admit you think they're all Grape-Nuts." Why was he playing dumb with her?

"I have to feed you, you don't have a car. Now I want to hear everything you learned today, lady. I don't want you withholding one stray thought. You listening to me?"

Charlie gave him a second-by-second re-creation of her afternoon leaving out no detail and making it as boring as possible. She even included the wonderful messages on the T-shirts Jack offered for sale at the Earth Spirit.

The sheriff had taken the chair beside her and was showing

signs of drowsiness when she, lifting the wine bottle they'd emp-tied between them, wrapped up her discourse with, "What's all the gunk left on the bottom of the bottle? Wait, I know, don't tell me, that's the—"

"Structure. See, our vineyards are young, our vintners still learning the soil and climate. But more and more often now you pick up a bottle of the local stuff and it blows you aaa-way."

He leaned too close and Charlie drew back. "How many wives have you gone through, Wes?"

"Three too many. And three divorces. And never again do I get into that."

"Good plan. Just cooking for you would be an experience."

He grunted. "Would you believe my last wife wouldn't even cook? Big-deal career woman."

"I can believe. How many kids, three?"

"How'd you know? One by the first, two by the second. But no more. Cops shouldn't marry."

He was leaning again. When this man leaned it was like Mount St. Helens about to tip over. Charlie slid out the other side of her chair. "How did Frank explain his wife's riding her bike at night?"

"They had a fight."

"Your kids live with their mothers?"

"I pay support for two of them. Oldest, I can't deal with."

"Well, I deal with and support one. If you'll excuse me," Charlie grabbed the last of the cherries and headed for the telephone.

"What's going on down there? I told Grandma you'd better have that cat in the shelter by now." Charlie could hear a rattling sound in the background. "Is that the cat or Doug?"

"Oh, Mom, you should see him. He's cracking me up. He's sticking his cold wet little nose into my neck." She squealed and the rattle deepened. That was the cat.

"Tell her you and the cat have already bonded." That was definitely Doug.

"Will you get that kid out of the house, Libby? It's a school night. Where's Edwina?"

"She's over at Maggie's. She didn't want to be here when you called. In case you're in jail, I suppose. Have they arrested you?"

"Not yet."

"I wish I'd taken Tuxedo's picture before and after. Now he's silky and fluffy and jumps around and his little pink mouth smiles." Libby had found the creature in the MacDonald's parking lot on the way to a friend's house and rushed him home to be nursed by a doting grandmother. "He was so bedraggled and forlorn. He's done nothing but eat since I brought him home."

Charlie hadn't known her daughter knew words like forlorn. She made an effort to be reasonable. "He could belong to somebody, honey. Cats do wander."

"This is a kitten, Mother, not a cat big enough to wander. He's obviously abandoned. But we've put 'found' signs around the neighborhood and notified the animal shelter."

"That's not you I hear talking. Somebody's feeding you lines. Is it Doug or Edwina? Is it Maggie? If she's there I want to talk to her."

Libby Greene delivered a quick, sharp exit line and broke the connection. Her mother sat staring at the receiver as if it could talk on its own.

The mammoth hand of the law lifted it from hers and replaced it. The hand's owner sounded genuinely concerned. "You choking on a cherry pit, Charlie? You look awful."

"My daughter just told me to fuck off."

"It's just a word, not a bullet. You'll live. Can't be the first time you heard her use it."

"Never on me, not that way. It sounds so different coming from your own daughter." Charlie decided to give up swearing. "I don't want her to be like me."

"You're not so bad. No great detective, but quite a woman, and it sounds to me like a great mother."

"I don't want my daughter to be a mother at sixteen." And Charlie lost it right there. No one was more surprised than she was. She pushed away from the consoling arms of the law and made another dash for the bathroom, this time for a tissue.

"I don't figure you," the sheriff of Moot County said when she returned. "You see a dead woman pulled from under your car, face suspicion of murder, and then break up over a smart-mouth teenager on the telephone." He had a curious way of grinning, the sheriff. The humor was all in his eyes and his mouth stayed closed with one corner turning down in a wryly self-deprecating manner that would have passed for a smirk on anyone else.

His smile suggested that his size was no big deal, that he was in reality no threat, just a good-natured guy. It tempted you to join in. Charlie was wiping dumb tears off her face and could feel the corners of her mouth tilting upward when his beeper went off, startling them both.

"Mind if I use your phone?"

"Might as well, made yourself at home every other way."

But he was already talking, "This is Bennett. Yeah? Where? On my way." He headed for the door. "They've found the gun. See you in the morning and you stay put, hear?"

"Sheriff, you can't leave me. The tide's up, I haven't got a car, and I haven't had dinner."

"Bought you all kinds of food today in Chinook."

"And you just ate it."

He came back down the hall and stared from her to the table, opened the refrigerator door, slammed it, and stood indecisively as if searching for a retort that just wasn't there. "Anybody ever tell you you're a pain in the brisket?"

Chapter 8

Charlie sat in the Moot County Bronco and watched Wes Bennett lumber about in front of the headlights. She'd been ordered to "stay put" again. Lights, flashing on the tops of the Bronco and the squad car parked a length or two ahead, bounced off the thick forest on either side of the road like a frenzied invasion of aliens.

Charlie rolled the window down and the night filled with the sounds of sea wind and tree creaks. And of too many men standing around snorting and talk-growling. A woman deputy joined the melee and added a nervous giggle.

They were on the road that swung down off Highway 101 to the village of Moot Point. Charlie could see the lights of the last retirement trailer in front of the squad car ahead of her. A section of the ditch and roadside had been cordoned off and was getting a good flashlight search. The air coming in the window was chilly and smelled a lot like Paige Magill's greenhouse.

Charlie was about to roll the window back up when a man marched into the various circles of light and demanded to know who was in charge. The uniforms present pointed at Wes as if cued. The civilian, nearly bald and dressed for success, had the nose and general shape of Frank Glick. He expressed his ire with jerky arm motions and volume rather than explicit language but his aim was clear. He informed everyone that he had some clout with the government in this state and was so appalled that an innocent old woman could come to such a mean end in Oregon, he had a mind to use his influence in Salem to see that pressure was applied where appropriate and justice speeded up. And where "for Christ's sake" was the woman who had run over his poor old mother? This man was of an age to be a grandfather himself.

"Your mother was not run over, Mr. Glick, she was shot. We are just now inspecting a weapon thrown in the ditch here that could be the murder weapon." Wes was called away by an excited official and Georgette's son began to pace.

He was acting like a pompous ass, but Charlie felt for the son whose mother had been murdered. At Georgette's age her offspring must have been all too aware of the statistics on life span, but they couldn't have been prepared for a bullet.

When Wes climbed back up to the road the man was at him again. "Well, Sheriff, where is this woman who did not run over my mother but who shot her then? I understood you had her in custody. I've already been to the county jail in Chinook and they claim she isn't there."

Wes was rocking on his feet again. "As of this moment, we do not know the gender of the person who pulled the trigger, Mr. Glick. Your mother was shot. Her bicycle may have been run over—"

"All right then," the male Glick said dangerously, "where is the woman who ran over my mother's bicycle?"

"As of this moment," Wes said, "we don't know who ran over the bicycle either, only where it was found. Now if you'll excuse me, I have an investigation to conduct."

"You will definitely hear more from me soon, Sheriff, and from Salem." Georgie's son pushed his way through milling cops and stalked off toward his parents' home and presumably the telephone lines to the state capital.

The sheriff of Moot County crawled in beside Charlie and gave her hand a fatherly bear squeeze. "Am I glad to see you sitting here behaving yourself. I was going through internal spasms out there worrying you'd do something stupid."

"Excuse me?"

"In that stuff my second wife reads you would have jumped out of here all holy-like to explain to Glick the second that you were the one under whose vehicle the dead woman was found and then go into tantrums about being innocent. And then he would have gone off like a regular guy, ignoring your explanations and then you'd have run off to solve the case while I was looking the other way doing something dumb."

"Did she tell you the plot lines? Did wife number two read her books aloud to you? How do you know all this? Did you read her books too, Wes?"

"That's not the point, Charlie." They tore off around the people and the squad car to careen to a halt in front of the first retirement trailer in sight. They could have almost walked it as fast. "But since I had to bring you along, I want you to know how pleased I am you are a sensible girl . . . woman . . . person."

"Human being?"

"That too." He jumped down to the road and then leaned back through the open door. "Listen, I got to run in here, take care of a few things. Then you get dinner, I promise."

Charlie was weighing the pros and cons of believing what he told her, what she would have been thinking if she were in his shoes and had to manipulate everyone properly to get the job done—when a shadowy face appeared in her window wearing Paige Magill's smile and dimples.

"Charlie, are you and the sheriff dating already? You work fast. He's the most eligible bachelor in the county."

"He told me he's been married and divorced three times."

"That's what makes him so eligible. Women figure he's hopelessly addicted." She glanced over her shoulder at the trailer. "Has he taken you to his house yet?"

"He has to take me out to dinner because I'm stranded with-out my car until it's been investigated enough." Charlie dis-obeyed orders and climbed down to join Paige. "Who lives here?"

"Mary and Norma. They found the gun. Jack's been asking for you. He tried to call you at the Hide-a-bye."

"What are you doing here?"

"I was on my way to see Jack when I saw all the lights up the road. Mary and Norma were standing out here watching the commotion and then Georgie's oldest went thundering past. When the sheriff's car started toward us the ladies headed for their door and I dove for the shadows. Wes Bennett is a sweet old teddy bear and we all love him, but he's so into the cop thing—you know. Want to come to Jack's with me? He's really anxious to talk to you for some reason."

"I don't want to meet up with Georgie's son. He thinks I killed his mother. He went on a rampage up there, threatened the sheriff."

"I'll scout ahead, see if there's anyone outside. He might not even know what you look like."

Because she didn't want to miss dinner, Charlie tore off the bottom of a blank piece of paper on a clipboard hanging from the dash and used the pen attached to it by plastic coil to tell Wes where to find her. He'd be furious of course. Charlie figured he'd earned it.

"Tell me about Mary and Norma," she told Paige as they set off. She was willing to bet they were the two women trying to comfort Frank last night.

"Mary Hitch and Norma Nelson, widowed sisters living to-gether. They've been here for a long time, originally from Port-land and Eugene. I don't know which, where."

"Do they hate Michael too?"

"Shhhh, wait here." Paige scuttled ahead to check out the Glick house.

Charlie noticed a drawn curtain pushed aside an inch or two on Clara Peterson the bird lady's picture window, the pulsating color of a television screen flickering in part of the crack. A woman living alone would be anxious at night where a murder had taken place the night before. Anyone standing alone outside in the dark should be too.

Paige reappeared suddenly to pull on Charlie's sleeve. "Way's clear, Holmes. Follow me."

"Holmes?"

"Well, you ask more questions than the sheriff, Sherlock."

"Georgie was found under my car. Why is it everybody expects me to sit around and twiddle my thumbs at the Hide-a-bye like a good girl? Do Mary and Norma hate Michael, the painter, like Clara Peterson does?"

"Charlie, you're barking up the wrong alley. Everybody hates Michael. He's the ultimate jerk."

There was something about Paige Magill that Charlie's instincts didn't trust—but it wasn't her ability to judge people. The door to the Earth Spirit was locked, the windows darkened.

"Maybe he's not home. Maybe he's asleep," Charlie offered.

"Or on an OOBE. With all the wine he'd had at Georgie's celebration that could be fatal, Charlie. I'm scared."

"You saw him after he left the celebration? Where was this celebration held? And what's an OOBE?"

Paige scurried back to the hidey-hole under the stair. "It was up at the institute. Jack staggered into my house, demanding to use my phone to call his agent—big-deal drunk author like—and he became truly uncentered when you didn't answer. You realize half the people in this town write, but old Jack's got an agent. Oh, shit, the key's gone. Now I'm really worried."

"Isn't there a back door?"

"Good thinking." Paige scuttled off into the shadows and Charlie raced after her.

The back door was unlocked and led directly into the bathroom. The light was on here. The warning buoy burped an "ooowaaaa" just as Charlie closed the door behind her and checked out the tub/shower for her author.

"Ohhh, Jack!" Paige said from Jack's living quarters, sounding more dire than the buoy.

Charlie joined her to find the budding author spread-eagled on his paltry single mattress, his face lit from the bathroom, mouth gaping like he was trying to remind Charlie of the woman under the Toyota.

"Should we call nine one one?"

"No, and keep your voice to a whisper or you could kill him. Charlie, I'm almost certain he's on an OOBE."

"He looks dead, I'll run for the sheriff."

"No," Paige grabbed her wrist with surprising strength and forced her hand to just brush Jack's forehead.

"He's warm, almost hot."

"In the condition he was in tonight, this is the sickest thing he could have done."

"Paige, we have to do something—cover him up, call a doctor." Charlie bent to lift one arm hanging off the side of the bed, but the girl stopped her.

"Please, if we move him it might scare him and he could panic and get lost." She crossed her ankles, bent her knees outward, and lowered herself smoothly to the floor pulling Charlie down beside her.

"If we're just going to let him sleep it off, why can't we cover him up?" Charlie's client had removed his shoes but was otherwise fully clothed. Still, it seemed wrong to leave him on top of the covers like that.

"He's not here, Charlie. Just his body is. He's left it for a little while. And he doesn't know how to do this very well. He says it's really scary but he can't stop experimenting with it. The worst part is being afraid he can't get back or that something's happened to his body while he's away."

"How do you know he's not dead drunk or drugged?"

"Because he's so still. You even thought he was dead, period. The real Jack isn't in there. His body's waiting for him to come back."

"Paige, you either explain all this fast or I'm going to pull him off the bed, run out on the porch and scream for Wes Bennett, and then—"

"An OOBE is an out-of-body experience. The others don't

believe Jack can do it. But I know he can. And when he's gone he can still feel some things—like he senses his arm has gone to sleep or his body's getting cold. And he rushes back, but he can get disoriented and confused and panic. Then he has trouble getting back. He's never experimented with an OOBE when he's been full of wine before, that I know of. I don't know what effect it'll have, but it can't be good."

"Grape-Nuts."

"What?"

Charlie saw with relief that Jack's chest was moving ever so slightly but regularly. "You say the others don't believe he can do this OOBE thing but you know he can. How?"

"Well, one day Jack said he'd prove it with a controlled experiment. So Brother Dennis and I had a late dinner in my kitchen and talked about some dreams he was having and Jack came down here, got in bed, and as he was falling asleep he left his body and came up to my kitchen."

"What did he look like without his body?"

"We didn't see him."

"Then how do you know he was there?"

"Because he called afterwards and told us almost everything we'd talked about. Brother Dennis said Jack was listening at the window outside in the dark. But he couldn't have been because Rose was the control part of the experiment and she stayed out in the store the whole time and peeked in Jack's room every few minutes. And she says he did not leave the Earth Spirit. But Brother Dennis says it was either a trick or someone's lying."

Charlie was inclined to agree with Brother Dennis. "Rose at the restaurant? Is she in all this New Age whatever-it-is too?"

"She's flirting with it. She realizes she needs centering. And also she's naturally psychic and doesn't know how to deal with that."

Jack Monroe's body moaned, twitched. Charlie looked away from Paige's plump sincere face to find him staring at her. "Jesus, Charlie, where've you been? I was looking all over for you."

Chapter 9

Charlie's dinner that night was like a trip into the past. She'd eaten so much Kentucky Fried while growing up that she hadn't touched it since. Edwina hated cooking and cleaning up afterward and the Colonel was made to order.

But the greasy, salty, aromatic, spicy, tangy combination of original recipe, coleslaw, potatoes, gravy, and fluffy biscuit with yellow petroleum product to dribble across it was irresistible this late at night. She and the sheriff dined at the first scenic overlook they came to on Highway 101 on their way back from Chinook's fast-food strip.

Sea and sky were blue-black now except for where the moon glittered on ridges of rolling foam. The couple in the car next to them disappeared from view.

They ate in silence because Wes refused to discuss what Mary and Norma had said to him and was predictably pissed that she had not waited docilely in the Bronco for his return. Charlie yearned to share the funny story of Jack's OOBE, but the sheriff's attitude now and his sexist remarks earlier made that impossible.

Jack had even claimed that when he was out of his body he had visited her cabin at the Hide-a-bye and, finding her gone, had rearranged some of her things to prove he'd been there. Charlie wondered how he could move things without a body that had hands on it, but in the interest of client relations she kept quiet.

Wes Bennett had come pounding at the door of the Earth Spirit before Charlie could discover what Jack Monroe was so anxious to discuss with her that he'd committed "OOBE" to do it. First thing in the morning she'd call the office and then trot along the beach to the village and talk to Jack.

Sheriff Wes Bennett finished off the last drumstick, dropped the bone into the bag, and tore open the little square packet of alcohol-soaked paper washcloth. He cleared his throat of grease and gravel.

"I can't—" he paused to wipe each finger carefully and to swivel the inside of his lips across his teeth repeatedly and then to clear his throat some more, "I can't give you your car back now, like I'd planned to—"

"You didn't tell me you'd planned any such thing."

"—now that we have a weapon to trace. And now that I know I can't trust you to cooperate with the sheriff's office on this investigation. There will be a deputy outside your cabin in the morning to guarantee you stay there. Understood?" When she didn't answer he added, "Charlie, I've done everything I can for you, more than I should considering the questionable position you are in. And I know there are things you know that you're not telling me. Why I do not know. But I do know my patience is at an end." The most eligible bachelor in Moot County backed the four wheel out of the paved overlook with such drama the couple next to them sat up again to watch.

It might have been because of the heavy hit of the dinner or because of the sheriff's latest power play but Charlie felt like she had a lead basketball in the pit of her midsection by the time she crawled into bed her second night at the Hide-a-bye.

She resigned herself to a sleepless night after an exhausting day and was about to get up and get some aspirin when it seemed like too much effort to disturb the basketball.

That tingly feeling began to overtake her as it sometimes did when she was about to fall asleep so she decided to lie still and concentrate on not thinking, on just relaxing and breathing. It was rather pleasant the way those tingles could just engulf the body like tiny bubbles in the blood, zipping around everywhere.

Of course there was another sensation that often accompanied this one. A less pleasant sensation which made her feel as if she were soaring helplessly, unable to stop or to order her direction. She remembered telling friends of this once at a college party and discovered it was not at all an uncommon dream. Which was a comforting thought that settled her more comfortably with the tingles now.

Charlie was idly wondering if this could be what Jack Monroe experienced when he thought he was having an OOBE when something hard came up out of the bed and struck her shoulder. She tried to sit up but, in her panic, couldn't seem to find the proper leverage. Rolling over quickly onto her side Charlie pushed herself up with the other arm.

That's when she realized there was something wrong with the window. It was too low on the wall. She could see amazingly well in the darkness but it took her a moment to figure out that she was looking up at the top of the lamp shade on the unlit lamp on the bedside table. And then at the top surface of her bed. It must have been five feet above her. There was even someone in it, completely defying gravity. Someone with hair like hers . . .

The hard thing banging on her shoulder was the ceiling.

Charlie was bobbing upside down near the ceiling.

"Oh, no, I'm not." She knew a grease-induced nightmare when she saw it. "I'm waking up right now!"

She dropped with a terrifying rush and came to a stop nose to nose with the dark form in the bed. It was Charlie all right.

Knowing this was a dream kept panic at bay but it hovered as close as she did. Charlie rolled over to face the ceiling, high above her now, and that's all it took. She was together again. Probably more than anything because this time she was awake for real.

She lay there a long while, alternately hot and chilled in reaction to her dream, before feeling herself begin to slide into a more natural sleep. Charlie was certain now that this was what Jack Monroe was actually doing when he thought he was OOBEing. Should she tell him? He and Paige clearly believed it was something else and their minds would probably be closed to any rational explanation. Still . . .

It wasn't until she'd showered and dressed the next morning that Charlie thought to check the cabin for things Jack thought his bodiless person could have rearranged for her. She wasn't surprised to find nothing misplaced.

Nor did she find any sign of a deputy outside the cabin to keep her there. That could be because it was too early or because the threat had merely been a bluff on the part of a sheriff who specialized in them. But she started off for Moot Point quickly just in case. She'd call the office later.

The tide this morning was higher than when she'd passed this way yesterday, but it was passable if she hugged the cliff and no rogue wave came along to grab her. She still preferred it to the longer route through the bushes to the lighthouse.

Charlie had just reached the safety of the path edging up the cliff from the beach when Frank Glick started his descent from the curve above her. It was an informal footpath with little room for passing and she was too surprised to move anyway. She'd caught him by surprise as well. When he looked up from the careful placement of his feet he nearly lost his balance at the sight of her and had to grab for weeds on the bank next to him to steady himself.

"So they're still lettin' you run around loose, are they? No wonder Randolph couldn't find you in jail. Or did you break out? You read about that all the time in the papers."

"How often?" She backed up to let him pass.

"How often what?" He went right on by and Charlie could see through the thin beard why he wore one. He had almost no chin.

She changed her course to follow him. "How often do you read of women breaking out of jail? Or committing murder for that matter?"

"Happens all the time. You women are getting so independent you think just being female will get you out of anything. Women do every terrible thing on earth men do."

"But what are the odds, Mr. Glick? Considering we outnumber men, what are the odds that any crime is committed by a woman?"

"Well, now, all abortions are, aren't they?" He jogged to the right and into the shadow of the bank under the Hide-a-bye. "Half the kids are staying in cabins up there and if they see me they'll come down and insist on trying to coddle me and then they'll start weeping again. Drive a guy nuts. Appreciate them all better over the telephone."

Charlie trotted along beside him. If he felt like chatting she felt like listening. "Don't you want to weep too? Don't you miss her?"

"Course I miss her. After all these years ain't nobody else going to know how I like my Cream of Wheat cooked for breakfast, you can be darned sure. She even picked out my shirts and my underwear at the store. When she mended something, it fell apart before the mending did. Think I want to go out and buy toilet paper and write checks for the bills and all? Hell, I been retired practically longer than I worked. My wife took care of things I wasn't about to. Now who's going to do all that? And who'd of thought she'd be stupid enough to get herself shot so's I'd be in this predicament, anyhow? No understanding women."

"If you think I shot your wife, why aren't you afraid to be walking the beach with me?"

"I'm no crazy old woman on a bicycle you can just go around shooting because you feel like it."

"Frank, did Georgette's bike have lights for night riding?"

"Hell, no, had enough fancy junk on it anyway because fancy

Brother Dennis said she'd better have it. That long-haired queer wasted more of my retirement money than the government. Him and that Jack Monroe with all those stupid books and tapes and rocks." They skirted the next headland and he moved closer to the water.

"What did you argue about night before last when she went out to ride her bike?"

"I'd been saving up, on the sly like, these articles about how watching sports on television is good for a man's health and how decaffeinated coffee pumps up his cholesterol count and how margarine is more dangerous than real butter because it's made of stuff they don't have to tell you about on the package and how real sugar is natural too and that red meat is good for the prostate." He laughed deep and rich and all his shaggy eyebrows lifted into little tents over his eyes. He tapped her shoulder conspiratorially. "Been saving them for I don't know how long. Then I springs them on her all at once. You'd of thought I hit her. Those old lips got tighter and that old back straighter than a flagpole. I had her then."

Yeah, but you don't have her now. "So she just got mad and left? Jumped on her bike? In the fog? In the dark? With no lights?"

"She got mad and left. That's all I know. It got later and later and finally I put on my slicker and went looking for her. She's old, you know, never know what an old woman will do. They're not rational anymore. Found her and her bicycle dead under your car." He stopped to stare down at Charlie and the sea breeze blew his wispy hairs all in the same direction. "Ain't fair. I don't even know what size undershorts I wear."

They walked on in companionable silence, his pace impressive, Charlie forgetting to worry about whether he was the murderer—spouses often were but generally not at this age—or even that he would make a grab for her body. "Do you think you should walk clear to Chinook this morning, Mr. Glick? Your family will worry."

"Man can't get any peace back there. Just because I'm old don't mean I enjoy being treated like a kid."

If this section was any indication, the Oregon Coast was one clean, deserted, long, beautiful beach after another separated by rocks and headlands with passable footpaths. Even the birds gleaning the wet sand or sunning on the dry appeared little bothered at their approach. The surf had left few footprints from yesterday in its wake, giving the illusion of treading virgin sands. The experience was unreal but Charlie still wasn't ready for the wreck of the *Peter Iredale* when they suddenly came upon it.

She'd been lost in thought somewhere, seeing it from a distance but not really taking it in and then she was standing next to it, stopped in her tracks while Georgette's husband continued on without her. The *Peter Iredale* was not on the rocks but embedded in the sand, broken in two, and upright. It was rusted metal bones with the wooden flesh vanished to holes. Even most of the bones were gone, but what was left was so out of place on the pristine beach it was haunting.

There was no fog this morning. Charlie saw no sailors in the wreckage as she had in Mad Michael's painting. But Charlie Greene turned on her heel, letting a seventy-nine-year-old bereaved widower walk off alone, and ran back the way she'd come. For the first time in her life Charlie wondered if she was in need of a dream counselor.

By the time she arrived at the village some of her reason had been restored and, rather than rush up to Paige's greenhouse so early, she stopped at Rose's for a bagel and a think.

Sheriff Bennett and Randolph Glick arrived just as her cup was being refilled. They sat on either side of the table next to hers and glared at each other in obvious anger and as enemies.

Both noticed Charlie at the same time, and when the murdered woman's son realized who she was both men were transformed into buddies bonded in righteousness.

Chapter 10

The sheriff of Moot County demanded to know how Charlie had escaped her cabin at the Hide-a-bye and the eldest of Georgie's children wanted to know where Charlie had buried Frank's body. And both pretty much at the same time.

"Now it's my father," Randolph shouted. "What is it you have against our family? Sheriff, arrest this woman."

Rose brought Charlie an unsolicited orange juice and a surreptitious wink. The coffee was fresh ground, the orange juice fresh squeezed, and Charlie sensed she was in all-natural, organic trouble. She tried to convince herself she wasn't particularly intimidated.

"When I left the Hide-a-bye there was no one there from your office so I thought you'd changed your mind about my having to stay," she lied to Sheriff Wes. That earned him a venomous look from the firstborn Glick who didn't have much of a repertoire when it came to expressions. Then Charlie explained to Randolph that she had last seen his father walking purposefully along the beach toward Chinook.

"He finds you all too coddling and irritating and resents your treating him like a child and he wanted some fresh air." Not to mention hot beef sandwiches, young female figures, chocolate malteds, and to discover the size of his jockeys for all Charlie knew.

"He can't be off on his own at a time like this." Frank's son was on his feet. "Who knows what he'll do?"

Both men headed for the door, Wes bellowing for Charlie to stay put until he could send Deputy "Whatever-her-name-is" to pick her up.

"We don't have many murders around here," Rose said, watching the door sweep shut behind them, "but I don't recall one ever going unsolved since Wes Bennett was elected sheriff." She wiped thoughtfully at the ring the orange juice glass had left on the oilcloth. "Most counties can't claim that."

Charlie slipped ample payment under her plate and stood, planning not to wait for Deputy What's-her-name, gambling— merely on the basis of that wink—that Rose wouldn't try to stop her and no one else would want to get involved either. She counted five customers and two waiters.

The proprietress had dark hair with gray roots and dark eyes that squinted up at Charlie myopically. "But it seems to me if you'd killed Georgie you'd be long gone. He must think so too."

Rose slipped the cash from under the plate and into the stretched-out pocket of her stretched-out cardigan, turning her back on Charlie's exit.

"Do you have a degree in psychology or anything?" Charlie followed as Paige Magill sprayed mist from a special hose on the hanging plants at the greenhouse windows.

"A master's is all." The dream counselor snipped off a dead blossom between two fingernails and tossed it at a plastic garbage pail. "There's lots of people out there counseling with less. But if you want to know the truth, Charlie," the backdrop of bright flowering plants and deep green ferns diffusing the light around her gave Paige an ethereal quality all out of keeping with her jeans and work shirt, "I've learned most of what I know since I came to Moot Point. You've had a dream, haven't you? One that bothers you. Just let me put on the teakettle and we'll talk about it."

Charlie sincerely did not believe in dream counseling or that dreams meant anything, but she wanted to learn as much as she could before the nameless deputy grabbed her off the streets and hauled her back to the Hide-a-bye. That was the only reason she sat in the darkened kitchen drinking that strange earthy tea, surrounded by the earthy smell of the greenhouse, telling this Paige Magill about her uncharacteristic reaction to the wreck of the *Peter Iredale*. Wasn't it?

"But your reaction on seeing Michael's painting of the *Peter Iredale* wasn't as strong as seeing it for real?" Huge almond eyes had narrowed to slits as Charlie talked. All the place needed was a cat and a broomstick. "Even though in your dream there was fog too, but today was clear?"

"Doesn't make sense, does it? When I saw the painting in the Scandia it made me uncomfortable but I didn't know why. When I saw the real thing this morning I remembered the nightmare that brought me up out of bed my first day here."

"You really didn't remember that dream yesterday when we talked? I thought you were holding out on me." Paige opened the almond slits to wide and leaned across the table. "I can't help you, Charlie, unless you tell me the truth. What did you dream about last night?"

"I dreamed I was bobbing against the ceiling looking down at myself in bed."

Paige sat back in her chair, drew a knee up to hug, and wrinkled her nose, satisfaction deepening her dimples.

"Everybody does that," Charlie insisted. "It's the first dream that's haunting me."

"And nobody from the village was in your dream?"

"No, I would have mentioned that."

"As your dream therapist, I'm going to tell you something at no charge. Because I want you to keep coming back. You know about therapy? If you don't keep needing it, the therapist will starve." Paige Magill giggled, then put both feet on the floor and took hold of Charlie's hands on the table. "Those dreams are connected, Charlie."

The man in the lumberjack shirt practicing t'ai chi yesterday was in a dirty lab coat this morning chasing a German shepherd toward Charlie as she reached the road after leaving the green-house. Expecting a sheriff's deputy in a car, she was run over by the dog instead. It uttered a parting growl and bounced off her chest. Its pursuer shouted for her not to move, he'd be back in a moment.

Charlie was sitting up resting her elbows on her knees and her forehead against her palms when the dirty lab coat knelt beside her, its owner puffing and shaking his head. "Lost him."

"May he rest in peace." Charlie pushed herself to her feet and the lush green world swam for a moment. This had to be the holistic vet Clara the bird lady had mentioned.

"I'm Doc Withers," he said. Charlie shook the hand he offered to support her.

"Charlie Greene. Sorry about the dog. I hope he doesn't get run over on the highway."

"Eddie'll head for home. But I'll have to sedate him to get him back here for surgery. Infected dewclaw. I'm the local animal doctor." Doc Withers was as tall and almost as gaunt as Frank Glick. His dark-rimmed glasses were too small for his face, and he had on worn Levi's under his lab coat. "You're Jack's agent, huh? What kind of books do you agent?"

"I don't do animal books," Charlie answered quickly.

"That's a shame. There needs to be one available on proper holistic health medicine for small animals. Listen, I have to call Eddie's owner and warn him to be on the lookout. But won't you come in for a cup of coffee? Least I can do after letting my patient knock you down that way. I've never met an agent before."

Charlie's first reaction was to say no, because she needed

another client like she needed a vent hole in her forehead. And she needed more caffeine even less. But she accepted. Charlie did need to get off the street before Wes's deputy discovered her. And here was another member of the community willing to talk.

Charlie found it curious that the prime suspect in Georgette's murder was invited so graciously into homes in such a small place where everyone would know of her involvement. She said as much to Doc Withers when they were seated in the cubicle he called a kitchen. Three cats, two parakeets, and a puppy watched her every move. The place looked immaculate but smelled of incense and pet potty-training.

Doc leaned his chair back against his oven door. "That's because we're so gullible here. We believe we're all one in spirit so it's hard to be suspicious of others. We love everybody like we love ourselves because we're all bites off the same cookie. Of course explaining this way of thinking is damn near impossible. When it hits you, you know. And I can see by your expression it hasn't hit you. Don't worry, when you're ready it will."

"Some people don't find it that hard to separate themselves from Michael the artist."

"Poor guy, talk about the Dark Ages. When awareness hits him, he's going to be so dumbfounded he'll probably have a heart attack." Doc Withers shook his head and then nodded it, rocking his chair in jerky rhythm. "But I'll admit that man's hard to relate to now."

His glasses had one bow affixed by a circle of wire where a tiny screw should have held it on. His hair looked like he'd cut it himself, impatiently, different lengths wherever it became a nuisance. Sort of like Michael's but much shorter and with no pretense toward artistry.

"Of course, here you just walk into my house without questioning whether or not I'm the murderer too. I mean you don't know me. And if you didn't kill Georgie somebody else around here did." He wore hiking boots like Frank's and an awkward smile.

Everyone in this place seemed so nice, so friendly, so "centered." Yet one of them . . . "Why would anyone want to shoot an old woman on a Schwinn?"

The holistic animal doctor shrugged and brought his chair down on all its feet to pour her more coffee. Charlie felt her bladder wince. "Wes Bennett asked me that and asked me that," he said, "and the whole thing is so out of sync with Moot Point I come up blank every time I think about it. I mean this place is so laid back—"

"I've heard Georgie was a little overly interested in other people's business."

"That's small town anywhere." But his smile straightened, a hint of confusion replaced its reflection behind the glasses as he considered what he'd said. Then he shrugged off the discomfort and started nodding again. "I know, I know. Murder happens in small town anywheres too."

"Could she have been something even in the fog? Come across someone doing something they'd kill to keep secret? Was someone just target shooting and hit her by accident?"

"Why would anybody go target shooting in the fog at night?" he asked.

One of the cats crawled uninvited onto Charlie's lap, turned itself around three times, and curled up to make a warm spot. Charlie watched its tongue take a few swipes at a paw and then it snuggled into a purr.

Her host stood to peer over the tabletop. "I've never seen Mortimer accept a stranger so easily. You must have a way with cats."

"I don't even have a way with kids." The creature sounded a lot like the one named Tuxedo who had kidnapped the affections of her daughter. "What kind of secret could the village have worth murdering for?"

"We aren't a united community. Lots of loners and individuals live here. But the people who own guns tend to be those living outside of awareness at this point, the retired laborers on pension who still hunt, that kind. Why are Georgie's colleagues in the search for expanded consciousness any more suspicious than merchants, or the widows of retired loggers? We're actually a pretty peaceful lot."

"The widows hunt and carry guns?"

"Well, probably not. But weapons are still lying around the house."

"Where did Michael the painter come from? How long has he lived here in Moot Point?" Charlie watched the gears change behind the dark-rimmed glasses. "I met him yesterday and I realize the population here is diversified but even so, he doesn't seem to fit in."

"Town's full of artistic types of one kind or another. A lot of people are jealous of Michael because his paintings sell for fabulous prices. An engineer with a steady job and benefits might make more but that kind of job doesn't exist near enough to here to provide us with other types to envy. Just because many of us are working toward higher consciousness in which envy doesn't exist doesn't mean we've reached it yet. Do you understand?"

Charlie didn't but continued, "Why does it seem like Brother Dennis runs this place? I've met him and frankly charisma doesn't quite answer my question. But it's like everybody's studying with him. Like he's a guru or something."

Chuck Withers studied with him too and he too had relocated to be near him. "Not that much veterinary business around here, but I make house calls in Chinook."

"But what exactly do you study? Why do people relocate to be near him?"

"Mostly transcendence, overcoming perceived reality, looking at the world through a child's eyes again but with an adult's acquired experience. . . . Haven't you ever passed by something for the thousandth time and suddenly seen it for the first? And realized that was only a crack in your clouded perception? And wondered what it would be like to open up to the world that way permanently? We study trying to do that. It's not easy but it's worth relocating for."

Charlie had the feeling that the man's sudden eloquence was due more to rote learning than to his own vocabulary and inspiration, but she couldn't fault his sincerity.

He showed her his surgery in the made-over garage, assuring her he used it only after all nutritional, psychological, and physical therapy techniques had been exhausted. He seemed proud of it though. It was modern and stainless steelish and smelled better than his house.

She left with a book proposal in a padded envelope, unable to think of a way to gracefully refuse it after accepting his hospitality and then grilling him. Georgette's calico nearly tripped her as Charlie stepped outside. She'd have known it anywhere by the accusation in its eyes.

"Frank's too distracted right now to feed her," Doc explained, picking it up. "Critters around here know where to come when there's trouble at home. Poor thing's trembling."

"She doesn't seem to think as well of me as Mortimer did."

"She should, her name's Charlie too. Talk about your coincidence." Charlie the cat rode Doc's shoulder into the house for a meal, staring back wide-eyed at Charlie the agent until the door closed between them.

Chapter 11

A white car with an emergency-light bar on its roof pulled to a stop in front of Rose's down on the first terrace, so Charlie headed uphill. And, as she had yesterday, she came to Brother Dennis's wooded lot. There was more to it than she'd thought— cabins with porches off in the trees, several ancient vans, an old round-topped house trailer, bird feeders hanging quaintly from tree limbs. But the sound of traffic up on 101 behind the compound undermined the illusion of cozy isolation.

The car with the light bar moved slowly away from Rose's and turned up a street toward the next terrace. Charlie stepped into the trees. She felt a little silly, but the thought of being imprisoned in her cabin while everything happened without her, of not knowing what might be said or done that could raise her ranking on the suspect list, was intimidating.

"Wes Bennett is a trained professional. He has real detectives, crime specialists, laboratories, computers. He probably knows methods and procedures you can't pronounce."

"His job is to maintain his winning streak and find a murderer for Georgie. My job is to make sure it isn't me."

"By not following his orders you're probably slowing him down and making things worse for yourself."

"Ex-football-player Marine types are not into losing. And elected officials can't be. And being cooped up at the Hide-a-bye, knowing nothing about what needs defending, is hardly going to be a winning situation for me. I'm just trying to talk with as many people as I can before I have to go back and be cooped."

"He is here to defend and protect you."

"Unless someone convinces him I'm the murderer while I'm pining away in my cabin with no information about this strange place and the strangers in it to use in my defense."

"It's only natural that the sheriff has to keep an eye on you until he has more evidence. But even Rose can see he doesn't really suspect you of murder and it's obvious by the way everyone's so eager to talk to you, nobody else does either . . . except maybe Gladys. She's the only one who's shown sincere fear of you. Let's face it, you're paranoid."

But Charlie backed deeper into tree shadows as the sound of an engine ground up the mountainside. An olive brown UPS truck roared into the semicircle of drive in front of the octagonal monstrosity. Its horn blasted three short ones and the driver pushed square boxes out onto the gravel. No one appeared from the house, but a dog in high fury erupted like a champagne cork from the trees on the other side. It didn't touch ground until it was at the door of the truck. The truck promptly bolted toward Charlie, passed her, and tore off down the hill—leaving her once again facing Eddie of the infected dewclaw.

She wondered if he lived here, because it was clear that this dog was not into loving or transcendence or higher consciousness. This dog was into growling and snarling.

"Knock it off, Eddie, right now!" Charlie said in her take-charge, no-nonsense tone and gave the creature a glare calculated to melt railroad tracks.

This dog was not into intimidation either. His tail didn't wag. His eyes didn't blink. His hind feet were set wide apart, his back end hunkered slightly in full preparation for leaping. The only thing on him that moved was the panting of his chest and the expectant drool dripping off his tongue. Eddie's teeth looked strong, clean, well used. The steady growl seemed to operate on its own.

Instead of going dry as she would have expected, Charlie's own mouth filled with saliva that demanded swallowing. She was afraid to move even that much. Perhaps it was empathy with the drooling mouth in front of her. Eddie had freckles on his gums. He had lots of gums, Eddie. Charlie wished mightily that Deputy What's-her-face would drive up, kick Eddie in the freckles, and haul Charlie off to the Hide-a-bye.

Just when she knew she would choke on her own spit, a sharp whistle sounded from behind the house and Eddie blinked. He looked away and then back at Charlie, undecided. It took a second whistle before he split. Charlie heard Brother Dennis scold the approaching animal, whose posture went suddenly contrite with head down, tail curled between his legs.

The man shook his finger as though at a naughty child and scratched the dog's ears, ruffled its neck fur, patted its rump. Tail up and wagging, Eddie tagged along behind him around the house, Charlie following in the trees and at a distance. She'd wanted to speak to the man without the dog present and hoped to see him tie Eddie up and go back into the house, and then she could go knock on the front door.

Brother Dennis did even better. He opened the gate on a dog run with chain-link fencing on the sides and across the top. Eddie's tail went down again but he obeyed the finger pointing him inside. Charlie turned to move back the way she'd come, careful to be out of his sight before she left the trees.

The house was not one of those domes the hippies of old built to live in, in communal peace and poverty, but a suggestion of that style was there. Except for the windows the whole place seemed covered with wooden shingles growing moss. Charlie didn't know why she'd had the impression of an octagon. To prove that she would have had to circle the house and count the wings. She was not about to offer Eddie that thrill.

A second floor perched on the center of the sprawl. It had

windows all around, calling to mind a head with eyes, and wore what looked like a one-room cupola on top like a hat. The roof on the ends of the wings dipped almost to the ground rising in between to allow first-floor windows and an occasional door.

The jumble of boxes from the UPS delivery still sat on the drive. The boxes were all the same size and shape—square. *Chinook County Printers and Bindery* was listed as the sendee on all, and all were addressed to the *Moot Point Consciousness Training Institute*. Books, self-published. Charlie looked at the envelope full of proposal she was already carrying and sighed. Maybe she should quit while she was ahead.

But now that Eddie was safely incarcerated, maybe she should talk to the guru of Moot Point, Oregon. How often did anyone get such a chance for free? Self-publishing was a lot more expensive than it looked because you had to find your own outlets. This octopus of a house offering lessons on transcendence and consciousness training would be one of them, but these operations were probably pretty expensive too.

Charlie knocked on the door of carved wood and wondered why there were no students here now. It was June, and no small business no matter how sublime could afford to waste this season. The door slid silently open on its own, showing her a darkened entryway.

"Hello?" she called and took a short flight of stairs to a platform overlooking a sunken gymnasium or auditorium with cushions and those web-and-aluminum chairs without legs. Television monitors hung from the ceiling, all running the same picture like home-appliance departments at Christmas.

Each monitor showed a head shot of Brother Dennis exposing his stained fillings, his eyes boring into Charlie's from eighteen different directions. Charlie took herself and Doc Withers's book proposal down the five steps to a legless chair and relaxed for the first time in hours.

Brother Dennis talked, smiled, squinted, nodded, blinked, winked, cajoled—all wise and serene and convincing—all silent and in living color. Charlie yawned. Eddie barked savagely, but far away in his Hide-a-bye out back. Exercise mats lined the walls, stacked under the windows facing the sea. They looked like the naptime cushions Libby'd had in day care, but these were longer, fuller, not as sticky.

She felt the last of the adrenalin rush from her confrontation with Eddie drain peacefully away and must have dozed, because she was startled aware suddenly by voices in midconversation.

". . . agent, if you can believe Jack Monroe. No, I haven't seen her since yesterday." Brother Dennis's voice seemed pitched too high for the compelling man on the monitors above her but Charlie recognized the soothing tones and softened consonants of a man trained to speak distinctly yet without suggestion of threat. "But if I do I'll let her know you're looking for her, Linda."

"Seems like everybody's seen her but me. Wes'll platter my head and stick an apple in my mouth." This Linda spoke with a drawl that sounded more like low blood pressure than region. She had to be What's-her-name. Charlie sat very still and very quiet.

"Saw a sheriff's car down at Doc's. Wondered if it was you. He's been seeing a lot of Gladys, Doc has. But I expect you know that."

"Yes, Dennis, dear. Now you phone the dispatch the minute you see that woman and ask them to notify me." Linda said it slow and insulting. Her shoes scraped the step and soon a car door slammed. She threw more gravel on her takeoff than the UPS man.

Brother Dennis winked at Charlie on the eighteen TV screens and mouthed the answers to questions she'd never asked. She lip-read the word "universe" several times. Off-screen, he grunted and swore under heavy boxes hauled in from the drive, up the lower steps across the platform to more steps, and along the floor above to drop them with a thud and return to repeat the sounds, his breathing growing less meditational by the minute.

Charlie lost count of the number of trips he made but waited until he'd kicked the door closed, then rose like a Phoenix from her floor seat. He stood panting and sweating on the platform hallway with stacked boxes in his arms, staring down at her with wonder and suspicion.

Brother Dennis made no rush to call "the dispatch" and notify Deputy Linda of Charlie's presence. Instead he showed her around the Moot Point Consciousness Training Institute—his gentle and benign condescension gradually returning.

"Why aren't you having seminars now? Seems like summer would be a great time," Charlie asked as they explored a bookstore and reading room filled with the local guru's publications and tapes.

"We've got a two-day, a three- and a five-day all overbooked and that's just for starters. Searchers begin arriving tomorrow. The whole village is gearing up."

"Sounds like Georgie's murder was poorly timed."

"You'd know more about that than I."

"Oh, come on, you don't think a total stranger dropped in to town to murder an old woman. I don't see you yelling for Linda the deputy."

A twist of his hair had loosened from the leather clasp of his ponytail. Holding the clasp in his teeth, he deftly gathered all the flat-black strays and imprisoned them once more. "Three wings are dorms. One male, one female, and one for couples. But it's not unusual for two of the dorms to be taken up by single females. Women are more transformative."

Each "dorm" had plaid spreads and matching curtains for those lucky enough to have windows. Each pair of beds shared a dresser, a tiny closet, and a rocking chair and were partitioned off from their neighbors. Each two partitions shared a tiny bath. Colorful rag rugs sat next to every bed on polished wooden flooring. Brother Dennis explained the rugs were handwoven by ladies of the town and on sale for students at the craft center next to the Scandia. "Many searchers buy so many rugs and other crafts they send them home UPS rather than take them on the plane."

"Do they fly into Chinook?"

"We arrange with a van service to bring them over from Portland International. Some people from Oregon or Washington or Northern California just drive it. There's a row of tourist cabins along the main street they can rent and two bed-and-breakfasts we sometimes fill with searchers as well."

He didn't show her the upstairs, which he shrugged off as his living quarters, recording studio, and storage. The dining room was cavernous, with trencher tables on a flagstone floor. Couches, chairs, and floor pillows grouped around a fireplace. But the kitchen was no bigger than Charlie's.

"Rose caters our meals," he explained.

"Sounds like Moot Point relies on your institute for its livelihood."

"A good portion of it—your client, for example. Jack Monroe's a lucky man. His son has an agent to share with him, and his store has a built-in clientele coming to town eight months a year."

"Even in winter?"

"The storm season has an aura all its own," he said ominously. "It might appeal to murderers more than summer."

They stood toe-to-toe before the great stone fireplace. There was no question of standing nose to nose. Charlie refused to bend over backward to challenge his stare and lose more of the advantage.

"The odds are," she informed the third shirt button up from his belt buckle, "that Georgette was shot by a male of her acquaintance. Not a total stranger with no motive."

"We don't know you are a total stranger or have no motive, but we have just established that it is hardly in the interest of an inhabitant of this village to have something so disquieting as murder done here. Therefore it must have been an outsider like yourself who shot that poor old woman." And with that he stalked off.

Chapter 12

"Therefore it must have been an outsider like yourself who shot that poor old woman," Charlie mimicked to a tree on her way off the institute compound. Something about Bro. Dennis was formidably convincing even when you knew better. Even when you were only staring at his shirt button. Charlie would hate to have him testifying against her on a witness stand. These were all things she wouldn't have known had she not disobeyed the sheriff and avoided Deputy Linda, she pointed out to her nagging rational self.

Why would anyone eager to entice "searchers" keep a man-eating dog in the backyard?

Charlie clutched Doc Withers's book proposal and searched the lower terraces for a Moot County sheriff's car. It was just backing down a driveway on the second level. She waited until it meandered over to Jack's store and then she headed for the last place Wes Bennett's little watchdog had visited, figuring that would be the safest bet at the moment.

Speaking of watchdogs—drawn drapes and a high crescendo

of doggy ferociousness bounced against the windows on three stories of the redwood, glass, and deck creation when Charlie rang the chimes. That was all that happened. Keeping an eye on the black-and-white-and-blue sedan with the light bar, still parked in front of the Earth Spirit, she followed a deck around to the back door. The grating din of what sounded like ten or fifteen yipping, slavering ankle biters begging for a swift kick in the incisors erupted now on this side of the house. Some human to answer the door did not.

Behind the house and to the right was one of those ostentatious three-car garages. One for her car, one for his car, one for the boat? Pickup? Motorcycle? Servant's car?

Above was an apartment with its own deck along the front to face the Pacific. And beneath the deck rose a flight of redwood stairs. And down by the sea Linda the law backed her black-and-white-and-blue away from the Earth Spirit.

The space above the garages held an artist's studio and apartment, both on the lavish side—Charlie was used to starving writers. Michael Cermack was not a starving painter. He was, if you could believe him, a gold mine of information. He was also still an asshole.

Charlie had stumbled across Gladys Bergkvist's little place on the hill, and the proprietor of the Scandia Art Gallery rented out her "loft" to visiting artists.

"More like leases it for next to nothing," Michael said in a bored-to-tears tone, lifting palms and eyes upwards in an appeal to the deities for a clue as to the mentality of Gladys and her ilk. One had to bear so much in life. "But then she'd have to, wouldn't she, to lure anyone with options to this backwater?"

Visiting artists lasted as long as they could bear it or as long as their work sold at the Scandia to tourists and students of consciousness-raising. "Gladys and Olie, of course, take an enormous commission. But since so much is provided and there's so much space and privacy to work, they're hard to refuse."

Olie, pronounced with a long "O" in the Scandinavian manner, was Mr. Bergkvist. But his wife was the one with whom everyone had to deal because good old Olie was on the road most of the year looking for artists and products for the gallery. "At least that's the excuse. My hunch is he can't stand the gloom of the rainy season—which is most of the year. And he can't abide Gladys—which is most understandable."

Michael had welcomed Charlie into this place with undisguised delight. He'd been visited by the sheriff's "lady dogsbody," sworn truthfully he'd seen nothing of Jack Monroe's agent, and then had been astonished to notice Charlie prowling around the Bergkvists' house. He'd known who she was from the dogsbody's description. "If you hadn't come up, I'd have come after you," he'd said and drawn Charlie into his lair.

She was seated now on a poofy couch, and he poured them both glasses of wine the size of iced teas. But these held no ice. "Nothing much happens in Moot Point, you understand."

Charlie just sat and listened, nodded and sipped, unable to believe this could be the same man who'd found her existence such an insult the day before at the lighthouse.

"But you know," her host said, "Olie's usually back by mid-June. He's late this year."

"How long have you been here?"

"Three years this month. About two years too long. Don't tell Gladys, but this has to be my last summer. Ennui can stifle the art inside as well as the man outside."

Charlie shrugged—as if she knew all about art and artists. People expected as much from agents.

Olie was a high liver who had discovered Michael at a New York showing. "I'd been discovered years before of course, but this sounded like a much-needed vacation from the routine and stress of the real world."

Charlie thought three years sounded like an incredibly long vacation from any world. But she made her living working with life's dreamers so she smiled, nodded, sipped. What would Sheriff Wes give to be hearing this bird sing?

Not all the little pieces of "structure" had settled to the bottom of the glass. A few ended up on her tongue. Must be Oregon wine. But after a few sips the taste grew very pleasant, relaxing.

Michael had shown Charlie the studio half of the loft first—skylights and the smell of oil paint and the stickiness of plastic sheeting covering the floor. The compelling, disturbing seascapes were banished to one corner and shrugged off as "crowd pleasers," "hack work" necessary to earn a living—art with a sneer for the subhumans who knew what they liked.

Michael's passions were the massive canvasses that hung on the walls and that she could only describe as slash and burns—fiery slashes of bold color that changed perspective when you moved to either side of them. Some reminded Charlie of animals and birds, but in a vague way—perhaps a beady bird eye suggested above a possible beak by the brush strokes—then when she looked again, they didn't. Charlie didn't know what she liked, but she found these paintings as disturbing as the seascapes.

And that surprised her because the man himself appeared so shallow. Libby was always chiding her for judging people too quickly, being too impatient to discover the mysteries behind the face and the style of dress. While Charlie insisted pink and green spiked hair and leather and chains were not necessarily meant to conceal profound minds or sincere hearts.

Maybe Charlie was too impatient with the people of Moot Point. Maybe if she didn't look deeply into one of them she'd be accused of a murder that person committed. Or maybe she'd just shrug off some important piece of information it would be to her advantage to have. Or maybe she wouldn't beat Wes Bennett to an important clue—or the solution to Georgie's murder even.

Now who's the dreamer? her nagging other sneered. But Charlie took a slightly deeper sip of her drink and gave Michael the asshole all the flattering attention she could fake.

He rose to uncork the bottle again and stood peering out the glass front of his loft. "The law is now zooming off to the light-house in hot pursuit of you."

Today he looked like a mad, if handsome, scientist or maybe a surgeon. The dark hair in that ragged, arty cut. The high cheekbones and satyrlike brows. The smooth swarthy skin so unusual in this sallow population more accustomed to rain than sun. The white lab coat worn for an artist's smock and liberally smeared with shades of Michael's favorite color—red.

The yappy dogs started off again next door, mercifully muted by the walls of two buildings and the distance between them. "People seem to have a lot of pets in this village," Charlie said, hoping his delight at fooling the deputy would keep him feeling chatty. He was the type whose moods would change quickly. "How many dogs do the Bergkvists have?"

"Five." He waved all the digits on one hand and flounced back into his poofy chair. "Five miniature poodles, every one of which I'd give the earth to throttle with loving care and exactitude. Gladys has given them fanciful, regal, ancestral, papered, registered, purebred, and blue-blooded names. I call them Eenie, Meenie, Miney, Moe, and Joe."

"Do they bite?"

"No, they nip. Nip, nip, nip—playful, don't you know. But mostly they get sick. And therein lies the tale." He leaned toward her and widened his eyes as if about to tell a small child a bedtime story of ghosts or princesses.

Charlie felt herself responding in spite of herself. "Tale?"

"Sick animals require a doctor." He laughed a laugh every bit as evil as his eyebrows. "An animal doctor."

It was Charlie's turn to laugh. "Doc Withers and Gladys Bergkvist?"

"Impossible, you say? She must have at least fifteen years on him?"

That's exactly what Charlie had been thinking. But she remembered Brother Dennis's insinuations to Deputy Linda a short while ago.

"I'd say more like twenty." Michael Cermack Heathcliff

Nureyev sat back looking pleased with himself. "Some men pre-fer motherly types. Safer than a lot of what's available these days."

"What does Olie Bergkvist think of all this?"

"He certainly has no right to judge her, from what I've wit-nessed of his travels. But then when one travels three fourths of the year . . . still . . . how could he expect the sauce for the goose and the gander to be that different? However, the Bergkvists are good Lutherans whatever else they might be. That may give him the illusion of leverage in the mating game. But I always know when Eenie, Meenie and the rest are sick because they broadcast the arrival of their doctor. Miniature poodles, you see, tend to become ill only at night. I have no-ticed the emergency is usually over by morning. I, too, keep strange hours."

"Wouldn't the neighbors notice his car here all night?"

"Unless the downpour is outrageous, no one drives around the village. It's small enough to walk most places. And he's a great man for walking, our vet. Especially at night, when others hover inside where it's dry and warm. He comes to the back door and no one would suspect if it weren't for the dogs. They're always yapping their heads off anyway. So I'm probably the only one who notices. He generally leaves at first light."

"He's not the only one out at night. Georgette Glick was riding her bike in the fog the night she was murdered, in the dark, without a light. You'd think someone her age would worry about breaking bones." Why did you hate her?

"If she was being chased by someone with a gun, she probably would be worried about a lot more than broken bones." A slow smile drifted across his face and he lifted his glass to her. "That's what you're up to, isn't it? Playing detective?"

"It's my car she was found under. I'm a suspect in the murder of a complete stranger I'd never seen alive. How would you feel?"

"Decidedly uneasy."

Charlie sensed her time was running out here, so she threw

all her questions at him at once. "Can you tell me anything that will help? Paige Magill said you hated Georgette. Why? Why does Brother Dennis keep a ferocious dog when he wants people to come and stay with him? Why isn't there any blue and green paint on your smock from the seascapes? Do you own a gun?"

Michael the artist set down his glass and then took Charlie's and set it down too. They were both nearly empty, even of structure.

"I'm not used to wine this early. I shouldn't have blurted out all that," she apologized, but he took her arm, lifted her from the poofy couch, and walked her into the studio toward the door. He clearly no longer found her or her situation amusing.

"Paige Magill is a witch. Old Georgette was a bitch, who had to know everything about everyone. In fact, you remind me of her. I told her often just where it was she could stick that nose of hers and leave it. I know nothing about that old crackpot's dog. His motivations would be a total mystery to me if I chose to take the least interest. I have a separate smock, as you call it, for my hack work." He took it from a coat tree by the door and held it up for her. There were indeed seascape colors in drips and smears all over it. "And yes, I have a gun. Would you like to see it, too?"

"Oh, well, no, I believe you. I mean it's not necessary."

"Oh, but I don't mind at all. Maybe it will save you another trip and me from another of your visits." He crossed to a row of stacked cupboards and began to paw underneath a pile of colored paper. He tried another shelf and then the next cupboard, finally pulling things out onto the floor. When he turned back toward Charlie the irritation with a lesser being and the jaundiced sneer were gone.

So, apparently, was Michael the artist's gun.

Chapter 13

Michael's expression had gone from blank surprise, to confusion, to storm warning in less time than it took Charlie to turn on her heel and scoot out the door. She was down the stairs and down the drive to the street (to the tune of Eenie, Meenie, Miney, and friends) before she paused to look back. He did not follow her. He was probably still searching for his gun. Was it registered? Had it shot Georgette Glick?

Charlie was not accustomed to drinking that much wine without food and certainly not this early in the day. She made it down to the main terrace and was taking deep breaths of what she hoped to be sobering sea air when she nearly ran into the bird lady, who carried a large paper bag held out in front of her.

"Here now, are you ill?" Clara Peterson set the bag down on the bottom step of the Community Center as Charlie grabbed the railing, embarrassed at how she must reek of wine.

"I just didn't see you. Lost in thought, you know. What's in the bag? It smells wonderful."

"Cranberry bread fresh from the oven."

"Cranberry bread, how interesting." Charlie looked over her shoulder. No Michael. "Well, good to see you again. I'll never forget your bird presentation . . . lecture . . . talk."

"Have you eaten yet today?" Clara asked in the soft concerned voice of the teetotaler and glanced at several women carrying crockpots into the Center. They were trying to avoid the loose weather stripping on the threshold while staring at Charlie. "We all enjoy guests. It's the senior potluck dinner. We get so tired of each other, guests are welcome. And I think you need some good wholesome food in you right away."

"Dinner? It's only lunchtime." And the black-and-white-and-blue was barreling down the road from the lighthouse. Charlie took Clara's arm and the bag and rushed them all into the Community Center. "I just love cranberry bread."

Once you reach a certain age, Clara explained, the big meal of the day ought to come at noon and a light supper sits better at night. Since this was a Saturday, all those who could cook brought their favorite dishes for a potluck. The rest of the week, except for Sunday, a hired cook prepared the meals. "Sundays we just snack or drive into Chinook for an outing after church," Clara explained. "But Saturdays are best because you get everyone's specialty."

Everyone's specialty tended toward soft, smooshy, salty, sugary fare—hamburger patties smothered in canned-soup sauce, tuna noodle casserole leavened with soggy potato chips, Jell-O, mashed potatoes, canned string beans or corn, and homemade pies and cakes heavy with meringues and frostings. To Charlie, with one too-small bagel and one too-large wine in her, the buffet looked like a soup kitchen might to the destitute. To her thighs it meant disaster.

But Clara was right about the popularity of guests. One table against the wall held the hot dishes, plastic trays and silverware, glazed paper plates, and a coffee urn. The rest of the long tables were strung end to end with metal folding chairs for seating. Except for the few men who sat silently at their own table but turned often to eye Charlie, everyone crowded into Charlie's

row. A couple of men did sit next to wives in the sea of maca-
roni and bosoms, looking like they longed to join the bachelors,
but most of the assembled were women who watched her every
move and slid questions off their tongues with the next bite
raised and ready to enter.

"You the one that girl deputy's been asking after?"

"You a real estate agent?"

"What's that Jack need an agent for?"

"You from California? Hear everybody's getting skin cancer
down there from too much sun."

"You shoot old lady Glick?"

"How much did old Frank pay you for it?"

Laughter all around. Charlie chewed, mumbled meaningless
sounds through the food, shrugged.

"Suppose we should call that snotty deputy?"

"Let the poor thing eat, she's my guest," Clara insisted.

"Wonder if Frank will start coming back to the dinners when
his family leaves. He sure liked your chocolate pies, Elsie."

"Remember the fights them two used to have? It was a relief
when they stopped coming."

"Never saw a man who could put away mashed potatoes and
gravy like he can."

"Ain't you going to put margarine on it or nothing?" This
was the babushka lady who lived next to Doc Withers's animal
clinic on the other side from Paige. She still wore her scarf
knotted under her chin and sat directly across from Charlie.

"On a tortilla?" Charlie looked at the warm paper-thin flour
tortilla she'd just rolled up.

Laughter again. Clara Peterson nudged Charlie's shoulder
companionably. "That's not Mexican, dear, it's *lefsa*. Made out
of potato flour. Sort of a Norwegian flatbread."

A plastic tub of petrochemicals slid down the table and
stopped in front of Charlie's plate. Plump, healthy, wise, grand-
motherly faces beamed as she spread plastic fat on her thighs.

"I remember back when it was thick cream and brown sugar
we rolled *lefsa* around," the babushka lady said wistfully. Her
name was Mrs. Olafson and she was only one generation away

from the old country, she informed Charlie. Mrs. Olafson had made the *lefsa*.

"Won't find that in no fast-food joint," one of the bachelors said, and then looked quickly back to his plate when he realized he'd admitted to listening to the old biddies who'd cooked and brought his food.

Mrs. Olafson's given name was Irene and Charlie was working up the nerve to ask her a leading question about her neighbor, the animal doctor, when someone else asked an even better one.

"So, do we have that place ready for the guests, Irene? Himself says they start arriving again tomorrow. Been missing my programs. And my knees won't take no more floor scrubbing for awhile I can tell you."

"Don't have to do nothing more but pick up our checks. Place is spitless."

"Spotless," Clara Peterson informed Irene kindly and slid a slice of cranberry bread onto Charlie's plate, whispering that cranberry bread was much better tasting than *lefsa*.

So the Consciousness Institute also provided widows with cleaning jobs. Was there anything in Moot Point that didn't depend on Brother Dennis's talents of persuasion?

"I suppose you eat across the street at Rose's sometimes," Charlie said, "when you aren't in the mood to eat here. Or in the evenings."

General disbelief and still more laughter.

"At her prices?"

"Would you rather be eating things like sprouts and tofu and cement doughnuts right now?"

"Bagels," Clara Peterson corrected Irene in a tired voice, "they're a bread also, but from a different culture just like *lefsa* and tortillas."

So Rose depended on outsiders for her business too.

"She's half Italian, you know, Rose is."

"Irene."

"Well, it's true." Irene made a face at Clara and then looked over her eyeglasses at Charlie's plate. "You didn't hardly take any to begin with and you only ate half of that. What's the matter, you don't like good food?"

"It was the best meal I've had in months and months. You all cook so well. Really, I ate more than you realize." Charlie realized everyone else had finished long ago, even those with mounded plates who'd gone back for seconds. These people didn't waste time eating. "Thank you all so much and, Clara, thank you for inviting me. It was sweet of you."

"Aren't you going to have any pie or cake?"

"What are we going to do with all this food?"

"Here, you old coots take a plate of stuff home with you, warm it for supper. And Clara, you taking some over to Mary and Norma?"

Dirty disposable dinnerware was soon whisked into plastic garbage bags to enhance the landfill, elderly gentlemen shuffled out carrying heaped plates covered in plastic wrap, and Charlie offered to help Clara carry similar ones to Mary and Norma.

"That's the least I can do for such wonderful food." And Mary and Norma were the ladies who found the gun in the ditch last night.

"Well, I suppose there would be less chance of mushing things together if the plates were carried separately. That is if you're sure you feel . . . steady enough."

It turned out there were three plates because the slices of pie wouldn't fit on the dinner plates. It looked like enough food to feed Mary and Norma for a week.

Clara explained that her neighbors usually came to the Saturday potluck but were feeling tired after all the hubbub over their finding the gun the day before. "Oh, dear, I forgot that you . . ." She pushed her trifocals higher on her nose with the back of a wrist because her hands were full. "But . . . you didn't even know Georgie."

"How did Mary and Norma come to find the gun in the ditch?" Charlie asked quickly before suspicion turned the conversation in the wrong direction. "Were they out walking like Frank?"

"I know you're going to think we're all a bunch of eccentrics here, but they like to clean up the roadsides. Most evenings after supper, if the weather permits, you'll see them out picking up litter and collecting cans and glass for recycling. Everyone needs something to do."

"Gladys wasn't at the dinner either," Charlie noted as they passed the Scandia. "I suppose she has to mind the store."

"Oh, my, she wouldn't be seen at the senior citizens' dinners —not that she isn't of age. But she thinks if she doesn't admit it no one will know. And the weekday dinners are subsidized and she really isn't at all poor. But I feel, and so do Norma and Mary, that the more numbers at those dinners the more likely funds will continue to be provided for them. And there are some who really depend on them for a decent meal every day and others who are shut-ins and the rest of us carry meals to them. So it's a very important service we all should support. Gladys and Olie don't believe in subsidizing anyone less fortunate than themselves." Clara Peterson's lips tightened and she led Charlie up three steps to the front door of her neighbors' trailer house.

Charlie had kept her head down hoping she wouldn't run into any member of the Glick family or the sheriff's department and was surprised to have made it this far. Clara knocked. The sound of the TV within indicated the sisters were home.

"They have a new VCR," Clara apologized and knocked again. "They record all the late night shows they can't stay up long enough to see and watch them on weekends when their soaps aren't on. I can't stand soap operas or Johnny Carson myself. I like the mysteries on PBS and nature programs." She opened the door and stuck her head inside.

Charlie didn't watch soaps and neither did Edwina, but Libby set the VCR to record something she called *Days* to watch after school, and by the time Charlie got home was often still hashing it over with friends on the phone.

Inside two straight-backed women stared at Charlie with disbelief, obviously recognizing her as the woman questioned in

Georgette's trailer home the night of her murder. And still their eyes kept sliding back to the TV placed in front of heavy drapes that shut out distracting reflection and a view of the Pacific that would be worth several fortunes if located in Southern California.

The trailer was inexpensively furnished (Kmart veneers and plastic), a little worn, everything in varying depressing shades of brown. Mary, the taller of the two, tried to keep one eye on David Letterman and one on Charlie while setting up TV trays on metal stands. Norma, the plump one, popped a dinner into the microwave and the other into the refrigerator for another meal. The sisters reminded Charlie of birds. Norma's movements were fluttery, almost apologetic—her expression timid, apprehensive—while Mary's movements were jerky, her eyes beady and suspicious. It was decided they would accompany Clara to Georgie's memorial service at the church on Monday. Charlie found herself outside without having said more than "hello" and "good-bye."

"They don't mean to be rude, dear, it's just not a good time for a visit," Clara explained and sketched quick biographies of the sisters as if to make up for the fact Charlie hadn't been able to get anything out of them.

"They grew up on the coast and after their husbands died decided to combine widows' pensions and social security and move back. They have something like five grown children between them. Raised their families, one in Eugene and one in Portland as I remember. One's husband worked on the railroad and the other's at a grocery warehouse. Those two tend to blend together in the memory so."

Charlie wondered if a similar bio sketch of Charlie Greene someday might be, ". . . never married, one child (smirk), worked as some kind of agent in California, I believe."

She left Clara to prepare for a trip up to the birds and headed for the Earth Spirit. Since the deputy had already visited Jack, his place might be a good haven about now.

But the startling onset of a siren behind her told Charlie her luck had finally run out. A car pulled up beside her and the wind-down of the siren that close to her ear had to be one of the scariest sounds Charlie had ever heard.

Linda the law sounded scary too. "Your name by any chance happen to be Charlie Greene?"

"Hi . . . uh . . . how you doin'?"

"Not so great, thanks so much for asking. Now you just slide that sweet little ass into this car before I kick it into the Pacific."

Chapter 14

"Think you're pretty smart, huh? Following along behind me to places I'd already been, figurin' I wouldn't look there again." The deputy snorted and reported to the dispatcher who linked her immediately with the sheriff. "This is Tortle, sir. I have apprehended the suspect. Want me to bring her in to the courthouse?"

"Jesus, what took you so long? Can't do a simple pickup? Your orders to take her to the motel stand. And Tuttle, stay with her. She goes into the crapper, you go into the crapper, hear me?"

"Sounds like I got you in a lot of trouble." Charlie grabbed the armrest as the black-and-white-and-blue screeched onto 101 and headed north. Deputy Tortle looked to be close to six foot and every inch was slender, muscular, fit. Right now every inch was also furious. It can be hard working for men in any field, but for a female in law enforcement it had to be something else. "At least you haven't read me my rights."

"Don't you count on that lasting, lady," Linda said and her lips continued to move without sound as she probably chewed out Charlie, Wes Bennett, God, and fate. "And don't figure the sheriff's so sweet on you, you can get away with what you want. That man puts his work before everything."

"Okay, I admit I was working to avoid you. Can I at least tell you why?" Woman to woman? Charlie thought but knew better than to say it. "Suppose you shut me up in the Hide-a-bye and the murderer of Georgette Glick goes about hiding his tracks and planting mine and I can't do a damn thing about it? Now be honest, what would you do if you were me?"

"If I was innocent, I'd let the proper authorities investigate and prove that I was innocent and the murderer was guilty, that's what."

"The proper authorities are not out trying to prove my innocence. The proper authorities don't give a shit about me no matter whatever it is you imagine between me and your sheriff."

"If you are innocent, Ms. Greene, we will uncover the facts to prove it."

"What if those facts were planted by the murderer to make it look as if I was the murderer? I am trying to defend myself. Is that so wrong?"

"Then they're obviously not facts and that will come out in court and your lawyer will defend you." Linda groaned behind clenched teeth. "Lord save us all from the paranoid."

"I am trying to nip this thing in the bud before I need to call a lawyer. Can't you see that? Wouldn't you?"

"You are interfering in a murder investigation, lady, and make no mistake, since you are a suspect that is not going to sit well in places where you need all the friends you can get. Understand what I'm saying?"

Linda Tortle handled the car expertly even when seething. They shot into the Hide-a-bye drive, but braked smoothly within inches of two startled tourists wobbling up the grade on mountain bikes. Linda's hair was long and bottle-bleached with a shaggy perm, and corralled in a fall in the back by a comb clip. Charlie wondered how she fit the Smokey the Bear hat hanging from the dash over it. Little red blood vessels ran toward the corneas in the deputy's eyes, as they did in Charlie's, to feed them oxygen under contact lenses.

Heavy clouds tumbled down the Coast Range from the north and Charlie could see rain falling out to sea when they pulled up in front of her cabin. The air smelled of fish and pine and rain. Two suspicious-looking nine-by-twelve manila envelopes lay up against her door.

Linda picked them up and glanced at the one Charlie carried. "What, you collecting these things?"

It was Charlie's turn to groan behind clenched teeth. The maid had been there to make the bed and tidy up. She'd closed the drapes on the view and when Linda opened them the sky and the sea blended together in shades of dirty aluminum. Surf frothed against the rocks out on the point. Rain spit slantwise at the windows. Charlie shivered. She hadn't been warm since she'd left LA.

Too late to call the office. Sometimes her boss was in on Saturday mornings, but he wouldn't be there by now. Charlie's mood was beginning to reflect the weather and she didn't really want to talk to her daughter or her mother.

"Great way to spend a weekend, huh?" Charlie matched Deputy Tortle's glum look and sat at the table to open the ominous envelopes. As she'd suspected there was a completed screenplay from Brother Dennis and a novel proposal from Paige Magill. Paige's offering had a little note attached—*Thought you might like something to read if Wes keeps you shut up in your room this weekend.*

Charlie explained what they were and why she'd been honored with them and stuffed them back in the envelopes.

"How do you know they aren't any good?" Linda asked.

"I just don't have time for any more clients. And the agency doesn't handle screenwriters who don't live in LA."

Linda sat in a kitchen chair, long legs stretched in front of her. Everything about her was long—eyelashes, feet, hair, nose, body. She folded long fingers across her belt buckle and stared at Charlie and then out to sea. "Doesn't seem fair. How do you get clients if you won't read their stuff?"

"Referral mostly. And believe me, finding clients is not the problem. Selling the work of those few you can take on is the problem, getting top dollar for it is the problem. There's so much more product than there is demand, agents are running for cover."

"Still doesn't seem fair. And do you have one single shred of evidence that somebody is trying to frame you for Mrs. Glick's murder?"

"Just one. That somebody shoved her body under my car."

The sheriff's deputy studied her so hard for so long, Charlie changed the subject in desperation. "What about you? How'd you get to be a deputy?"

Charlie had about given up hope the woman would answer when finally Linda said, "I was a secretary in the courthouse when the county law establishment got orders to get some females on line to avoid charges of sexism. Janitors in the building made more money and had more fun than I did."

Linda Tortle passed the tests and got the job. She trained to shoot, use a variety of martial arts, think clearly in a crisis, and act tough. "But what I really need is a degree in psychology."

The job turned out to be handling female suspects like Charlie, searching women, talking to schoolchildren about the evils of drugs, making brownies for colleagues' birthdays, trying to sweet talk suicides out of it, nurturing women and children yanked from hostage and abuse situations, delivering news of death and injury to families, and consoling male colleagues who were having relationship or career problems.

"Or getting too old to get it up on demand?" Charlie asked.

The deputy choked back a guffaw that bounced her hands on her belt buckle. "I can see you too are a working woman," she said, but to be safe added, "whatever else you might be."

They watched the storm turn the surf angry, roil metallic clouds across a gray sea that thudded against the coast so hard it rattled the windows.

"Mind if I turn on the TV?"

"No," Charlie told her, "but if you do, I'm going to go lock myself in the crapper."

"Mind if I use your phone then?" Linda didn't wait for an answer any more than her boss had last night. "Hello, Peety? Hi, honey, Gramma there? No, I don't want to talk to her. Just want to be sure you aren't alone. I don't know when, but we'll do something tonight, okay?"

"You have a kid too," Charlie said when Linda had finished, and knelt to light the paper log in the fireplace.

"Yeah. He's eight. Hottest thing to hit the planet in this century even though his father's the jerk of the decade. You?"

"Libby's fourteen. I'm praying she's not going to get hot."

"God, if Peety'd been a girl I'd of jumped off a bridge. I was hell on roller skates myself and I don't know how my mom survived."

They sat in front of the fire and turned their backs on the cold and storm outside.

"On second thought," Charlie said, "I have the written words of three possible suspects in those envelopes on the table. I might not need these writers for clients, but you might find some clues for solving Georgie's murder. Or at least to get a better feel for these people. It'd be something to do."

Brother Dennis had a lot of nerve dropping off a script after insulting Charlie only a few hours ago. She wondered if Paige might do his typing and have had it on hand, left it with her own at Charlie's door and would tell him later. It was untitled and just had FILM SCRIPT at the top. But it was more of a treatment with some dialogue and camera angles thrown in. It was awful.

A mature man (Mitch Hilsten was suggested) finds himself alone and destitute on a deserted and unnamed beach, his old van broken down and his spirit with it. (Violins, sea gulls, surf sounds.) He takes a handgun from under a seat in the van and loads it, and as he sits in the sand facing the sea—obviously about to commit suicide—his troubled life flashes before him and the audience. The usual divorce. The nasty wife takes his son from him. He can't hold down a job. He travels across the country looking for a meaning to it all and ends up on this beach with a gun in his hand.

And strange things begin to happen. A German shepherd comes running down the nameless beach, licks the nameless man's face, and knocks the gun out of his hand.

Charlie read it first and handed it over to the deputy who, when she reached the part about the dog, said, "I feel like I'm reading somebody's diary."

"You haven't seen anything yet," Charlie told her.

(Lots and lots of violins.) Dolphins come swimming up almost to the shallows, stand on their tales (sic) and make dolphin sounds. Farther out whales cavort by, spewing joyous spumes. Closer in, sea lions belly along the sand toward him, cormorants dive, pelicans swoop, swallows streak.

This is where the deputy forgot her determination to remain distant from the suspect and leaned across to slap Charlie's knee. "And through all this the dog just lays there with his head on the guy's lap?"

And then the grand finale (violins cut out and drums take over) and a huge wave builds up, rushes the beach, swamps everything, and for just a moment—through some trick of photography—man, dog, wildlife, beach, and wave blend into one. (Fade out of drums, and a chorus hums some piece Charlie couldn't even pronounce.) The wave recedes leaving only the man and dog and van, dripping but undisturbed. For the first time, the man wears a smile. His eyes "reveal a knowing, a perception, a serenity and inner peace so unlike the tortured soul he had been earlier." Fade out with the chorus, fade in with eerie flute music as the camera "backs away" to reveal a pink, rose, and lavender sunset and the man on the beach tossing the gun into the ocean while the dog "cavorts joyously."

"We talking box office here or what?" Deputy Linda hadn't stopped giggling for the last two pages. She slipped the script back into the envelope and wiped her eyes. "How come there weren't any mermaids? Not even a flying saucer. And no mention of the guy having trouble getting it up. That would have added some pathos there."

"Everybody's a critic."

"Brother Dennis is a dreamer all right. But I don't know what the village would do without the institute." Linda squinted thoughtfully into the fire. "I keep waiting for the Japanese to buy him out. They bought up Rose's, you know, let her run it, make her dress up the staff. But she dresses herself sloppier than she ever did just to spite them. At least Jack Monroe's still holding out. And the Scandia. Japanese own most of the business district, vacant lots and all. Keep wondering what they're going to do with it. Good thing the lighthouse isn't for sale."

"You seem to know a lot about the village and the people."

"I've lived in Moot County all my life. It's not that big. Took a seminar at the institute in one of my weaker moments. Sort of a month of weekends for the employed locals during slack time in the tourist trade. I was still a secretary on a five-day week."

"I take it you didn't become one with the universe."

"Nah, it's sort of like a religion without God. There's a real strong appeal there though. Idealistic as hell, unattainable, but appealing."

"Appealing how? Why is it unattainable?" Why did it seem everyone talked around it, couldn't explain the theory directly?

"It's not the kind of philosophy you can sum up in a sentence or two, or that you can learn in an hour. You are a part of everything, everything is a part of you—rocks, birds, dogs, the universe . . . so you look at things differently. While you're under the spell it's wonderful. But it will never work unless everyone feels that way and is willing to work at it every day, always. It's pie-in-the-sky, Charlie Green." Linda hesitated and then met Charlie's glance head on. "It's also the only philosophy I ever heard that was complete enough to make sense."

"Want to read about *Holistic Health and Nutrition for Your Pet* by Charles W. Withers, Doctor of Veterinary Medicine? Ought to be a nice contrast to *Middle-aged Male Figures Out the Mystery of his Navel*," Charlie said uncomfortably.

"I don't know if I can stand any more preaching by that asshole. You know Doc sleeps with ducks in his bed?" Deputy Tortle blinked realization that she was cavorting with the enemy and revealing far too much of her personal life. She grabbed Doc Withers's proposal, which was probably the only marketable possibility in the bunch.

Charlie picked up Paige Magill's novel proposal. It concerned the murder of an elderly woman in a small village and the disturbing dreams of a visitor from Los Angeles, California.

Chapter 15

"Didn't you bring extra?" Linda Tortle leaned against the doorway of the bathroom of cabin three at the Hide-a-bye Motel, arms and ankles crossed, eyebrows looking just plain cross.

"I can't find them. The maid was here. But why would she move them? She didn't anything else." Something had gotten into Charlie's eye and she'd had to remove a contact lens. It was of the flimsy disposable kind and she'd torn it. She never traveled without a spare for each eye, but the little zipper bag with the eye drops and rewetting solution and spares was no longer tucked away in her cosmetic kit. "Why would anyone swipe prescription lenses?"

That deep impatient groan again. It seemed to come up from Linda's knees. "You just misplaced the damn things. I can get along on one in a pinch, can't you?"

"Looks like I'll have to." Charlie went back to the fire and Paige's proposal, feeling uneasy. Now she had one lens instead of four. She hated not having a backup for something she was this dependent upon. But the deputy was right. Her contact eye soon took over the distance work, while her uncorrected eye did the close-up. But it would tire of reading soon enough. She remembered seeing the little zipper bag with her eye supplies in her cosmetic kit this morning. Or was it yesterday morning?

Unlike Brother Dennis's screenplay, Paige's mystery proposal had a title, *Death of a Grandmother*. There were two completed chapters and the rest was summarized. It seemed more an attempt to needle Charlie Greene than it did to interest an agent in handling a book. Paige was a far better writer than the local guru, however.

The story varied some from the real thing. Gertrude Geis, the grandmother, was found dead on a Pacific beach by a woman named Patsy Prudhomme. Patsy was on vacation from her smog-choked home in Los Angeles and one foggy night while wandering on the beach (for no reason mentioned) she tripped over Gertrude's body. "Even in the thick fog, Patsy realized immediately it was no driftwood log that had tripped her up, but the cold dead body of a woman." So Patsy hies for the nearest communal gathering of lights seen "wavy through the fog-shrouded air" and raises the "alarum." She pounds on doors next to lighted windows from behind which come the sounds of life—"television sitcoms, blenders, dishwashers"—but no one will open to her.

"That Paige Magill's an asshole," Deputy Linda decreed when she'd given up on holistic pet medicine and nutrition and begun to pick up pages of *Death of a Grandmother* as Charlie finished them.

"She sure writes and plots fast though." Charlie admired anyone who could get this much material down in a couple of days without any glaring sics while running a greenhouse-dreamhouse business.

Finally, poor Patsy gains entrance to the studio of a dashing young painter who calms her down with a glass of wine (and his dashing profile) while he calls the authorities. Who arrive to find no body on the beach but—and this is the hook at the end of chapter one—they do find Gertrude's body beneath Patsy's "little foreign-made" car.

Charlie sat back and let one eye water while she stared at the dying fire, suddenly aware that the storm had given up outside, and inside her unwilling companion was thinking of young Peety. When she said as much, Linda put down her reading too and looked at her watch.

"I never learn. I promised we'd do all kinds of things. Today was supposed to be my day off. First Saturday off in months." She eyed Charlie grimly and leaned forward with her forearms on her knees, hands dangling toward the floor between her legs in a curiously masculine pose.

"I know the feeling," Charlie said. "This job wasn't supposed to entail much travel—one of the reasons I took it. But I find myself on airplanes more than I'd planned. I've been lucky to find sitters and friends. Libby's been through the whole schmear —day care, preschool, nursery school—even went to my local high school with me so I could graduate. Volunteer ladies came in to take care of the infants of teen mothers."

"No father in the picture at all?"

"Not since the moment of ecstasy." Charlie laughed and was surprised at how little bitterness she heard in that laughter. Charlie's own father had even died, shortly before Libby was born.

"No thought of abortion?"

"I was too stubborn. Anyway, now I have a daughter who won't accept a sitter in the house because she is a baby-sitter herself and is too old and sophisticated to need one. She knows everything, is totally able to take care of herself, and believes I'm paranoid like you do. Her grandmother happens to be visiting right now or I'd be having panic attacks."

Peety Tortle's father was threatening to contest Linda's custody of their son and she worried he'd get worked up sometime and decide to kidnap him. "One of the reasons I trained so enthusiastically for this job. He's a slob, drunk half the time. I don't want Peety around that shit." And then Linda said with a certain lack of sympathy for Charlie or herself, "Life's rough on single parents, isn't it?"

"At least you don't have the stigma of unwed motherhood dragging at you."

"What stigma? That's so common nowadays, nobody blinks." The deputy was not about to give Charlie an advantage here either. "Libby and I are right, you really are paranoid."

"Edwina, that's my mother, says it's always been common because most single mothers are "common"—read slut, whore, whatever. And that they never make anything but disasters out of their lives and mess up the lives of their unfortunate offspring as well." Charlie had been out to prove Edwina wrong since she was sixteen.

"Looks like you've made a pretty good recovery," Linda stood and stretched, opened the sliding door, stuck her head out into the foggy gloom, and brought it back in, "unless of course you're sent up for the murder of Georgette Glick."

"Or set up."

Linda came back to her chair, little beads of mist clinging to fluffy bangs. "Like who? Can you honestly see Brother Dennis setting anybody up for murder? Or even Paige Magill, who God knows is capable of a lot? Chuck Withers is obviously too stupid to figure out how to do anything that complex. And Jack Monroe wouldn't want his agent behind bars."

Charlie sensed she was getting to the deputy and pushed harder, asking every question she could think of about the residents of Moot Point.

Linda Tortle was anxious to get home to her son and equally anxious to stay personally uninvolved with a murder suspect. But she was bored and also liked to gab.

According to Linda, Paige Magill slept occasionally with both Brother Dennis and Jack Monroe and reveled in the estrangement that caused the two men. "Heard they used to be close friends. Now they're competitors and competition of that sort is not well thought of in the teachings at the Moot Point Consciousness Training Institute. Whether she knows it or not,

Paige Magill is into power and I'm talking heavy. She enjoys every minute of it."

Which also went against the grain of the teachings of the institute. Charlie tried to fathom how this gritty, logical female deputy could ever have been attracted to the institute in the first place.

And Doc (Charles, Chuck) Withers was a brain-dead asshole from the word go. He let any critter take over his house, bed, or attention span (which was none too long) the instant it came into view.

"Has he ever been married or anything?" Charlie asked, remembering Brother Dennis's insinuations when Linda confronted him while Charlie hid in a legless chair at the institute that morning.

"Fortunately for the planet, no."

"How did you meet him . . . and all the others? When you were a student at the institute?"

"Well, then, yeah, but I've been back here a lot since . . . complaints about dogs and anything unimportant they can send a woman after."

"Dogs like Eddie?"

"You've met Eddie?"

"Yes, and I'd like to file a complaint. Right now. He attacked me twice today, once in front of the veterinary hospital where he escaped while Doc Withers was trying to do surgery on an infected dewclaw and shortly after on the grounds of the institute."

"Somehow you don't look attacked."

"I was knocked over, threatened, growled at, intimidated and drooled at by a dog running loose. What more do you need?"

"You're complaining because Eddie drooled at you? Didn't you just read this screenplay?"

"You know that village a lot better than you want to let on, don't you? Especially Doc Withers."

Linda the deputy stood and switched on an overhead light. The fire was out, the battle lines drawn. The fog was a darker gray. "And you still think you're a detective instead of a suspect, don't you?"

"You don't believe anybody you know in Moot Point would be capable of murdering Georgie Glick, do you? So I'm the easiest answer, right?"

"Lots of people are capable of murder that you'd never suspect. Maybe you. It's not for me to say. Where are you going?"

"To look for my contacts." Charlie dumped her cosmetic kit on the floor and put everything back one item at a time. As she already knew, they weren't there. She pulled her luggage out from under the bed and searched linings and pockets. She looked inside her shoes, in coat pockets. She searched the three drawers in the dresser and the one in her nightstand. Nothing.

"Maybe they're still in your car." Linda ran her hands over the high shelf above the clothes pole and came away with only dust. "Maybe they fell out of your luggage."

Charlie didn't think so, but it was possible. She was about to pick up the telephone to call the motel office and have them question the maid, when it rang. It was Jack Monroe with his deep jerky voice. It sounded like he'd just won the lottery.

"How's it going, Charlie? Say, if you're looking for that little paisley colored purse thing with the eye drops and other mysterious packets in it, it's under the bed. Told you I hid something. Remember?" He laughed so hard he started to cough. "Oh, and tell Linda she's got no call to be so hard on Doc. Just because she can't stand to crawl into bed with a man who sleeps with ducks that's no excuse to mean-mouth him."

"Jack, how do you know all this? Where are you?"

"Home. Hurried back to my body to call before you two tore the place apart. Tried to talk to you while I was there but neither of you would pay attention. Oh, and Charlie, don't worry, I'll find you a lawyer if it comes to that, but I don't think it will. We got a book here or what?" He hooted this time and broke the connection.

Charlie stood looking at the receiver until the deputy took it from her hand and cradled it. Then Charlie repeated every word

Jack said. Then she explained about Jack Monroe's supposed OOBE's.

"Jesus, I knew old Jack was into some strange stuff, but running around without his body?"

Then they both rushed to look under the bed.

Leaning up against the inside of the plastic wheel on the metal bedframe at the head of the bed on the nightstand side was the small zippered paisley bag in which Charlie kept her eye supplies.

Neither she nor Linda said a word as Charlie looked through it, went to the bathroom to wash her hands, and inserted a replacement for the lens she'd torn. They were back sitting in the recliners in front of the dead fire not looking at each other when Linda snapped her fingers and grinned.

"He's got the place bugged. I don't know why, but that's the answer. Damn you, Jack, I'll get you for this. And those ducks were dirty and mean." She said it loud enough to be picked up by hidden "bugs" and jumped up to run her hands along the fake mantel and under the chair arms and under the table. "Don't you see? When he snuck over to hide your contacts he planted the bugs."

Charlie felt the goosebumps subside on her arms. The last time she'd felt this relieved somebody had told her Libby had been born and she could stop pushing. "Thanks, he really had me going there."

They were both running their fingers over and under and around everything and giggling at each other when Charlie asked, "What does one of these bug things look like? How big are they? What exactly are we looking for? And did Doc Withers really sleep with ducks . . . and you? At the same time?"

They were standing about three inches apart, laughing into each other's faces like the world's best friends, when they realized Sheriff Wes Bennett had walked through the door and stood in the short hallway staring at them, wide-eyed and open-mouthed.

Chapter 16

"Don't you ever knock?"

"Don't you ever lock your doors?"

"Sheriff, the suspect has been here all afternoon and has had contact with no one," Linda's drawl was even more pronounced when she was nervous, "except Jack Monroe on the telephone and me of course."

"Of course. Surprised I didn't find the two of you in bed, so cozy are we here. Tuttle, I want you—"

"Tortle, sir." Angry red flared everywhere uniform or hair didn't hide it.

"Linda Tortle," Charlie added, feeling the warmth of anger diffusing her skin too.

"Deputy," the sheriff compromised, "write up your report and be back here by six tomorrow."

"Sheriff, she was supposed to have today off to be with Peety and you wouldn't let her. She should spend tomorrow with him to make up for it."

"Peety? You get married again, Tuttle . . . Tortle?"

"I can handle my own affairs," Linda warned Charlie. "Sir, I think you should know about the telephone call from Jack Monroe. It came just—"

"Write it down, Tortle, hmm? Back at the courthouse, please? In your report? I'll read it tomorrow first thing."

Deputy Tortle left them with a series of snaps—a snap in her eyes as she looked from Charlie to her boss, a snap of her teeth as she bit down on what she couldn't say, and a snap of her heels as she grabbed her Smokey the Bear hat and headed for the door. Charlie wanted to go after her and make amends but knew better. She liked the deputy, hated to see her treated this way, and was about to vent her indignation on Wes Bennett when she noticed him studying her again, this time with his eyes so squinted he could have been staring into the sun.

Charlie sipped some kind of Oregon-grown wine and watched Sheriff Bennett cook dinner for the chief suspect. It reminded her of her first night in Oregon with Jack chopping and stir-frying for her. Except then she hadn't been a suspect yet. Then it was olive oil, now it was corn oil. Then it was tofu and seaweed, now it was thin strips of sirloin and onions and peppers.

Why wasn't the sheriff worried that if Charlie ever got to court, her lawyer would pounce on this little "date" that wasn't a date like the proverbial chicken on a June bug?

They were up above the fog in the sheriff's mountaintop eyrie. Having been born in Colorado, Charlie would never be convinced anything low enough to have trees on top could be a mountain. Mountains had bald jagged rock on top. Foothills had trees. But she didn't say as much. Had this been a real date, that would have made wonderful verbal fencing material.

But on the way here he hadn't unclamped his jaw long enough to clear his throat. He had stared steely-eyed at the road and gripped the wheel like he was practicing strangling techniques. Charlie had braved the tension enough to risk, "Come off it, you don't really think I'm a suspect here? What are you so frosted about? Just because your deputy and I were laughing when you came in the door. Just because I nosed around the village for a while—"

"Oh, but you're wrong, Charlie Greene," Sheriff Wes Bennett uttered the only words he would relinquish on the entire trip. "You are my *chief* suspect."

Wes's house reminded Charlie of Gladys, Olie, Eenie, Meenie, Miney, Mo, and Joe Bergkvist's house in that it was largely redwood, decks, and windows. But this was a smaller, less opulent version, more of a bachelor pad version. Still, he lived pretty well for a sheriff with child-support payments. The place reeked of raw wood and the damp fire trying to survive in the rock fireplace, of the fajitas, frijoles, and south-of-the-border spices.

As they ate, Wes loosened up enough to tell her that under the fog to the west was a stunning view of the lights of Chinook and the Pacific Ocean. To the east was a stunning view of the Coast Range.

Right now they seemed to be floating on dark moonlit clouds like flying on a jet at night. But instead of having to peer through tiny portholes onto a scary life-sustaining wing, they were surrounded by windows. The floating view, the spicy food, the wine, the massive man across the butcher-block table were all heady stuff. Charlie caught herself wishing this was a real date. And then she remembered his treatment of Deputy Linda, set her own jaw, and offered up not a word.

Wes rose to uncork another bottle of Oregon red and slam it down on the table between them in a gesture Charlie identified with childish-male gauntlet slapping. She reached for the bottle and poured for them both.

He grunted, did his malevolent squint again, and jabbed his fork in her direction. "You are in a who-o-le lot of trouble, lady."

"You've got sour cream on your chin."

He wiped his chin and threw his napkin on the table and

then his fork at the plate. It bounced. He took a slug of wine and swished his teeth with it. People really could flare their nostrils. "Think you're real tough, don't you?"

"Michael Cermack's gun is missing." Charlie wanted to reach for her wine glass but didn't want him to see her hand shaking.

"Who the fuck is Michael Cermack?"

"The artist I told you about meeting yesterday. His paintings take up most of the Scandia Art Gallery. He lives above the Bergkvists' garage in a studio loft. I asked him if he had a gun and he said yes but when he went to show it to me, he couldn't find it. He seemed furious, but then he's a moody, arty type so it's hard to tell."

"You just walked up and asked a total stranger if he had a gun in a village where a woman had just been shot to death."

"I asked him a lot of other things first. Do you know Olie Bergkvist?"

"I couldn't pick him out of a lineup, but I know who he is." The sheriff looked disgusted, thwarted, drowning in the unreasonableness of the moment, but at least the massive hands were bringing food to his mouth again instead of encircling Charlie's throat as she'd sensed their urge to do.

"He's usually only home in the summer months, but this year he's weeks overdue." She reached for her wine glass and took a quick gulp.

"What's that got to do with the murder of Georgette Glick? Or the fact some painter can't find his gun?"

"I don't know. You're the professional law enforcement type here. You yourself said this is all a puzzle. Yesterday on the dock, remember? I'm just helping you find some of the pieces."

"Wharf."

"Wharf. Did you find Randolph Glick's randy old daddy in one piece this morning?"

"Yeah, I remembered what you said and we finally found him at the only little old café in Chinook that still makes hot beef sandwiches with real mashed potatoes and gravy, not that packaged glue you—you think you're real smart don't you?"

More like desperate. "Brother Dennis's institute is overbooked and the searchers begin arriving tomorrow. The village will probably be swamped with strangers walking all over and haphazardly destroying clues."

"Searchers?"

"Searchers of cosmic consciousness and transformitiveness." Charlie was in too deep again. She poured him more wine and changed the subject. "Do you know what an OOBE is?"

Coffee in front of the fire. Wes finally got the one in the fireplace roaring. Must have used half the wood that empty Japanese ship had wanted to take home. And Charlie was finally warming up sitting next to him. Not that her host had thawed much but he was so big, he radiated warmth no matter what his mood.

"Why is it," he said, "just when I think I am communicating something relevant to you, you get weird on me? Would you explain that? We have important things to discuss."

But you haven't read me my rights yet. Whatever it is, and obviously something I don't want to face up to has happened, you're not that sure. "Read Linda's, I mean Deputy Tortle's report."

"So you misplaced your contact lenses under your bed and that means Monroe walks around out of his body? I don't know what you're trying to pull here, and frankly, Charlie, I don't know why, but this stuff is—"

"Wes, you don't misplace something from your cosmetic case in the bathroom across a hallway, into a bedroom, and under a bed. And if there were no bugs in cabin three, and your deputy and I couldn't find any, how could Jack know what we had just been talking about? I mean *everything* we'd just been talking about."

"You don't honestly believe in this OOBE stuff."

"No, but I think it's got to be another piece of the puzzle."

"Charlie, you can't take every little piece of gossip and trivia you overhear in the village and plug it into the murder of Georgette Glick. It doesn't work that way. You can have too many pieces for a puzzle."

"But the more pieces you have, the more likely you are to find the right ones."

"Shit, what do I have to do, draw you a picture?" And he stomped off around a stairway and into a room she'd only glimpsed on entering. It looked to have an odd combination of uses. She'd seen a cluttered desk, a television, a rowing machine, and a bench press.

Wes came back with two oblong boxes and shook them. He set one down, took the lid off the other and handed it to Charlie. The box had a picture of four horses running across a summer pasture, manes and tails flying, a corral and fence in the background, a mountain ridge and cloudless sky behind that. 1000 Pieces, proclaimed the lid.

The sheriff dumped all the pieces on the rug at Charlie's feet. He picked up the second box and repeated the process, moving slowly and deliberately as if demonstrating a simple procedure to an imbecile. The second box had only five hundred pieces and the lid depicted a mountain stream splashing merrily among rocks and wildflowers. The sheriff got down on his hands and knees and scrambled the puzzle pieces together methodically with big blunt hands, all fifteen hundred of them.

Then he leaned forward on all fours, his head hanging over her lap like a woolly Saint Bernard wanting attention. "Charlie?"

"What?" She very nearly patted his head.

"Wouldn't it have been easier to assemble either one of these puzzles if I hadn't mixed them up like this?"

"Oh."

"Oh, she says. Jesus!" The Saint Bernard stood up into a two-legged sheriff, those blunt hands clenched into fists.

"But what are you going to do with this mess?"

"What am I going to do? I'm going to dump this mess in the garbage can." That low rumble of a chuckle came out strangely mirthless. "Because, Charlie Greene, both puzzles are ruined now. Because there are too goddamned many pieces to make sense out of anything now. You can't separate one from another. Any chance any of this is soaking in?"

Charlie was saved by the telephone. Wes stomped off into the weight-lifting television office and she stared at the puzzle pictures on the lids.

"Oh, Christ, not again. Whadya mean he . . . no, no special privileges cause his dad's a cop. If anything, make it harder on him . . . no, I'll call his mother. And thanks, Harry." The door closed on the next conversation and all Charlie could hear was the defeated tones of a beleaguered father. Welcome to Parenting 101, Charlie thought.

When he came back he poured himself a brandy and downed it in one gulp like a Hollywood cowboy on a saloon set. "That kid's going to keep at it until he kills me. Him and his mother too. And what's his mother say? She says, 'Life just doesn't live up to Joseph's expectations anymore.' Who ever told him it was supposed to, is what I want to know. Charlie, what are you doing?"

"I'm separating the puzzles. See, if you look closely at the colors in the pictures you can see different shades of greens in the grasses and blues in the skies. The other colors aren't the same at all, well, maybe the fence in the horse one and the rocks in the stream one could get confusing but—" Charlie's voice broke in a squeak when he kicked the boxes with some of the separated puzzle pieces already collected in them across the room.

He lifted her off the couch by her upper arms. Her feet were dangling. He asked reasonably, "Why are you doing this, Charlie?"

"Because I don't want you to tell me the important things we have to discuss. I don't want to know why I'm the chief suspect. I had the awful feeling those fajitas were a last meal. I don't want to hear the bad news."

He lowered her gently back to the floor, but kept a hold of her shoulders, which was good because she didn't think she could stand on her own.

"You're going to have to."

"I know. Don't let go."

"I won't."

"So what is it?"

"The revolver in the ditch? It was the murder weapon like we thought. We got fingerprints off it. Your fingerprints, Charlie."

Chapter 17

"That can't be," Charlie had insisted all the way down the mountain. "I would know if I had handled a gun. I've never touched one in my life."

"Prints don't lie, Charlie, and they were very clear."

"Then why aren't you taking me to jail instead of back to the Hide-a-bye?"

"Because the prints were too clear."

"Now you're the one not making any sense."

"I know. The damn thing was in a ditch choked with damp grass and weeds that hadn't dried out since the fog blanket the night before."

"How could the prints be perfect then? Wouldn't they get smudged?"

"Not inside a plastic bag with a Ziploc top that was zipped."

"Somebody (supposedly me) shot an old woman on a Schwinn, put the gun in a bag to keep it dry so the sheriff's department could find the prints on it, and threw it in the ditch, maybe four hundred yards from where the body was found under my Toyota. Isn't that a little bizarre?"

"Well, it's not way up there with walking around without your body—but it certainly raises questions. The old sisters who found the bag—"

"Mary and Norma."

"Mary and Nooormma, said that's what caught their attention. The bag had dew on it and their flashlight made it sparkle. They used a flashlight because they like to pick up litter on their evening walks and bottles and cans show up better that way when the light's not good."

"I know."

"You know what?"

"That Mary and Norma pick up roadside litter. I learned that today when I was picking up all those useless puzzle pieces that mess up your murder investigation."

"Well, did you happen to pick up how your fingerprints got on the murder weapon?"

Charlie wasn't legally under arrest this particular minute only because there was such a fishy smell to the whole business. But a deputy—male and fortunately not poor Linda—was already parked in a car at the cabin door with a bag of sandwiches and a thermos of coffee. Wes informed her that man would stay there all night to see that she did too. "You're costing the county a lot of money."

"You don't really believe I did it or I'd be in jail." She followed him as he inspected the closet, peered under the bed, pulled back the shower curtain.

"I've seen people like you who I would have sworn incapable of a serious criminal act. And they've proved me wrong. Shit, my own kid's screwing up every life he can touch and he looks to be as innocent as a newborn lamb. I can't say what you did or did not do yet, Charlie, but for all the chauvinist pig redneck you think I am, remember that if you were a man you'd have been in jail the minute those prints were verified. Don't tell me women don't have privileges." He peeked out at the fog on the balcony, closed the sliding door, and locked it.

He turned to find Charlie barring his exit by standing in the center of the entrance hall, arms outstretched, hands flattened against the wall on either side.

"Why aren't I in jail?" She felt about as effective as a canoe would have felt blockading that Japanese cargo ship in the harbor at Chinook. "You don't put women in jail? Moot County is an unusual place. It has nothing to do with the fact the evidence is fishy?"

"That, too."

"And?" Why was he doing this? He could be an incredibly likable oaf. Why did he have to bait her this way? "I mean besides the fact that I'm not knock-kneed, cross-eyed, and forty pounds overweight or the fact there's no motive?"

"Well, the courthouse is old," he conceded with an impatient shrug, "and there's only a couple of holding cells available for females and they're occupied at the moment. And there could be a motive I don't know about yet. Charlie, those prints will stand up with a jury."

"And why only a couple of cells for women? Because they don't even begin to constitute half your perps, right? Unless you're going after women who smoke, drink, or swear when they're pregnant, right?"

"Perps? I knew you'd been reading that female police junk just like Doris. I somehow had you figured as a little more intellectual." He picked her up, set her down in the bathroom doorway, and stalked out into the fog.

"And I somehow had you figured as a lot brighter," Charlie called after him and slammed the door. This time she locked it.

Actually what she'd been reading were statistics on the ratio of males and females convicted of serious crimes or even suspected of them. It was all part of a documentary Sid Goldfine had helped script for PBS and she'd seen several versions of it. Frank Glick was right. Women were capable of most all the crimes men were. Women's prisons were overflowing too. Charlie had always accepted that men were more likely to commit a crime. It was a sort of given like boys will be boys and the testosterone thing. But the difference in the number of violent and serious crimes committed by male and female had surprised Charlie.

Right now she stood chilled and alone, the daily paper log already used up, damp fog hovering at the windows, and the deputy outside with his sandwiches and coffee. Charlie was too shocked by her fingerprints on a gun she'd never seen to even attempt sleep. She decided to take a hot shower and crawl into bed with the rest of the proposal on *Death of a Grandmother*. If that didn't put her to sleep *Holistic Health and Nutrition for Your Pet* couldn't miss.

She was down to stripping off her bra and panties before she thought to wonder if Jack Monroe could be standing around without his body scrutinizing hers.

Charlie stood under the hot water until it started turning cold on her. Instead of relaxing, as had been the plan, she allowed the fact of those prints to really soak in. First of all, it was impossible. Second of all, she couldn't go to jail for murder because of Libby and because she had a job. Even by now Edwina and Libby were probably at each other's throats. They got along fine only as long as they had Charlie to gang up on and flay between them. And how would she ever explain this to Richard Morse of Congdon and Morse Representation, Inc.? And what about all her writers? It wasn't as though no one depended on Charlie.

By the time Charlie stepped out of the shower, she was so worked up Jack Monroe could have been standing there completely visible in his body and she'd have just flipped him off on her way past.

She might as well forget sleep for a week. Oh, and she could hear Edwina already, "I told you you'd end up in a bad way. Wreck every life you ever touched." Well okay, she'd borrowed that from Wes Bennett but it sure sounded familiar.

By now Charlie was in her nightshirt and in bed and so hot under the collar she had to throw aside one of the blankets— only in Oregon or maybe Alaska would there be two blankets on a bed in June and a quilt for a bedspread.

Chapter Two of *Death of a Grandmother* started off with Patsy Prudhomme meeting the big handsome Sheriff Lester of the unnamed county. He questioned Patsy and immediately hauled her off to his bachelor pad on a mountaintop overlooking the Pacific Ocean—instead of to the courthouse for fingerprinting. Paige Magill might have her mystery and her romance genres confused but she sure had visited the home of the sheriff of Moot County.

The lurid details of the fictional encounter would have been funny if Charlie had not just returned from that mountaintop herself.

Of course when Paige was up there, she hadn't been a chief suspect in a murder investigation. Charlie went back over the lurid parts again. Nah, Sheriff Bennett wouldn't have served Patsy (Paige?) California wine and not even bothered with dinner before screwing. No fajitas, no frijoles, no nothing but grunting and some truly incredible positioning! No phone calls about disturbing kids, no mention of former wives and present responsibilities. Just panting and sweat and ecstasy.

"Damn near make you want to go out and commit murder just to get arrested by Sheriff Les."

Charlie didn't know that there was ever anything between Wes Bennett and Paige Magill. And if there was, they were both well of age. What she should be thinking about is how those fingerprints found their way onto the murder weapon. Did fingerprints never lie? And why, if the sheriff thought he had any case at all, would he confide to her things like the Ziploc bag and the too-clear prints? There must be something very wrong with those fingerprints.

"There are five totally unexplainable things here. How did the body of Georgette Glick get under my car? How did my fingerprints get on the murder weapon? How did my lenses get under the bed? How could I dream of the wreck of the Peter Iredale before I ever saw it, either in Michael Cermack's painting or for real in its grave on the beach? And how am I going to get out of all this?"

"You're just tired. It's very simple. The murderer put Georgette

under the Toyota to frame you rather than someone he knew. And somehow he got you to touch the handle of the gun without knowing it. Either that or he could somehow transfer the fingerprints from something else you knowingly touched. And Jack came over here while you were away and moved your contacts because he wants you to help him convince the people at Morton and Fish that he really can OOBE. And the Peter Iredale is probably much photographed because it is so accessible and you probably saw it in a National Geographic or even a poster store and subconsciously registered that it was located on the coast of Oregon, so when you came up here your mind connected the two and threw you a dream about it before you saw it on the beach."

Sometimes Charlie's rational mind simply astounded her. But it didn't usually work this efficiently until after her first cup of coffee in the morning. "And the last one? How am I going to get out of this?"

"Relax and let the law do the investigating as I've said all along. You're well aware of the sheriff's attraction to you. He'll find the answers to clear you. He knows his job, he likes you, and all you're doing is making it harder for him by mixing up the puzzle pieces."

Charlie was right. She really ought to listen to herself more often. She sighed, stretched, reached up, and turned off the lamp on the bedside table. Just for kicks she slid out of bed and to the window, pulling a crack open where the short drapes met in the middle. The deputy was drinking coffee and reading a magazine under the patrol car's inside overhead light. He must have a powerful battery.

Back in bed, snuggled under both blankets now and cuddly warm, Charlie had almost drifted off to sleep when her eyes popped open. "That still doesn't explain how Jack Monroe knew everything Deputy Tortle and I said."

She and her rational mind began chewing it over again. Charlie just knew the answers lay in all the little puzzle pieces she'd collected. If she believed everything people told her— Paige Magill played Brother Dennis off Jack Monroe, Doc Withers slept with ducks and Gladys Bergkvist, Rose was a part-

Italian natural psychic who had to sell control of her restaurant to a Japanese concern, Brother Dennis practically supported the little community with his institute, Michael Cermack had either misplaced his gun or someone had stolen it to murder Georgette, sisters Mary and Norma wandered around after dark with flashlights to clean up the roadsides, Jack Monroe wandered around without his body, Clara Peterson—as sweet as she was—didn't really seem to approve of anyone except maybe Mary and Norma, Frank Glick let his wife go off on a foggy night on a bike without lights, Gladys Bergkvist did not associate with her poorer retired peers and did not believe in subsidizing them, Olie spent only the summer months at his home and was late getting back this summer, and you ate *lefsa* with margarine.

According to Paige's mystery proposal Paige knew the layout of Michael's loft as well as the sheriff's eyrie. Linda Tortle had attended the institute and she had had an affair with Doc Withers. And Georgette Glick was nosy. The gun was found in the damp ditch last night, so Charlie's prints (if they indeed were) must have gotten on it between the time Georgie was shot and the next evening. What had Charlie touched during that time? All kinds of things at the Earth Spirit and here at the Hide-a-bye, some at Page Magill's house and at Rose's. Probably a few things in Frank's trailer home, nothing she could remember at the Scandia.

The next thing Charlie knew she was sitting up in bed watching the door to the outside fly into the entryway through the open door of the bedroom, the sheriff following his shoulder right behind it and yelling her name. It was daylight.

Chapter 18

"This time you lock the door." Wes sat on the side of the bed, the deputy leaning in the doorway. They had rushed in, Wes searching the room for an intruder, the deputy with gun drawn heading to check the rest of the cabin only to come back and eye Charlie skeptically. "What were you screaming for?"

"I wasn't screaming. Was I screaming?"

Wes rubbed the back of his neck, rolled his head from side to side. Charlie could hear his neck cracking. "Not only am I losing sleep and the department is going to have to pay overtime for Tuttle and Olsen here, but we're going to owe the Hide-a-bye for a goddamned door, just because you decided to have a nightmare. You are a walking disaster area."

"Nightmare, that's it. I was having a dream."

"Great." He cracked his neck so hard Charlie winced and Olsen grimaced. "Get dressed. I'll take you to Rose's."

"No, wait, I sort of remember this one. I just don't remember screaming."

"There's a lady over at Moot Point who can really help you

out if you're bothered by dreams," Deputy Olsen offered. "Finally took my girlfriend there and after about five or ten sessions she ain't had a—"

Wes had stopped cracking his neck knuckles and turned, displaying the full force of his mood. The deputy nodded and took off. Charlie grabbed some clothes and headed for the bathroom before she received the same treatment.

They were the first two people at Rose's. She poured them coffee and juice and told them they'd have to wait for the grill to warm up. "And the cook."

Wes said, "I thought somebody was in there killing you."

"I was lying on the ceiling and having an awful time getting back to my body and my bed and panicking."

"At least you got enough sleep to dream."

"You don't look like you had much. Was it just me and the fingerprints or Joseph too?"

"Joseph his mother calls him, I call him Joe. She's married to a hotshot lawyer who's got his little balls all primed to get the kid off the hook with influence. As if poor old young Joe didn't have enough strikes against him without influence."

"Is it drugs or—"

"Rape." His coloring this morning reminded Charlie of the storm color of the sea yesterday. His eyes were streaked with red. Bloody dots on his chin and neck bespoke a hasty shave.

"Oh, Wes, I'm sorry."

"It's not the first time. I been on the phone all night trying to talk everybody into stopping long enough to think. Counseling is wonderful but it's not going stop the problem if the kid's running loose. There are victims out there who are not going to appreciate it."

"And I thought I had problems with Libby. It must be tearing you up."

"I know what you think of me, Charlie, but honest to God I only had him with me for four years. I swear he didn't get this off me. I walk on eggshells trying not to step on toes of small people behind me if I just need to back up. Or away."

"Where are Joseph and his mom and her lawyer?"

"California, where else?" Then he remembered who he was talking to and shrugged.

Charlie couldn't be sure whether the sky was going to clear today or not. It was a gray morning but the sun hadn't breached the mountaintops on the other side of 101 yet. The sea was still angry though. It flung foam halfway up bird-island rocks off the point and roiled and tumbled against the beach below the village to rattle Rose's windows. The fresh salty sea wind seeped through the walls to mix with frying bacon and fresh-brewed coffee—making Charlie long to come here sometime on a real vacation.

Even under his staggering load of worries, Wes managed to plow through his veggie-and-cream-cheese omelet and automatically reach for her half-eaten Sunday special. She cupped her hands around her hot coffee mug and allowed herself to enjoy the implied intimacy of that act without letting it show on her face. What would it be like to live with someone so familiar he didn't think twice about being that familiar? No way, Charlie Greene.

"Wasn't Deputy Tortle supposed to come baby-sit me this morning?"

"Oh, shit. I completely forgot."

"Only reason I remembered," Charlie said, "is she just walked in the door. She has spotted us and doesn't look exactly—Good morning, Deputy. Won't you join us?"

"Please don't get up," the deputy said.

But her boss was already on his feet with the last strip of Charlie's bacon in his hand. "Oh, Jesus, I'm sorry. I forgot all about you coming this morning. How'd you find us?"

"Woman's intuition," Linda answered pointedly, and added a slow blink, then a "sir."

"Right. Well, sit down, Tuttle, I'll buy you breakfast to make up for it." He was about six inches off the chair when he noticed the deputy standing straight and tall. And rigid. "Uh, Tortle, I mean. What will you have? Rose, there's another customer here. Put it on my bill."

"Deputy Linda Tortle," Charlie reminded him. His was a very selective memory. He knew who Rose was. But then again he had a codependency problem with food.

"Deputy Linda Tortle, I recommend the omelet of the day highly," Wes said magnanimously and settled with relief as Linda lowered herself into the chair next to Charlie.

Linda ordered French toast and bacon and, when the sheriff left, moved over to his chair facing Charlie, her expression warming not at all. "So, you must have really pissed him off last night. What'd you do, lock him out?"

"Who, the sheriff? No."

"When I got there this little man was fixing the door. Said the sheriff had busted it."

"Oh, that was because he and Deputy Olson heard me screaming."

"What were you doing, reading Brother Dennis's screenplay again?" She couldn't hide the grin that slipped into her eyes before she could lower those magnificent lashes on it.

"No, I was dreaming, and apparently woke up screaming just as the sheriff pulled up. I was dreaming I was having an OOBE like Jack does and I couldn't get back into my body. How was Peety?"

The long, stern face softened. "We got in a workout at the gym, dinner at his favorite hamburger joint, a movie, and made it home in time to catch a late one on TV. That's why I was late this morning. Not that anybody was there to notice."

"Does Wes treat all female deputies like he treats you?"

"There're only two of us. Mona knows how to blend in— you'll notice I didn't say fit in—and she knows how to curtsy without you realizing it. Quite an art. But then I don't suppose she has anything on you. Your fingerprints are on a murder weapon and you're walking around free."

"More like under house arrest."

When they reached cabin three at the Hide-a-bye, the maid was just coming in to clean and there was a note asking Charlie to come to the office and pick up the new key since the door had been replaced. When they left the office the sun was high enough to begin burning off the gloom hanging over the Pacific and to warm their shoulders when they lingered in open spots. Little birds chirped and sang and darted from bush to bush, their berry picking causing branches to jerk and tremble at odd intervals and spacing as though a confused breeze had come along to fondle only selected branches. Bigger birds called and crooned in the higher trees, leaving behind an echo something like a jungle sound track.

Charlie sighed and stretched. "Is there any reason why I have to stay in the cabin, if my jailor goes on a walk with me?"

"Usually I could come up with twenty in a minute, but I don't know how you'd get away from me. And a morning like this shouldn't be wasted. You make one suspicious move though and I'll put cuffs on you."

They walked down the stairs and along the beach, Charlie picking up shells and putting them down again. Large doses of nature could make her nervous but the thought of sitting around the cabin all day staring back at Deputy Linda was far more daunting. Something about Mother Nature Charlie didn't trust. The raw beauty here was undeniable, but even while her eyes took pleasure in it her ears were pricking to the vast ominous empty silence. Which was filled with sounds. Maybe that was it.

Seabirds "screed" and squawked on one side of her and land birds chirped and called on the other. Sun or no, the Pacific was all roiled up and thundering. There was no end of sound, but it was all a sort of floating background noise to the silence. She tried to explain some of this to her companion but got only a raised eyebrow and a frown. It didn't really make sense. Her fingerprints being on that gun didn't make sense either, but apparently it was true.

Maybe it had something to do with perception somehow.

Like that sign in the Earth Spirit, *To the blind all things are sudden.*

"What's wrong with those fingerprints on the gun?"

"Revolver. I don't see anything wrong with them. They're a lot easier to explain than Jack Monroe overhearing our conversation yesterday, unless you were wearing a wire or misreporting what he said to you over the phone. Both of which in the light of day look highly possible."

"What about the prints needs explaining? The sheriff said they were very clear and would hold up in court."

"They're backwards."

"Oh, backwards." Their pace picked up as the deputy seemed to feel a need for exercise. Charlie dreaded that the day would come when eating only half of what was on her plate and trying to fool her appetite with diet colas wouldn't suffice and she'd need to get in the exercise mode, too. Did they have Jazzercise classes in prison?

"Since I've already shot off my big mouth I might as well tell you what I think," Linda said finally, not even breathing heavily. "Backwards is no mystery to me at all. You shoot Mrs. Glick wearing gloves or wipe off the prints afterward, get rattled, and forget to wear gloves when sticking the weapon into the Baggie butt first."

"The prints were on the barrel? Backwards? Why would I put the gun in a plastic bag, why not just throw it into the ditch?"

"I don't know. That's not my problem."

"Why would I shoot that old woman in the fog anyway?" Why would anyone? It always came back to that.

"That's not my problem either. That's not my job. That's for the judge and the jury. But come the word on this radio," she clicked her fingernails on the black box hanging from her belt, "come the right moment, my job could be that of arresting officer. Is that clear, Ms. Greene?"

"Do you only just do your job, Deputy Tortle?" Aren't you tempted to think for yourself?

"Unlike a mutual acquaintance of ours, yes."

Charlie wondered if Wes Bennett had any idea of the trouble his consistently offended deputy could cause him in the next election. Linda might be able to lessen the risk to her job and Peety's future while still getting revenge by serving as the source of anonymous leaks to the media about her boss's private life and, at least on one instance, of his coddling a particular female suspect in a murder case. It was a man's world still, but thwarted women had long ago found ways to gouge chinks in its privileged armor.

The *Peter Iredale* was on them before Charlie was ready. That seemed always to be her introduction to it.

"Hey, you all right? Don't try anything flaky on me now," Linda warned.

Charlie sat in the sand, her heart pumping louder than the surf. "I was here last night."

"With Sheriff Bennett?"

"I keep coming here in my dreams," Charlie said dully. "And when I try to get back to the Hide-a-bye I keep hitting the ceiling on my back."

"You make one suspicious twitch and you're cuffed."

"I don't understand why that wreck has such an effect on me."

"Been there since 1906. Some stupid skipper beached it. Lucky it wasn't an oil tanker."

The iron ribs of the *Peter Iredale* were dressed in foam today as the breakers assaulted it. Early this morning it had been wreathed in a dim and foggy dawn but Charlie had seen it clearly. Early this morning the tide was higher and the ocean had been a somber oily color. Today it was a bright green, the white foam sparking in the sun, what remained of the rusty skeleton looking darkly out of place.

Chapter 19

Monday morning found Charlie still under the informal house arrest and on the phone to Congdon and Morse Representation, Inc. She'd called home earlier to find Tuxedo still in residence. Richard Morse was all for rushing up there and informing the authorities they couldn't railroad Charlie just to clear a murder case off the books.

"I have some influence in the world, after all. And where I don't I can find people who do," he said over the sounds of the remodeling job going on in the hallways. "Just because you're a single mother doesn't mean they—"

"Thanks, but to paraphrase a friend of mine, influence might not be the best idea at the moment." Charlie couldn't imagine what influence he thought he could have in a Moot County, Oregon murder investigation. "I'll keep you informed of what's happening and if I need a lawyer. Can you switch me to Larry?"

Not until further posturing, indignation, and reassurances of his support he couldn't. Charlie owed him enough already, but hearing it all made her feel a lot less alone in the world and she was grateful. She'd met Richard Morse when she worked as a Hollywood liaison for a large literary agency in New York, and he'd eventually convinced her to come out to California and work for him. It was nice to live in the sunshine again and Libby hadn't minded the move one bit.

Larry, her assistant, offered to come up and play Sir Galahad, too.

"That's sweet, Larry, I appreciate it, but I haven't really been charged with anything yet. Right now what I need is for you to start going through my phone log. The ones marked with asterisks are have-to progress checks." Anyone who thought the life of a Hollywood script agent glamorous would be surprised to watch one at work at her desk all day with a phone growing out of her ear. "Oh, and would you call Keegan Monroe and tell him his Dad is fine? I don't know if Jack thought to call Keegan."

They worked on an excuse (unavoidably detained out of town—let them think she was in New York) to reschedule a lunch with studio execs trying to screw David Hynd out of payment for certain hasty rewrites later dumped in story committee. And they discussed which of her phone messages he should answer for her and which should await her return.

Charlie sat back in the recliner and swiveled to stare out the front wall of window at another gray day. The sky was a lighter gray than the ocean and she could just make out the line on the horizon where they met. Coming straight at them at an immensely slow rate was a black-hulled ship with a light-colored superstructure and short puffs of black smoke issuing from its stacks. Charlie watched it while disjointed thoughts nudged each other for her listless attention.

Deputy Olsen sat at the Formica table contentedly playing solitaire. Today was Georgette Glick's memorial service and Charlie wanted to go, just to watch people's reactions. But her presence would probably infuriate Randolph Glick. Both Richard Morse and Larry reminded her of Randolph and his threats to Wes about his influence in Salem. They also reminded her of

Joseph Bennett's lawyer stepfather. She hadn't seen Wes Bennett since breakfast the day before. Deputies Olsen and Tortle had been taking turns as her baby-sitter and Wes had sent over groceries to stock the kitchen. It looked like she was truly stuck this time.

A speck broke the monotony of the horizon and gradually became another ship following the path of the first. Must have traffic patterns like an airport out there. The first ship turned its nose toward Chinook and now, with the long side facing her, Charlie could see it was dark gray instead of black. When the second ship reached the turning point it displayed a two-tone hull, red below and black above, and had "HYUNDAI" written across the side in giant white letters.

Watching the big ships passing made Charlie feel even more a prisoner.

Deputy Olsen looked up from his cards. "Want me to turn on the TV?"

"No, please. Daytime television drives me crazy."

"Too bad you don't have no VCR. There's probably cable if you want to watch a movie." When Charlie shook her head even harder he said, "I could call Linda, ask her to stop by the library for a book before she comes down if you want. Better yet, she could pick up some mysteries at Mrs. Peterson's just over to the point. She's got tons and she's usually pretty good about lending them."

"Clara Peterson? The bird lady?"

"The one lives in the trailer house between old Frank Glick and the widowed sisters who found the revolver." Deputy Olsen had borrowed some mysteries from Clara when he'd had to care for a dying mother who used to live a few miles south of Moot Point. "Mrs. Peterson's got bookshelves covering every wall where there's not a window. Wouldn't be surprised to find she's got boxes of them stashed away too."

Clara hadn't seemed the type to read mysteries, but she had mentioned she watched *Mystery* on PBS. Charlie sat up straighter. "Do you know the people at the village very well?"

"I got orders not to discuss the case."

"Not the case, just the people."

The deputy really preferred talking to solitaire and Charlie flattered him with rapt attention. She learned all sorts of unre-lated, probably useless things to mess up the puzzle and a morn-ing that had promised to drag flew by. Deputy Olsen, too, had lived three miles from Moot Point until his mother died just last year.

The Moot Point Consciousness Training Institute was in trouble financially. The deputy's brother was a contractor in Chinook and preparing to take Brother Dennis to court for outstanding debts dating back to the second or third renovation of the place. The main building had been built in stages and improved over the years. "Used to be a money-maker, and if he'd just paid off his bills instead of getting bigger and better, he'd have been all right. The Japanese are buying up everything in sight. It would be a shame to see the institute go, too, but what you gonna do? Guy can't pay his bills."

"What would the Japanese want with an odd building like that?"

"There's a lot of land with it. And with a prime view. I've heard speculation it could be turned into a fancy restaurant, maybe a luxury hotel built around it."

"Might not be so good for Rose."

"Probably close her down."

"Do you know Olie Bergkvist?"

"Seen him in church a few times. Big good-looking older gent. He's not around much. Usually Gladys comes alone. Got that painter fellow living over her garage. He's a kettle of fish smells, if you ask me. Something unhealthy about that whole setup. Olie spent a lot more time at home when his first wife was alive. So my folks used to say anyway."

Olie Bergkvist, so the deputy's folks used to say, had made a fortune off the used car business in Portland and then Chinook, but had always had a hobby collecting art. His first wife died of breast cancer about twenty years ago and their only child, a son, in an automobile accident five years later. A year before that Olie had married Gladys, a widow and schoolteacher in Astoria, and installed her in the house he built in Moot Point.

"I think she was Finnish before her marriages, but I can't remember for sure. Either that or her first husband was a Finn. And I believe she was an art teacher, but anyway he leaves her in control of the Scandia when he's away. Which is most of the time. Who better than an art teacher to watch it for him while he's gone?"

"Gladys came from Finland?"

"More likely her grandparents."

"Well, if the institute goes under, everything in the village, except maybe those living on social security and pension checks . . . I mean what little business there is will go under too, won't it?"

"Scary what's happening all over the country."

Charlie set out smoked salmon and hard rolls and cheese and deli potato salad for lunch. And tasty selections of locally grown cherries and berries and plums. Deputy Olsen kept talking while he ate but declined the salmon. "I get so tired of fish. In Texas, I suppose poor kids lived on beans. Well, in Oregon guess what we lived on?"

Rose came from Astoria too. Rose Kortinemi. "Finn mixed with Italian, if that ain't a fishy salad."

"Rose came from Italy or Finland?"

"Her father's family sometime back came from Finland." Deputy Olsen scraped a Bing cherry off its stem and seed. "Who knows where Italians come from?"

He was young and pale and pleasantly freckled and, Charlie had a totally groundless inkling, not nearly as tough as Deputy Tortle. If Charlie ever had to elude either one, she'd pick Olsen. If anything, Linda Tortle overestimated Charlie's capacities and nerve.

"You said yesterday morning you took your girlfriend to get help for her dreams to Paige Magill and it really helped her. Do you still think I should go?" Charlie rose to put the teakettle on and rummaged through the supplies to find Hostess Twinkies for the deputy's dessert.

"I wouldn't take out an IRA from the Magill woman, mind you, but Stephy certainly got straightened out at the Dream Emporium. And if you knew Stephy, well—"

"What does Paige Magill do? How long did the straightening-out last?"

"Got her to keep going over her dreams until she figured out what they meant. See, the dreams was telling Stephy something in her life was wrong and it was daytime stuff that was actually bugging her, but the dreams were trying to work it out. They finally decided it was because she was still living with her folks and her dad's always making her feel dumb. She moves in with me and she stops dreaming altogether." He reddened slightly when he thought about that and Charlie covered her grin with the pretense of wiping cherry juice from her lips. "It took a couple of months is all, her going once a week."

Stephy had been out of high school for five years and had worked her way up from stocker to checkout at a Chinook supermarket. Deputy Olsen droned on and Charlie's attention had begun to wander when suddenly he was talking about Paige Magill again.

"I hear she has lots of men friends," Charlie said, trying to catch up with the conversation and aim it to suit her.

He shrugged as if he didn't pay attention to that sort of gossip and squished the filling pulp out of his Twinkie to lick separately. Then he paused with a glob still on his lip. "Well, I did see her once in the little red Ferrari with that painter, Michael. He drives like he's demented which, if you listen to him at all, it appears that's just what he is. People like him shouldn't have a driver's license, let alone a Ferrari."

This sounded promising and Charlie was about to pursue it when someone knocked at the door. Her jailor went to answer it. It was Jack Monroe.

He was in his body.

He kept trying to peer over the deputy's shoulder or around it to talk to Charlie but was told no visitors. "But she's my agent and I just sold my book and—"

"I heard about that. Congratulations, Mr. Monroe."

"Thanks, but you see," and he raised his voice to be sure Charlie heard, "I've got this chapter here and I'd like her opinion on it. It won't take long. If you could just give us a few minutes."

"Sorry, but I'll give it to her for you."

Charlie groaned and rubbed the back of her neck like the sheriff had this morning. Needing constant reassurance each step of the way was the sign of an amateur. A professional, whether it was his first book or his fifth, did his own work and took his lumps. If Charlie praised the chapter, Jack would waste weeks daydreaming of glory and perhaps refuse to heed an editor's call for revisions.

"But my agent said this was the best part."

"Your agent's not the one buying the book, Jack."

If Charlie panned it or sounded a sour note he could very well be unable to complete the manuscript, so deep in despair would she have flung him. Charlie's favorite amateur clients had spouses or live-ins to inflict this torture upon by making them read and comment on the manuscript-in-progress every day and letting Charlie off the hook.

"I should look at this first," the deputy apologized when he brought the chapter back to the table, its author shut out in the cold, gray day. "Be sure he's not passing on some kind of information about the murder, you know."

"Deputy Olsen, be my guest." This was the very last time Charlie would allow herself to get horned into representing an amateur who did not have either a fall-over-dead blockbuster idea going for him or superstar status already established in another field, so help her God.

"You know, my Stephy writes a pretty mean poem. Maybe you should look at some of her writing. She's a lot better at typewriting than Jack Monroe too."

"Agents don't handle poetry, Deputy."

"Ooo-ob?" he asked, puzzled. "Ooooo-bee? What's he talking about?"

Charlie grabbed the first page, ignoring the misspellings and clumsy typing, and read about Jack's first experiments with out-of-body experiences.

He'd kept thinking he was lying on the ceiling and that he was asleep.

Chapter 20

When Deputy Tortle came to relieve Deputy Olsen, she found her colleague and Charlie deep in contemplation of OOBE's and Jack's chapter. Linda Tortle carried in still more groceries and put them in the refrigerator. Sheriff Bennett either assumed everybody ate like he did or wanted to make sure Charlie had no excuse to leave cabin three at the Hide-a-bye for the rest of the week.

"So what are you scheming now?" Linda asked once she'd shooed Olsen on his way and taken his place in front of Jack's chapter.

"I've learned that either Jack Monroe has the same dreams I do and thinks they're OOBE's, or I have OOBE's like he does and think they're dreams." At first, Jack wrote, he could never remember these dreams, would just find himself in a panic trying to return to his body. But then he'd visit a place and know he had been there in his dreams. The chapter ended with the hook, "And then one day I realized these experiences weren't dreams!"

"I've had this feeling of flying out of control and getting all tingly just as I fell asleep before," the deputy said after she'd read for awhile.

"I think everybody has," Charlie assured her. Jack made it sound as though at certain times in life and under certain circumstances, even in certain places, it was likely to happen to anyone, but that only he and a few others had recognized it for what it was and perfected a technique enabling them to do it at will and to have some control over destinations.

Charlie tried to think of what she'd tell Jack. Actually it wasn't bad for rough copy but a chapter does not a book make and she didn't have her copy of his proposal to fit this chapter into the total picture. For lack of anything else to do Charlie retrieved *Death of a Grandmother*. She'd read the sample chapters but hadn't finished the summary of the rest.

After Sheriff Lester and Patsy Prudhomme's steamy session in the sheriff's mountaintop home, he had to arrest her for the murder of Gertrude Geis. Seems that Gertrude was shot and Patsy's prints were found on the gun and the gun was found in the trunk of her car. Meanwhile, Patsy was having dreams very like the ones Charlie had described to Paige over teacups.

Once in jail Patsy was subjected to "horrid abuse" but couldn't convince her lawyer of that. And the sheriff refused to see her. This was all very generally summarized, but Charlie found it chilling. Which of course was the intent.

"Deputy Olsen let me call my family and my office this morning," she told Linda. "My boss claims you people will have to charge me pretty soon or let me go. He says—"

"You're not in jail, are you? You could be a prime witness being guarded by the department."

"Or a chief suspect nobody can quite believe committed the crime in spite of fingerprints on the gun."

"Revolver."

"Sheriff Bennett's just trying to keep me from mixing up the puzzles, isn't he?"

"If you mean from interfering in a murder investigation, yes."

"Did you tell him about *Death of a Grandmother?*"

"It's in my report." Deputy Linda rose to switch on the television, knowing better than to ask Charlie's permission.

Charlie made it about halfway through a talk show that delved into such deep and mind-numbing problems as, How do you feel when you're feeling feelings, before she jumped to her feet and insisted they take a walk.

"Why? The weather's crummy." Linda squinted up at Charlie as if trying to place her.

"Either that or let me call my lawyer."

Charlie was a little surprised to find herself strolling along the path to the lighthouse minutes later. "Never assume a door is locked to you," Richard Morse of Congdon and Morse Representation, Inc. had told her more than once, "until you have tried the knob, knocked, and then rammed it. People will always let you assume what it is most convenient for them to have you assume."

Charlie glanced at the tall authoritarian figure beside her. "Did you know that Deputy Olsen's brother is preparing to take Brother Dennis to court over long-standing bills?"

"Deputy Olsen was told not to discuss the case and so was I." But Linda's steps had paused.

"His brother's a contractor who's done a lot of work on the institute's main building and I didn't know we were discussing the case and I'm sure Olsen didn't either. We were just talking about Brother Dennis."

It wasn't so cold that they saw their breaths, but dampness on the chill wind insinuated itself through their clothes. It was hard to believe they'd worked up a light sweat walking the other direction the day before.

"The institute sells all those books and tapes, charges the earth for its seminars. The town's packed with searchers today and cars and—" Linda shrugged, "—sure seemed like a going concern."

"And the village lives off it, has grown very used to the extra, and sometimes the only, money other than social security and pension checks coming in. And most of the money from them is spent elsewhere, where there's services like groceries, drug and clothing stores, that kind of thing." Charlie thought of trying to raise Libby here and shuddered. And she tried to figure how this puzzle piece could possibly fit into the one about a seventy-eight-year-old woman getting shot off her Schwinn on a foggy night.

"Well, there're tourists."

"Who come in the summer months mostly, right? Just like the searchers. This is June and Moot Point doesn't seem that full of tourists. June is when an awful lot of people travel in this hemisphere."

"It's a long coast," Linda said defensively.

"And the long, rainy, stormy winters attract only a select tourist trade."

The trail with its chopped-off bushes on either side reminded Charlie of the arbitrarily contoured bushes of a maze in the garden of a mansion in Beverly Hills. It had once belonged to a silent screen star and was now the residence of kids little older than Libby who'd made it big in the video biz.

Long strong thorns and pale pink roses decorated much of the thick growth behind the fence—the bushes droned with bees.

The deputy turned away from the lighthouse when they reached the Porta Pottis and headed up another paved trail running along the headland. Here tall grasses and wildflowers threatened the trail—swaths of purple lupine, yellow daisies, and a large clump of white lace on a tall stalk.

Ahead, a line of bicycles zigzagged down 101, and behind them a solid wall of rain forest, pine and deciduous with bushy undergrowth choking the trunks, rose up the mountainside to be lost in cloud. Charlie could see how the bigfoot phenomenon started in such forests. If you saw something suspicious, you couldn't chase it down without a machete. And it would be a lot harder to shoot than an old lady on a bicycle in the fog.

Deputy Linda and the trail turned suddenly and swooped down off the headland toward the road that led to the Hide-a-bye. When they reached it Linda turned toward the sea and the cabins, but Charlie crossed it and picked up the path again on the other side. The deputy swore behind her but turned back to follow Charlie.

What was it Richard Morse often said? (The man overflowed with his own peculiar brand of homily.) "Your trouble, Charlie, is you keep thinking the system works. While thinking people work the system."

"What's so damn funny now?" Linda asked behind her.

This trail continued down to a small inlet and left them. Charlie's only recourse was to follow the trickle of water emanating from the rain forest through a sewer pipe under 101 as it headed for the sea.

Once she reached the beach she turned north and averted her eyes toward the bank of sand and clump grass on her right when she passed the rusty ribs of the skeleton ship on her left.

"Look, you said a walk, not a marathon," Linda complained.

The sea mist left the taste of salt on Charlie's lips and was so thick it looked like rain up ahead. But when they reached "up head" it looked like rain where they had been. Another headland stopped her finally. Sudsy breakers exploded against and over rocks, sprayed into bushes and shore pines that grew right down to the water wherever they found foothold. "Must be high tide."

"High enough." Linda Tortle squinted into the wind, her permed hair escaping the comb clasp in frizzy, gyrating streamers. "Time to go back."

She looked dangerous again, still, steely. They had a staring match. Charlie was angry too. She wouldn't have gotten this far if the Moot County Sheriff's Department had any right at all to keep her under surveillance without charging her with anything. She was about to say just that when a siren wailed in the distance and the deputy's radio went off up close.

"What the hell are you doing down there?" Wes Bennett's voice crackled from the box Linda had taken from the hook on her belt. The official Bronco crested a dune about forty yards back the way they'd come and hurtled down a sand road Charlie hadn't noticed, siren and lights at maximum flash and octaves.

Charlie sat in back this time, chain mesh separating her from the officers so she couldn't attack them from behind. The sheriff had been on an emergency run from Chinook when he spied them on the beach below.

"We'll drop her off," Wes interrupted his deputy's attempt to explain the walk on the beach. "You follow me in your car."

"She won't stay put. You'll have to lock her in somehow."

Charlie could remember watching her parents' heads from the back of the family car when she was a kid as they discussed her in the third person this way.

The sheriff made frustrated noises in the back of his nose and ended up taking Charlie with him. He made unintelligible sounds in answer to the unintelligible sounds coming in over the radio as they careened down off Highway 101 into the village of Moot Point, siren screaming, and Deputy Linda not far behind.

Charlie was startled at the number of cars and people on the streets. Frank and Randolph Glick in suits and ties stepped off the road to let them pass, peering in at her with surprise. Clara Peterson stood with Mary and Norma in their front yard, all in dresses and hose, white shoes and matching handbags. They must have just returned from Georgie's memorial service. But the town was crowded with informally dressed visitors, too. Several people stood on the porch of Jack's store, their hands cupped around their eyes to peer inside.

Out at the point in the parking lot below the lighthouse a third sheriff's department car parked crosswise and empty, its pulsers still flicking, its door hanging open. Several couples in windbreakers segmented by camera-bag straps stood looking over the edge of the parking lot to the beach below.

Next to them was a gaping hole in the guardrail.

Chapter 21

Wind scooted sand grains along the surface of the beach, just a tiny few off the top layer as it dried them. They made a whispering sound Charlie could barely hear over the roar of the surf. Foam from a wave that crept up on the red Ferrari left patches of suds in Michael Cermack's dark hair. He wasn't handsome anymore.

"I told you to stay in the car," Wes said as she walked up beside him, but he sounded defeated. And he hadn't locked her in.

The Ferrari wasn't pretty anymore either. It had bounced and flipped when it hit and lay crumpled on its top with Michael sprawled half out of it. Most of the breakers didn't reach farther than a few inches up the length of the car and, as she had come down the path, Charlie heard Wes order everybody away from it. He sent Linda back to the village to question everyone she could find about Michael's movements today.

"I want nothing touched and I want a full crime scene crew on the double," he'd told the other deputy. "Then I want statements from the witnesses in the lot and whoever is in the light-house." After missing Georgette's bullet wound a few days ago, he was taking no chances that this was more than just an acci-dent. His minions scampered, giving Charlie hard looks as they passed her.

Swallows with narrow pointy wings swooped and soared and darted among invisible hordes of insects. Their shadows winked across Michael's death scene without compassion.

"At least I can't be blamed for this," Charlie said and swal-lowed back unpleasant tastes. "I've been so well chaperoned lately."

She didn't realize she was leaning against Wes until he turned her around. "Keep looking at him and your nightmares are re-ally going to get squirrelly. I can't spare anyone to keep you out of trouble right now. Charlie, I need to be able to trust you."

"And I need a drink."

"Go back to Rose's and stay there. Don't wander around town, promise me. I'll pick you up or send somebody."

"I don't have any money. I thought I was just going for a walk."

He fished out a ten and added a handful of change. "Here, have one for me too." He gave her a very unsherifflike swat on the tush. "Now get out of here."

With the low backless padded stools you could swivel, Rose's bar was also the breakfast counter. The plastic pastry displays held pie now instead of cinnamon rolls, and on top of them plastic signs displayed pictures of cocktails sporting exotic fruit and names. In the slit in the center of the liquor bottles, where most bars had mirrors, the heads of kitchen people doing kitchen things darted about like the swallows. Rose served as bartender and handled the cash register at one end of the counter. But she kept peeking into the slit as if she'd rather be in the kitchen.

Charlie took the stool next to Gladys Bergkvist and ordered a vodka tonic. They were the only two at the breakfast-and-booze bar. She could have chosen one of the other stools. But the sheriff had said don't wander around the town. He hadn't said don't sit next to Gladys Bergkvist, the employer and landlord of the recently deceased artist who had probably owned the gun that killed Georgette Glick. The gun that had sprouted Charlie's fingerprints all by itself.

Charlie smiled. Rose and Gladys exchanged hooded looks. This was the only bar and commercial eatery in the village. In fact, Charlie hadn't noticed anyplace else that even sold groceries. She said, "I'm sorry about Michael."

Rose and Gladys put fingers to their lips and shook their heads in sync. Rose signaled with her eyes to the darting heads in the slit and mouthed, "Wait."

"For what?"

Gladys leaned into her ear, smelling like scotch. "Wait till the van's loaded. If they hear about the accident now they'll have to stop and discuss it. Food'll get cold."

Charlie answered her conspiratorial wink with a nod. Rose slipped back into the kitchen, where the darting picked up speed and the harried clang and clatter increased. "Van?"

"Takes dinner to the institute. They put it in containers to keep it warm and serve it buffet style up there." She flicked her wrist and clicked her bracelets uphill. "When it's over, everything's packed back here. No fuss, no muss."

Gladys's outfit today was a cranberry-and-beige flowered skirt with a cranberry-colored blouse, and the stones in her earrings, necklace, and bracelets were a deep expensive blue, mounted in the dull gleam of real gold. Charlie wondered why anyone bothered to murder old ladies on Schwinns or perhaps even artists in Ferraris when Gladys Bergkvist walked around offering a fortune for a simple mugging.

"So, what are the searchers having for dinner tonight?"

"Dill, spinach, tomato, and sprout quiche Dijon, asparagus artichoke vinegarette, fresh garlic-onion bread, and lemon honey yogurt Grape-Nut parfait, with a choice of fresh-ground Kona coffee or Celestial Seasonings herb teas. Same as the special on the board up there."

"Grape-Nut?"

"Gives it crunch," Gladys assured her. "Tomorrow, by six-thirty, Rose'll have scrambled eggs, fresh cinnamon rolls, fresh-squeezed orange juice, fresh-baked herb and bran buns with all-fruit sweetenings, hot bagels with cream cheese—the works—in that van ready to go. She and the help don't sleep much this time of year."

"No meat it sounds like."

"Not at the institute. Not allowed. But a lot of the guys, especially, crawl out the windows at night and hit here for cheeseburgers and fries. And before that, the searchers staying at the bed-and-breakfasts or the tourist cabins have come in for dinner."

"Bet you sell a lot of paintings at the Scandia when all the searchers are in town, huh?"

Gladys winked again. "And prints. Especially the seascapes. People want to take home a piece of the point after an emotionally satisfying and consciousness-titillating experience at the institute. There's usually four or five rich widows in each bunch that want the originals. Stuff's not art, it's photographs in oil paint, but they eat it up. And Michael's slightly spooky stuff just knocks 'em out." Gladys pondered that a moment, sprouted fresh tears for Michael, and went behind the bar to refill her drink.

Gladys's face-lift had not been successful. That had never been more apparent.

"Will Olie be able to find a replacement for Michael?" Charlie asked.

Wet mascara zigzagged down Gladys's pudgy cheeks and she shook her head, gulped scotch. Rose came around the partition from the kitchen, her face greasy with sweat and stress. The van must have left successfully loaded because the kitchen had quieted. Rose put an arm around Gladys's shoulders and squeezed. The dyed-black and bleached-beige heads leaned close together and looked back at Charlie with identical expressions.

"Sisters?" Charlie ventured.

"Half." Rose led her half sister back to her stool and fixed

Charlie another drink on the house. "Were you out there? Did you see Michael?" When Charlie nodded, Rose asked, "Was he really dead? For sure?"

Charlie nodded again, finished her old drink, and started the new, trying to push away the mind shot of Michael Cermack half out of the red Ferrari with surf suds sticking in his hair.

Gladys choked off a sob. "He must have been drunk."

It was the sheriff of Moot County who came to pick up Charlie. He looked the color of abused aluminum again and glanced pointedly from Charlie to Gladys to Rose.

"Hungry? We got a great special tonight, Sheriff." Rose pointed to the chalkboard behind her.

"It's got Grape-Nuts in it," Charlie offered. She thought it sounded pretty good. But Wes motioned her off her stool and led her to his car. "Well, anything sounds good if it means putting off going back to that friggin' cabin."

But to her relief the official Bronco roared past the turnoff to the Hide-a-bye.

"Was Michael an accident or a murder?" she asked.

"Don't know yet."

Charlie hoped she wasn't being taken straight to jail without passing go where, according to Paige Magill, she was due for some horrible abuse. Maybe she was just being lured back to the bachelor eyrie for some of the best-seller attempts at incredible humping featured in Chapter Two of *Death of a Grandmother*. Somehow that didn't sound so bad right now either.

But the Bronco zipped past the turnoff to Wes's house too. Just before reaching Chinook it left 101 and headed inland along a wide river cutting through the Coast Range.

"Mrs. Bergkvist looked drunk as a skunk," he ventured finally. "She say anything?"

"Did you know that Rose and Gladys were half sisters? That Rose caters all the food for the institute? That Olie Bergkvist is late in coming back this summer? That—"

"Frank Glick says Georgette swore she'd seen Gladys bringing

Olie back in their car from Portland like she always did about this time of year. But when she went by the house to speak to Olie the next day, Gladys claimed he wasn't back yet and Georgette must have been seeing things. That pissed Georgette royally."

"What did she want to talk to Olie about?" Charlie asked.

"Frank didn't know, but he said his wife was forever sticking her nose where it wasn't wanted."

"Sounds like she did it once too often." Maybe the murdered woman had wanted to tell Olie about his wife and the animal doctor.

"We're checking the airlines for a record of Olie's travels. According to Gladys, the last she heard from him was Buenos Aires. He didn't take a bus home. I personally do not believe he's missing or that Georgette saw him going by in the car or that he had anything to do with Georgette being shot. But since you insist upon raising so goddamned many questions I'll just go about following all the false leads you can find. If I didn't feel pretty confident you weren't the murderer, I'd think you were just trying to fuzz up the case."

They were driving along an estuary where a lowering sun turned the water a faint pink, where blue herons stalked about on stilt legs searching for dinner. The Bronco turned off onto a road leading out to a spit of land where a shabby-looking building of weathered wood hunkered at its end, surrounded by still, shallow water on three sides. It passed a diamond-shaped yellow sign with GARLIC XING written in black lettering just before pulling into a small parking lot, already half full.

Another sign, *Warning: Garlic in Use*, graced the door. Inside, strings of raw garlic bulbs hung from open rafters and draped the mirror over the bar in ropes like Christmas tinsel.

They made a meal of steamer clams and beer on the deck outside, coleslaw and great hunks of toasty garlic bread. They watched the pink on the water turn to red and whole herds of ducks take off and land just for the hell of it. The mountains in the background grew purple, then gray. They sat at crude picnic tables and the people around them spoke barely above whispers, if at all. The odors of pungent garlic, reedy water, and hearty mud melded pleasantly.

Charlie wiped grease from her chin with an oversized paper napkin and sighed. This was sure a long way from murder and the Hide-a-bye. "It's perfect here. Thanks."

Wes looked away from the water where something flapped and splashed and started perfect rings growing. A slow smile lifted one corner of his face and wrinkled up the corners of his eyes. "Beats sprouts and Grape-Nuts, right?"

"Right." Charlie sighed again.

The smile stayed pasted on his lips as it faded from his eyes. "Jesus Charlie, don't look at me like that, okay?"

"What do you expect, bringing a woman to a place like this, a knee in the groin?"

But this was just an interlude for a country sheriff with two recent deaths on his hands. After coffee in the bar he hurried her back to her cabin, refusing to say exactly when the Toyota would be returned to her. He did divulge that a preliminary on-the-spot check didn't show any damage to the brake system of Michael's car. "No skid marks on the parking lot. It's like he just stomped the gas pedal and flew off the cliff."

"Gladys thought he might have been drunk."

"We'll know soon. Watch some TV and get some sleep. I'll see you in the morning."

There was no baby-sitter deputy at the Hide-a-bye. Wes just watched her unlock the door before he drove off. Charlie got on the phone to Jack and was back in the village of Moot Point in twenty minutes.

Chapter 22

Jack persuaded Clara Peterson to rush over to the Hide-a-bye to pick up Charlie. Searchers wandered the village and business hours would extend until the streets emptied. Jack was happily ringing up sales when they arrived at the Earth Spirit, so Charlie promised to stop by later.

Once the skies cleared, night took a long time to settle in on the Oregon coast in June. The sunset had faded but it was by no means dark yet. Couples strolled the beach as well as the main street where electric streetlights were disguised to look like old-fashioned gas lamps. House windows lit the hillside in erratic polka dots.

The air was cool but soft, the ocean breeze gentle. Rose's was lit like a Christmas tree and the lights from its windows splayed across the beach below. The horizon formed a glow line on the edge of the sea, the lighthouse a phallic shadow against it. Charlie cut off a sigh. If the sheriff had work to do, so did she.

"Isn't it awful about what happened to Michael?" Clara said now, and Charlie realized the older woman had stopped beside her to take in the night. She'd spoken little on the way over, explaining that she rarely drove at night and had to concentrate on it when she did. Clara said she saw so poorly in the dark she really shouldn't be driving at all then. After riding the short distance with her, Charlie had to agree.

Clara had just happened to be standing by the cash register when the call came through, and that's how Jack had come to send her for Charlie. "I never liked the boy much but it's so sad when a young promising life is snuffed out that way. And on the same day as Georgette's memorial service. Things like that just don't happen in this little place. I understand he'd been drinking . . . Michael."

"As far as I know that's only rumor. Deputy Olsen told me you're an avid mystery fan besides being a bird-watcher." And Charlie soon found herself inside Clara's trailer home to see for herself. Deputy Olsen had not exaggerated. Bookshelves lined the walls from floor to ceiling with time out for heating ducts and windows. They were hard packed with paperbacks, spines out and where possible stacked three deep in horizontal piles on top.

It was a more colorful and diversified decor than wallpaper or paneling would have been. Certainly an improvement over Libby's bedroom walls which were covered with shelves that held a mass of once-colorful stuffed animals congealing, with the help of dust and smog, into a depressing gray.

"Mrs. Peterson, you even have them alphabetized by author. I'm so impressed."

Clara flashed her gold-filled smile and looked years younger. "I'm afraid I have two vices, mysteries and caffeine. And do you know what? I sleep like a baby. Most people my age don't."

"You even have one of my authors." Charlie had followed the alphabet around a corner and into the bathroom. It was not the location Charlie would have chosen, above and behind the john rather than in front of it, but there would always be a certain excitement about finding a book you'd sold just lying around someone's home. "You've got them all."

"Who is that? Oh, Lennard Shipton, yes. I do enjoy his Sheriff Tomlin books. Do you know if he'll publish another one soon?"

"I don't think there'll be anymore Sheriff Tomlin books. Len has had some sticky problems and gone into real estate to make a living. But we are marketing a new series proposal." Which didn't have a chance in hell, but this didn't seem the time to tell the bird lady that.

Charlie used the bathroom, and when she emerged, Clara was making coffee. "Then Sheriff Bennett doesn't think Michael had his accident because he'd been drinking?"

"He won't know until he gets lab reports or whatever. But he sure can't blame this one on me. I've been under lock and key for two days."

"Then it's possible his death was more than an accident?" Clara asked without taking her eyes from the stained Mr. Coffee pot, sucking and flushing, excreting dark fluid in a steady drip into its glass pot.

"He does seem a little young to have a heart attack and drive off a cliff. I expect they'll check his blood and his brakes pretty carefully."

"Artists are temperamental people. They often commit suicide." Clara handed Charlie a cup of coffee she didn't want, the cup and saucer a delicate china with a rose pattern—remnants of better days perhaps. "It's possible he shot Georgette and when his gun was found he decided to end it all."

"That would tidy up everything nicely, wouldn't it? But Michael didn't seem the type to kill himself. His self-esteem was way up there." It was pretty obvious Clara had heard rumors about Charlie's relationship with Wes Bennett and was not too skillfully trying to pump Charlie for information. "And you don't seem the type to shop at the Earth Spirit. Why were you there tonight when I called Jack? Or does he keep mysteries under the counter?"

"Oh, no." Clara smiled wistfully and gazed about her multicolored walls. "I was unofficially observing, and looking over the stock. He's going to hire me part-time in the evenings this summer so he can work on his book. I can use the money, and I don't fall asleep at nine o'clock like most people my age and then wake up at four in the morning when the world's not ready to start up yet. I begin work officially tomorrow night."

A rapping on the metal storm door startled Charlie into spilling coffee into her saucer. Some even dripped on worn kitchen carpeting. She grabbed a paper towel to blot it and when she rose from behind the counter Frank Glick was stepping up the little metal steps into the front room. Clara hurried to close the door behind him and they stood looking at Charlie as if they'd been caught in *the* act.

Charlie tried to envision Edwina, who was younger than either of them, having an affair. She couldn't and decided she'd misinterpreted that look.

Frank explained to Clara he'd had to get away from the "looney bin" next door, and turned to Charlie. "Seems like you're every place I look. I thought the sheriff would have you tied up somewhere by now."

"Now, Frank, I asked her in to see my mystery collection. Do you know I have one of her authors in the bathroom? I baked a lemon meringue pie this morning. The creamy kind that you like, not the Jell-O-y kind." She led him over to the little kitchen table and held out a chair for him, and he sat as if they'd done this often. "I took a couple of pieces over to Mary and Norma but there's lots left. And the coffee's made. Maybe Miss Greene would like pie, too."

"No, thanks, I've eaten." Charlie surreptitiously dumped her coffee down the sink and rinsed out the cup. She complimented Clara on her collection again and left her busily undoing all Georgette's nutritional priming of Frank Glick. He sure didn't look like a man who'd gone to a memorial service for his wife that day.

Outside, night had arrived for real. Street lamps and lighted windows looked even prettier. In front of the Glick's house Charlie could just make out two women sitting on the picnic table, their feet on the bench seat. One cried softly in the dark, the other hugged her and stroked her hair and looked out over her head to an all but invisible sea. Georgette's daughters probably. At least someone mourned the woman. Charlie wondered if there was anyone to mourn Michael Cermack.

"Brother Dennis must have started off this seminar with a bang," Jack confided when he'd hung the *Closed* sign and taken Charlie back behind the curtain. "Going to take me all day tomorrow to restock for tomorrow night."

"There's no basement or stockroom. Where do you keep everything?"

"In the shop. The walls are really the doors of storage cupboards if you take a close look." He gave her a smile and an irritating little nod that said he knew she hadn't noticed.

Before he could get in the question she knew was coming, Charlie asked, "Jack, have you seen Olie Bergkvist here yet this summer?"

They sat on the kitchen bar stools. He drank wine and she'd refused to. She was getting fed up with Oregon in more ways than one. "Gladys's husband?" Jack thought a moment. "I don't think he's back yet. Why?"

"Well, Michael said he's late this year and apparently Georgette thought she saw him coming into town with Gladys but Gladys told Georgette she must be crazy and . . ." Jack was looking at her, lips parted, ". . . you did hear about Michael?"

"Oh, yeah, listen, bad karma there. Wonder he lived this long." He was fidgeting up to ask the big question.

"Then you think he was murdered?" Charlie said hurriedly.

"He was a nobody. Who'd want to murder him?"

"Who'd want to murder Georgette Glick?"

"I heard big-deal Michael drove off the cliff because he was drunk. No mystery there. He drank like a whale." Jack poured more wine and turned to Charlie with the important things on his mind rolling to the tip of his tongue.

And she cut him off with, "Does Michael have any relatives that you know of?"

"Everybody's got relatives someplace. You feeling sorry for the guy or . . . Charlie, how about my chapter? Did you like it or hate it or what?"

"Well, I liked it. . . ." She watched his face come apart at her tone, which would not have earned her a cheerleader's job. So she sat up perkily and asked, "Do you really feel like something comes up out of the bed and hits your back and shoulders and then realize it's the ceiling?"

Jack Monroe perked up too, now that he could be the center of attention, and was off on a pitch that would have died in the hallway before it reached a producer's threshold. "Of course OOBE's are only part of my book but there's not much of substance been done on them, you know. There is one book out that covers it fairly well but it hasn't had much distribution."

He took her out in the shop and showed her a paperback with a spooky cover, *Out-of-Body Experiences*, by J. Paul Read. But there was another on the shelf below that caught her eye and she pulled it out. *Mentalphysics*, by Brother Dennis. There was a picture of him on the back cover, smiling broadly, his fillings retouched.

"You wouldn't be interested in that, Charlie," Jack said confidently. "It's self-published."

"But I suppose you sell a lot of them with the institute right here in town."

"I used to, but he decided to make the institute the only outlet so he sells them up there himself. Pretty soon I'll be able to sell my own book right here and everywhere else too."

"Is there bad blood between you because of Paige? I heard you used to be friends."

"And because of you, Charlie Greene." The intense blue eyes under the salt-and-pepper eyebrows probed hers until she had to look away. Jack Monroe may have been a Grape-Nut but he was not stupid. "We're still friends, just not as close."

"What's his last name?"

"Thornton. And you're more interested in him and what goes on in this town than you are in my book."

"I am implicated in a murder that happened in this town and I don't know anything about the place. Help me, Jack."

"Nobody really thinks you shot Georgette. You're being silly.

You didn't even know her. And it was Michael's gun. You didn't know him either."

"And my fingerprints were on it. And now Michael's dead. And I don't know what's going to happen next."

"Your fingerprints? But how . . ." He sat on a cushion and drew one up for her near a wall heater.

"You hadn't heard? I thought news got around here in seconds. And I can't imagine how unless I was tricked into touching it thinking it was something else. But there is definitely a conspiracy going on. So far I'm the only suspect. Now talk to me, please. We'll get back to yours, but let's concentrate on my problem for a while."

Jack agreed, obviously stunned by the fingerprints. Or could it be an act? Yes, Olie was usually back in Moot Point by now. No, Jack hadn't questioned the lateness of his arrival. "He's got to be seventy-five anyway. Man's old enough to come and go as he likes."

No, Jack didn't know of any kind of relationship between Clara Peterson and Frank Glick. "I'm not the nosy neighbor type, Charlie."

No, he hadn't gone to Georgette's memorial service today. So he couldn't fill Charlie in on people's reactions there. "I don't believe in churches and never go in one. Went to celebrate her passage at the institute and that's enough."

No, he had no idea who would want to shoot Georgette or why she'd be riding her Schwinn at night without a light and in the fog. No, he hadn't been aware of any suspicious undercurrents in the village that could have culminated in two deaths in so short a time. "Unless Michael killed her, felt bad about it, and committed suicide. I always thought he was a little nuts. But you're asking the wrong person, Charlie. You should talk to Rose over at the restaurant. She's psychic, you know. She doesn't want to be and she's half scared of it. But she can't help it. Surprised she hasn't figured it out already."

"Okay," Charlie stood up and motioned her client to do the same, "let's go over and ask her right now."

Chapter 23

But Rose Kortinemi wasn't behind the cash register or at the tables. One of the white-shirted young waiters with his short hair moussed to hard perfection blocked the entrance to the kitchen. Behind him a woman sobbed between long drawn-out groans.

Jack pushed the young man aside with one outstretched arm and the kid nearly bounced. Jack walked in and Charlie followed.

Gladys Bergkvist lay on the floor, her wet blouse half off and her skirt drawn up to expose a beefy thigh and hip. Her underpants and panty hose had been cut open, her skin an angry red all along that side from shoulder to thigh. Under the fluorescent lights, and against her Scandinavian and Oregonian pallor, the red patches resembled radiant blossoms just opening.

Rose knelt beside her with one knee on her chest trying to knot a kitchen towel around a pack of loose ice cubes before they got away from her. A waiter held Gladys's ankles to the floor.

Jack grabbed a towel and yelled for more ice. "Grease or water?"

"Water."

"When?"

"Just now." Rose had her ice pack formed and laid it gently across her half sister's burned arm.

"Call Paige?"

"She's on her way."

"Charlie, get over here and help me." Jack handed his agent an end of the towel to hold while a cook scooped ice into it.

"Are you sure you're supposed to use cold? Has anybody called an ambulance?" Charlie asked, the contents of her stomach starting to Jazzercise as welts and blisters formed magically on the victim's beet-red thigh.

Jack covered them with the second ice pack and asked Rose what happened. Gladys had apparently decided Rose's cook was talking back to Rose and had "waltzed" into the kitchen to chew him out just as another cook was lifting "a goddamn vat" of water off the fire because it was boiling over. Somehow they'd collided, Gladys taking the whole heat.

"She's been drinking all afternoon. I tried to get some food into her but she didn't eat much. God, I'm glad you're here, Jack." Rose moved the ice around gently on Gladys's top half.

Jack did the same on the lower. Gladys still moaned but she seemed to be calming. Maybe you did put cold on a burn. But with something this bad you also called 911.

"Has anybody called a doctor yet?" Charlie asked.

Jack's eyes met Rose's over the prostrate Gladys in a look that lifted four eyebrows. It probably said, "California." It's the look people from Texas get in Colorado, where Charlie was raised. The look Coloradans get in Wyoming, and everybody from the lower "forty-eight" must get in Canada.

Gladys's wonderful jewelry winked at Charlie from the corner of a chopping block behind Rose.

"Gladys isn't that big a drinker." Jack moved his pack and the welts and blisters were still there. But Charlie couldn't detect any new ones forming.

"It's Michael's dying. That was too much after Georgette and everything. Gladys has always been too sensitive."

Charlie was about to demand that medical help be called instantly—it would probably have to come clear from Chinook —when Paige Magill burst into the kitchen hugging a green spiky plant in a large earthenware pot. She slid across the floor in the water generated by the accident and the melting ice packs and came to land next to Jack.

"Knife," she demanded.

"I am serious about this doctor thing," Charlie insisted.

One of the cooks handed Paige a knife and she began slicing the tips of the plant spikes off and handing them around. Charlie found herself holding a drooling tip. Paige noticed Charlie then, and again that quick, provincial look passed among the insiders.

"Squeeze the goo out and smooth it on ever, ever, ever so gently," Paige ordered, between gasps for breath. She'd come on the run.

Gladys grimaced and squeezed tears out of her eyes. "Paige? Did you get here in time?"

"I think so, Gladys. And you are to think good thoughts. A nice cool mountain meadow. A cool stream runs through it and wildflowers dot the cool green grass alongside it. Can you see it, Gladys?"

"Yes," Gladys said, but weakly.

"Now feel it."

The leaf tips reminded Charlie of cactus and there were sharp barbs on the outside edges but she could squeeze the cool soft width of the leaves without getting pricked. The pulp oozed out in a stringy, treacly, colorless spit. It was slow going and Rose soon had most of the kitchen help and some from the dining room kneeling thigh to thigh, applying layer upon layer of the gross goo on her half sister. As soon as Charlie's piece of leaf spike ran out of stringy spit she was handed another, as Paige cut them farther and farther down.

Charlie looked up once at the man in the chef's hat directly across from her and he rolled his eyes like Wes Bennett did when pontificating on Grape-Nuts.

"Don't you think we should get some real medicine?" Charlie interrupted Paige's endless chant about the coolness of the rocks, trees, clouds, breeze, and insects. "This woman has been badly scalded." Real medicine came in bottles or tablets or needles, everybody knew that.

Several of the help from Chinook glanced at her as if they agreed but kept their lips clamped.

"Don't rub it in now, just drip it on," Paige said, ignoring Charlie, and continued the cooling liturgy with hardly a pause.

By the time the plant was nothing but oozing stumps, Gladys's red patches were fading to pink. The skin had probably died and was preparing to fall off, leaving Gladys even more exposed than she had been for the last fifteen minutes. But Rose put her half sister's clothing lightly back together and helped her up. She and Jack walked the patient out the back door. Paige hugged the amputated plant to her bosom and followed.

Charlie shrugged at the snickering kitchen help and went after them. It wasn't long before she realized they were walking Gladys home. No rushing her off in a car for medical assistance, no calling an ambulance. Oh, no, not in Moot Point.

Gladys hiccupped sporadically the entire distance but walked along briskly for someone who ought to have been on a stretcher.

Charlie stopped when she noticed the sheriff department cars and unmarked but obviously official vans on the concrete apron in front of the three-door garage. Michael's loft was fully lit above, and in the Bergkvist house next door Eenie, Meenie, Miney, Moe, and Joe waxed happily hysterical.

Charlie turned on her heel and stepped off alone into the dark.

. . .

The Moot Point Consciousness Training Institute was lit even more festively than Rose's, the semicircular drive festooned with flickering candles in paper bags, every third one having given up the ghost to the moist air. But the low slant of the tentacled roof of the main building deflected much of the light from the windows off at the woods at odd angles. Charlie was reminded of the Disney flicks in which animated trees came alive to terrorize fairy-tale maidens.

She listened for Eddie's barking and didn't feel better for not hearing it. If the sound had come from the back of the building she'd have at least had reason to hope he was kenneled.

But everything seemed so open, peaceful. A couple strolled past her and smiled. She could hear chatter and normalcy wafting from the open doors ahead.

If you've just been stringing plant spit across a half-naked scalded woman, walking uninvited into a group of perfect strangers seemed patently normal. So Charlie did.

The dining room/lounge area was filled with searchers and Charlie received a few curious glances, but these people were new to each other today and probably couldn't be sure they hadn't seen her before. They might think she was hired help from the village. Most of them had anywhere from ten to thirty years on her. All but two of them were women. Perhaps the men were out strolling with their ladies among the candles in the paper sacks or down at Rose's chuffing cheeseburgers.

Words like "aliveness," "lovingness," "psychecology," "synchronicity," "empowerment," "life force," "aromatherapy," "channeling," and "rolfing" permeated the air along with lingering odors of garlic and spicy teas. Doc Withers appeared carrying a tray of plastic wine glasses, and by the time he wove his way to Charlie there were two left. It was white wine, which she detested unless it was champagne, but she took one to appear as if she belonged.

"Ms. Greene, I didn't know you were into transformation."
Taking the last glass as his own, he set the tray on the corner of
the raised hearth and led Charlie off to the hallway leading to
the bookstore tentacle. "What did you think of it?"

"Well . . . it's a trifle sour, but it does have lots of structure."

"My book?"

"The wine."

"I was talking about *Holistic Health and Nutrition for Your
Pet.*" He looked as disappointed in Charlie as Jack Monroe had
not long ago.

"Uh, it's not my field of expertise but I do sense a great deal
of life force and lovingness. You *have* heard of what just happened to Gladys?"

"Gladys?" The boyish innocence, behind the thick glasses he
had constantly to push back up his nose against the law of
sliding sweat, was lost on Charlie. This was the man who slept
with ducks.

"Bergkvist. At the Scandia. Which reminds me, have you
seen her husband around yet this summer?"

"Something's happened to Olie?" he asked.

"No, to Gladys."

"What could happen to Gladys?" Mother figures were supposed to be invincible.

"You answer my question and I'll answer yours," Charlie told
him. "Isn't Olie due back in town by now?"

"I don't pay any attention to whether he comes or goes. Why
should I? What's happened to Gladys—Mrs. Bergkvist?"

"She just scalded herself in a vat of boiling water."

Doc Withers went white—which with these people wasn't
easy. "Did they call Paige?"

"She came with her spiky house plant and we all gooed
Gladys. I thought it was odd they didn't call 911 and an ambulance. Gladys is badly burned, although Paige tried to convince
her otherwise. They should even have called you in the interim.
You would have known more about how to keep her skin on

until they could get the poor thing to a burn center or something. But no, they call the local florist."

Doc Withers had relaxed noticeably. "Sometimes when I get in trouble with the animals I call Paige too. Where is Mrs. Bergkvist now?"

"At home with Paige and Jack Monroe."

"Oh, well, that's good." He finished his wine casually and set the glass down on the hearth. "I better get back to the clinic. Eddie's having a little stomach trouble after his surgery today." The holistic animal doctor disappeared down one of the tentacles—and not to the clinic, Charlie would have bet the Toyota, but to the home of Gladys and Olie Bergkvist.

"What did you do? Tell him his proposal stank?" Brother Dennis said behind her, and steadied her arm so she wouldn't spill the wine she wasn't drinking. He had a habit of sneaking up on people. "What did you think of my screenplay?"

"Well, it was certainly unusual."

"I could flesh it out more for you if you're interested."

"I'm sorry, Brother Dennis, the agency just doesn't handle screenwriters who don't live in LA."

"But that's so unfair. You can write anywhere."

A lady with tight gray curls and huge dangling earrings turned to give him a wine-loosened smile. "Serenity, brother, remember?"

"Did you hear what happened to Gladys?" Charlie changed the subject quickly. "She was scalded with hot water down at Rose's. Do you know of some way we could get in touch with Olie? He should know about this."

"Who's with her now?" Brother Dennis's hair was done exceptionally well tonight, glossy and buoyant. But his face was greasy. Charlie suspected he was under more tension than he'd care to admit to his searchers.

"Jack, Paige, Rose—but not Olie. Where do you suppose he is?"

"Argentina, I think. Are they still at Rose's?" He started for the door.

Charlie set down her glass and followed him. "At Gladys's. Nobody even called a doctor." When they were halfway down the drive, she said, "Looks like you have a good crowd, but I understand the institute's in financial trouble."

Brother Dennis stopped suddenly and Charlie ran into him. "As a matter of fact," he said, "the institute is remarkably solvent. I plan to begin a major expansion once the summer season is over."

Chapter 24

Apparently satisfied he'd put a nosy agent in her place, Brother Dennis gave a little "huff" and marched off toward Gladys's house with Charlie tagging along behind uninvited. But not told outright to bugger off either. She reminded herself of what had happened to a nosy lady named Georgette Glick very recently in this village. Had Michael been nosy too?

They came upon the Bergkvist house the back way, from the stair-step street above and probably the way Doc Withers had come to visit. Official activity still bustled about the loft.

Charlie had hoped to follow Brother Dennis right into the house but they met Jack Monroe just coming out. Jack offered to take Charlie back to the Hide-a-bye and before she could change his mind the door to the Bergkvist house had closed on her.

Linda Tortle was climbing into her car when Charlie and Jack walked down the driveway. She paused to watch them, returning Charlie's friendly greeting with a tired grimace. Peety Tortle had just spent another evening with Grandma. With any luck so had Libby Greene.

Jack's idea of taking Charlie home was walking along the beach. "But what if the tide's up? I'm tired," she protested. "Couldn't we drive?"

"My pickup's in the shop, as usual. But thanks to you, Charlie, and Morton and Fish, I'll soon have a new truck." They were in front of Rose's about then and he picked her up and swung her around. He was a very strong person for someone his age. "I might even buy a computer to do my work on and build a second story on the Earth Spirit to live and write in. And hire a full-time clerk to watch the store in the summertime so I can spend more time writing. What do you think?"

"Do me one favor, Jack. Don't spend a penny of your new-found wealth until it's in the bank. Don't project ahead from what you think might be coming."

"Why? I mean if you sell so many books, you're going to make so much money, and—"

"Sometimes we overproject." Charlie didn't know why she invariably got into this conversation. It never did any good. "There's money withheld for returns and things you can just never predict." Modern accounting didn't help a lot either. "Just don't jump into any big spending until you've got the cash in hand."

"Paige just told me the institute's expanding and you said it was bankrupt. Rose intends to build on an addition—"

"But rich Japanese own that."

"I just found out tonight that Rose is going to try to buy back their shares. And Paige is even planning to expand the Emporium. Moot Point is blossoming, Charlie."

At the mention of blossom, Charlie saw Gladys's burned thigh. "But the economy sucks here. It's so obvious, Jack."

"You California types assume things that don't exist for the rest of the world," he said in disgust.

"Just don't come carping to me when money you borrowed against doesn't materialize when you expect it to or at all."

He stepped ahead of her down the wooden stairs to the beach, confident and surefooted in the dark. She followed unsteadily with her heart in her mouth. Funny, she hadn't noticed this problem the other day when she descended these same stairs with Wes Bennett.

"Acrophobia?" Jack asked and took her hand to help her down the last few steps.

"Yeah. It doesn't bother me unless I think about it, or unless I'm on top of a skyscraper or a mountain and can't not think about it."

"You ought to talk to Paige. She's good at getting people to talk themselves out of phobias."

"Is there anything she can't treat? Jack, Paige might have talked Gladys out of the pain of those burns with all that cooling chatter of streams and rocks, but the pain is going to come back when Gladys thinks about it, and she's going to wear disfiguring scars for the rest of her life, if not come down with some terrible infection right away. Why wouldn't anyone call 911 and get help for her? I know you people are into alternative ways of doing things here, and I respect that, but tonight was really irresponsible. The mind can do wonders, I know, but there are limits. I've heard of people dying from being scalded. Paige is a florist, not an MD. And shouldn't someone contact Gladys's husband?"

"Paige is also a psychology major and a trained herbalist," Jack said as if that had anything to do with the price of pizza. "There's no reason to call Olie. Gladys will be fine. Aloe has proven itself in treating burns for hundreds of years."

"Aloe? Is that what that thing was? Jack, Gladys was really scalded. Don't you think if it could help burns that serious they'd use it in hospitals?"

"Anybody can grow aloe," he said patiently, as if finding her gullibility mind-boggling. "The pharmaceutical companies couldn't make any money off it. They certainly aren't going to test it and announce a lowly houseplant outperforms their expensive medicines. They use aloe as an ingredient in some of their salves and ointments. But nothing works as well as fresh-cut aloe applied immediately. By the time the emergency 'experts' arrive with all their expensive junk it's too late. Rose really should have one growing in the restaurant and handy. Of course I don't suppose most of her help would let her use it on them if they were in flames."

"Jack, if it was that great a cure-all, doctors would grow aloe among the ferns in their waiting rooms and run out and cut off a hunk when they needed it. Things aren't that simple." This sounded like another loopy idea from the great minds offering to treat cancer with avocado pits.

"Doctors won't try anything that hasn't had big bucks spent on pharmacological testing, government approval, and approval in medical journals. And nobody's going to bother to test something so simple and natural as aloe."

"I give up."

"You stick to being a good agent and don't mess with things you know nothing about. Wouldn't hurt you to be a little less judgmental. Damned depressing to see someone as young as you are keeping such a closed mind."

Properly reprimanded, Charlie slogged along beside him, surprised at how well she could see the sand when all else seemed so dark. It reflected a dull glow that cast shadows off the rocks at the end of the point and highlighted the surf suds to remind Charlie unpleasantly of Michael. But the wreck of the Ferrari had been hauled away and so had he. The tide covered all traces of the accident scene and she and Jack had to walk up tight against the cliff to round the point. He reached down to pick up something white caught in the rocks. Jack had pretty good eyesight for a man his age, too.

"Looks like one of those boxes Rose packs for tourist picnics," he said. "People come here for the scenery and leave trash and don't see the dichotomy. I could live to be a hundred and never understand that way of thinking."

"This is where Michael died." Charlie shivered and he put an arm around her shoulders. "He was half out of the car and his eyes were open and the ocean sort of snuck up and left foam in his hair."

"Why didn't Wes leave you up in the parking lot?"

"He did. I just didn't stay put."

The birds out on the rookery rocks were quiet now. Jack and Charlie walked quietly too. Until Jack asked, "Find your contact lenses?"

"Yes, and right where you put them when you snuck into my cabin while I was gone. Then you call me up and expect me to believe you did it when you and your body had temporarily parted. Jack, I may be younger than you are, but I wasn't born yesterday."

"All right then, tell me how you liked Brother Dennis's screenplay? And Paige's *Death of a Grandmother?*"

"If I was as gullible as you think I am I would suddenly realize you couldn't have known Linda and I were reading them shortly before you called. But, since both authors are friends of yours, you could have read both offerings before I did and have been aware that somebody left them on my doorstep. And you could also easily have known enough about Linda and Doc Withers, and that relationship, and the ducks too, to have guessed what she might have told me of them. You didn't have to crawl out of your body for any of that information, Jack. I'm your agent, we're supposed to be on the same side, remember?"

When Charlie entered cabin three the phone was ringing. It was Wes.

"Just checking to be sure you're in and safe."

"Thanks again for the steamers and beer."

"My pleasure, lady." There was a new intimacy in his voice. "Where are you?"

"Home finally, and too old and tired to gaze into those big eyes of yours, let me tell you. See you for breakfast. And Charlie, lock your door tonight?"

"I thought you were worried about me wandering around outside, not about somebody wandering in. What's up?"

"I don't know. That's what worries me. There's bad stuff going down at Moot Point, and I don't have a clue as to what it is. Now you know how tired I am to even be admitting that."

"Michael's death wasn't accidental, was it, Wes?"

"No lab reports in yet, but it doesn't look like it. We may have an extremely clever murderer operating here. Then again we may have an amateur so dumb he can fool you just because you can't imagine anybody that stupid still up and walking."

"See you for breakfast," Charlie said and growled.

She hung up on his groaning. And realized it was too late to call home again. "Edwina and Libby Greene, I'm counting on you both. Don't let me down now."

Charlie stopped soaring and began to fall. She'd done this before and hated it more each time. She felt weak with nausea and sweat, terrified at breathing that wouldn't regulate, and panicked by adrenaline that rushed to push her into action while total helplessness clamped over her like a body cast.

This time it would be a relief to arrive at the *Peter Iredale* and come so unglued she'd wake up screaming at the Hide-a-bye.

"I can't take much more of this. Let's just get it over with." And the body cast tightened. "It can't get any worse than this."

But it did.

This time she wasn't alone. There were "things" out here with her. Charlie had lost control of her body, her dignity, her breathing, and for all she knew her bladder. But she could lift her eyelids. The black was pitch. But the things were here. And they were megatimes worse than anything she'd even imagined before. They reveled in her terror, their glee silent but pervasive in the dark. The more delighted and victorious they became, the stronger they reeked.

Charlie couldn't see a thing. But she almost knew what they looked like. They just didn't look like anything she knew, so they didn't relate to anything. She couldn't explain them even to herself—amorphous, omniscient, so dangerous it was incomprehensible. She'd be a fool not to struggle to escape them, and a worse one to even try.

The word "evil" kept popping up in Charlie's brain with the adrenaline bubbles.

Charlie sat in the recliner rocker wrapped in the god-awful Hide-a-bye quilt that passed for a bedspread and stared into the fire of the day's pressed log. Her stomach hurt as it always did when she went on vacation longer than a weekend. Charlie had been born with a man's stomach. It liked the routine of a regular job, a little good sex didn't detract, and a home with the regular perks—cleanliness, orderliness, happy children, patio barbecue, and all the rest—but not a lot of surprises.

Charlie's stomach had the misfortune to come wrapped in a woman's body, a woman with a messy life. Once she'd finished her education and become a responsible, gainfully employed head of household she'd tried everything she could think of to ensure her stomach a comforting life-style. And sometimes for as long as a month or two she'd think she'd succeeded. Then something would happen or a series of little somethings would pile up, at first in her job—but as her daughter grew, increasingly at home. Still, this was the first time Charlie and her stomach had become involved in murder.

She rocked herself and hugged her stomach and tried to gain warmth from the bedspread and the fire. But she was cold from the inside out. Charlie'd awakened to find herself in the entry hall, checking to be sure she'd locked the door. Now she waited for something to come down the hall, something like whatever kept you afraid to look under the bed when you were a kid.

"See? I'm putting my whole arm under there. There's nothing," Edwina would say and poke the flashlight under there too. "Can't even see anything. Come down here and look."

"Whatever it was probably skittered into the closet before you turned on the lights."

Edwina, who'd worked a long day before having to come home to work a long night, had looked very old and tired on those occasions, Charlie realized now.

When her turn came, Charlie, who'd put in long days herself, merely pulled up the covers on her bed and let Libby in beside her. "They're under your bed again, right?"

"Yeah, what are they?"

"Damned if I know."

And Charlie and her daughter would snuggle together against the bogeyman. It had worked splendidly. But in all fairness, Charlie hadn't had a husband in her bed to complain, as had Edwina.

Chapter 25

"Charlie, stop it. What's the matter with you? It's me, Wes. Remember?"

Charlie's throat was raw, drier than a hangover. The body cast clamped around her torso again, the helplessness. No, it was Wes. "Put me down."

"Will you behave yourself?"

The fire was out, the quilt bedspread on the floor. Daylight streamed into the room. And the sheriff's square face was bleeding.

There was blood under Charlie's fingernails.

"Last night you growled at me on the phone. At dinner you eyed me like I was some kind of meat. This morning you come in for the kill." Wes did look hurt and confused. He'd had to get the owner of the Hide-a-bye out of bed to give him a key. "After I knocked and pounded and shouted, that is. Couldn't raise anybody but the neighbors. Probably still standing outside in their bathrobes waiting for the sheriff to haul out another body."

Charlie couldn't seem to do anything but stare from her fingernails to his face and back again. At this particular moment he was the last person in the world she wanted to hurt.

"You must have been dreaming again. I know. Hey, it's okay." He grabbed a paper towel from the roll by the sink and soaked it under the tap, held it to his wounded face. "But you weren't screaming this time, so I figured you were already dead."

Charlie took the towel from him and wiped and blotted the blood until the lopsided grin returned. Then she painstakingly kissed each wound to make it better.

It was some time later that Charlie, wrapped once again in the Hide-a-bye quilt, sat on the couch to call home while the sheriff used her shower. Edwina wanted to know why, as long as Charlie wasn't in jail, she couldn't come home right away. "Tell them you're a single mother with a child to care for, for Pete's sake."

Libby's music, friends, and television/telephone/eating habits were driving her grandmother up the wall. Grandmothering was fine in theory, but in reality Edwina had to get to the desert and back to work. Charlie tried to think of some comforting words but came up blank. She finally insisted her mother wake Libby instead.

"Mom, you in jail?" came a voice still slurred with sleep that managed to tug at a string connected somehow to Charlie's heart.

"Not yet, honey, but this is important. I want you to help me remember something, okay?"

"It's not even eight o'clock. Like, I haven't had my first diet Coke yet." The voice had moved suddenly from sleepy to incredulous, putting a perceptible slack in the attendant heartstring. "What do you mean remember?"

Charlie described the wreck of the *Peter Iredale* as best she could without letting the panic it evoked into her voice.

"Is there a picture of anything like it in the *National Geographic* on the end table? It's called the *Peter Iredale* if that helps."

"Just a minute," Libby said, incredulity melding into disgust. Charlie could hear her whisper, "She's freaking out, Grandma." There was a buzz as Charlie's only two living relatives whispered back and forth. *"Peter Iredale"* rose to the top of the buzz and Libby came back on—live. "Grandma's looking. This have anything to do with the murder?"

"I don't know. I keep having nightmares about that wreck and I'm going to feel a lot better if you tell me it's just something I've been looking at at home and not seeing. Do you remember anything like that at the poster store on the mall or any place else we might have been together?"

Libby didn't, and disgust had given way to suspicion when, after a slight pause, Charlie's daughter asked, "You got a boyfriend in there with you?"

Charlie glibly lied that it was only the television, and turned from the direction of the shower where Wes was sounding off like a teenager's boom box. Charlie just knew Randolph Glick, whose car was parked outside the cabin two doors down, was on the phone even now to the authorities in Salem about this latest impropriety.

"You don't watch daytime TV," Libby said, sweetly this time, "remember?"

"I do when I'm alone in hotel rooms, just for the noise and companionship." Which was true. "Has Grandma found anything?"

Knowing full well the search had come to an abrupt halt at the mention of a boyfriend, Charlie cuddled the mouthpiece tighter into her shoulder and shielded it with the bedspread even though Wes Bennett and the shower had turned themselves off. Charlie was helpless to stem the tide of guilt washing over her at the thought of her mother's reaction.

She hadn't even had time to bring up the subject of the goddamned cat before her two female relatives decided they could find or remember nothing about the *Peter Iredale* but would keep looking and call her back.

Sheriff Wes had dressed and brought her a cup of instant coffee before he noticed the change in her mood. "You switching Charlies on me again, Charlie?"

"I called home while you were in the shower. Libby thinks I'm 'freaking out.' Do you think I'm freaking out, Wes?"

"Well, let's see now." He pursed his lips and gingerly fingered the scratches she'd left on his face. They'd turned into welts. "I've been here what, little over an hour? In that time you've tried to claw me to death and love me to death. And right now you look about ready to cry at the sight of me. It's possible you're freaking out."

They ate cornflakes and fruit sitting on the balcony bench, their feet up on the railing. "Tell me," the sheriff broke into her nagging thoughts, "was it the clams last night or the guilt over inflicting serious wounds upon my big mug this morning that made you so cuddly and sweet all of a sudden?"

Charlie stopped crunching flakes to stare up at him.

"I'm not trying to be insensitive or macho or anything," he assured her. "I just want to know if I did something right for once . . . I guess."

"I'm sorry, I don't know. I just needed you."

"Jesus, don't apologize." He laughed rich and deep where she'd never heard more than a chuckle before. "You want to talk about it? Your dream I mean? Hell, you want to talk bad dreams, talk to a cop—life we lead."

And Charlie did, feeling less guilty and more silly by the minute. When she finished they were both grinning.

"Shit," the sheriff said, his breath rich with the odor of plums, "there's a murderer running loose, you've looked upon two dead bodies since last Thursday, found yourself all but under arrest, and you're dreaming about a shipwreck almost a century old?"

Charlie had to keep reminding herself that, although she had an alibi for the time of Michael's death, her fingerprints were supposedly still on his gun. And that gun shot Georgette Glick.

And the highest-ranking officer on the case had just slept with her. She felt guilty again. How this man managed to keep his office was beyond her.

"If I just knew I'd seen the *Peter Iredale* before, I could rationalize these stupid dreams, make sense of the senseless." Charlie tried to explain to them both why Jack's OOBE's disturbed her so.

"He's just dreaming himself and trying to make a book out of it. I told you about the people around here."

"But Jack's and my dreams are identical, Wes. That chapter he gave me to read would have sounded a lot less plausible if I hadn't dreamed I'd experienced something similar."

"We all get tingly, floaty sensations sometimes when we're falling asleep," he said. "We all have nightmares."

"But how could I have them about the *Peter Iredale* before I saw it? That's the one thing that keeps coming back to drive me . . . to freak me out."

"I wish there was only one thing about this case that freaked me out. But I remember standing on the beach years ago and this couple from Florida were taking pictures of it and making a big thing about running across a familiar landmark. They recognized it from a picture. That's a pretty famous wreck, Charlie. Odds are you did see it before you came to Oregon."

He'd made her feel better yet again so, to be fair, she admitted she hadn't stayed at the Hide-a-bye when he'd dropped her off last night, but had gone back to the village instead. If she shared everything she'd learned with him perhaps between the two of them they could make some sense of it all.

"I knew about Mrs. Peterson's walls being covered with books," Wes told her. "I was there before you were. Doubt it means anything." He said it offhandedly but defensiveness had added an edge to his tone. Maybe he was changing sheriffs on her.

Charlie hurried to tell him of the scalding at Rose's and Dr. Paige's treatment with aloe. "I wonder if they ever called a doctor for Gladys."

"No law says you have to call for medical assistance if the

victim is an adult of sound mind and doesn't want it. What's this houseplant again? And how do you find out all this stuff, most of which is useless, by the way?"

"Tagging along, being an unofficial observer. I don't believe in amateur detectives any more than you do, Wes, but I can see how they might be places and learn things an official wouldn't." She'd noticed the spark in his eyes when she mentioned houseplant. "You still haven't told me how Michael died."

"Lab reports aren't in yet. But we think it was poison. There were fairly obvious signs plastered around the inside of the car and elsewhere which I won't go into since we just ate."

"Thank you." She licked sticky cherry juice off her fingers and went on. "Jack tells me that, contrary to obvious economic indicators, the institute plans to expand and Rose is going to buy back her shares from the Japanese investors and Paige hopes to build onto the Emporium. Doc Withers has marvelous plans for a pet clinic that is so poor he has to make house calls in Chinook and shuffle wine at the institute in the evenings. The economy has mysteriously picked up in the village. Noticed any such changes in Chinook?"

That gave him pause and he finally shook his head no. "But I did check it out with Olsen about his brother getting ready to sue the institute for unpaid bills and found out that was old news. Brother Dennis has paid up and Olsen's brother's in the process of preparing a bid on more improvements. That was another one of your puzzle pieces that didn't fit. But I checked it out, took you seriously, and investigated your suspicions." His contentment had vanished. He lifted an empty coffee cup to his lips while his eyes searched this small section of the Pacific Ocean as if for the reason why.

"Let's get a second cup at Rose's," Charlie suggested.

Wes insisted on making a private phone call first.

"How's Gladys this morning?" Charlie asked Rose, accepting the coffee being poured and realizing the same stomach that had given her so much trouble the night before felt happy as a jaybird after an early morning recurrence of a nightmare, a later morning comforting by the sheriff of Moot County, and the requisite guilt trip. No explaining stomachs.

"She's cool." Rose poured coffee with one hand, and stifled a yawn with the other.

"Cool? I saw those burns last night."

"That Paige ought to be an MD." Rose bent close to squint at Wes's face as she filled his cup. "Looks like you should make an appointment with her, Sheriff. Either that or stay away from California women."

"Rose, where did Michael Cermack eat usually?" Charlie asked. "Did he cook for himself or drive into Chinook? There's no deli in Moot Point."

"We do breakfast, lunch, and dinner seven days a week. Why should he cook? We pack picnic lunches to eat on the beach and even carry-out. Rose's takes care of Moot Point. Who needs a deli?"

On the street outside, Wes stuck his hands in his pants pockets, rocked on his feet, and said casually, "I'd already figured out that's where Cermack got his lunch to take up to the lighthouse, unofficial investigator. But nice try." He wrinkled his nose in good-natured condescension, as only a man who'd made love with a woman before breakfast would have the nerve to do.

Then he watched her face as Deputy Turtle drove up in a gray Toyota and stopped in front of them. Charlie's gray Toyota.

"You're not to leave the county, understand," he said. "Me, I'm feeling the need for some of that 'unofficial' investigating you keep telling me about."

When the sheriff slid into the county Bronco wearing his facial scars and a complacent smirk, his deputy said under her breath, "Jesus, you two play rough."

Chapter 26

As Charlie and Deputy Linda stood watching the Bronco wend its way up to Paige Magill's Dream Emporium, Charlie felt suddenly empowered by the return of her wheels. "Could I give you a lift, Officer?"

"I'd thought maybe Himself would give me a ride back to Chinook, but it doesn't look like it. If it wouldn't be too much trouble?"

"None at all." Charlie patted the top of the Toyota. Once inside, she stroked the steering wheel and sighed. For all the freeway hours she'd cursed having to sit in it over the last two years, it felt marvelous now. Deputy Linda folded herself into the passenger side and slid the seat back as far as it would go.

"I don't care for these little Jap cars myself, but I'll say one thing—this sucker rides smooth as butter," she said once they were out on 101. "Got to get me a new car. My old Pontiac's rusting out."

It was a blustery, bright blue day. They let the wind in to tangle their hair and talked about their kids and about their mothers. And then the conversation turned to the sheriff, un-professional on Deputy Tortle's part and unwise on Charlie's.

"You're not in love with him or anything, I hope."

"Just attracted I guess," Charlie admitted.

"Yeah, well he's got three exes who'll tell you not to get involved. Why do I have the feeling you already are?"

"Has he given you any indication of when I can go home? I mean if he gave the car back—"

"Soon as we figure out how your prints got on the revolver probably, and maybe know more about how Michael died. I think he gave you back the car because he doesn't think your snooping around will hurt the case. That would be one reason I could think of. Or that you're not in any danger now. Or that without charging you with anything he can't hold onto the car any longer. Or that, left on your own, you might do something to implicate yourself as the killer. Or," they'd pulled up at the curb next to the Moot County Courthouse and Linda unfolded herself out, then leaned down to finish the sentence through the open window, "that running around loose you might flush out the killer. That'd be my guess."

The drive back to Moot Point didn't look as bright. The sheriff was probably using Charlie and letting her think she was using him. The guilt set in again. Charlie decided guilt made sex better at the time and lousy later.

She could see the wreck of the *Peter Iredale* from 101. From here it looked tiny and inconsequential. How much stock could she put in those crummy dreams anyway?

Once back in the village, her first stop was the Earth Spirit. Jack was just opening up and he looked terrible.

"Writer's block?" she asked half in jest and half to belay the dark look on his face.

He rubbed at an unshaven chin. "Bad OOBE last night."

She trailed him to his living quarters where he lifted a coffee mug and swirled the liquid around his mouth like TV cowboys once did whisky. "Worse than a bad trip in the days of chemical blowout."

"Where do you go, Jack, when you leave your body?" Charlie crawled up on a kitchen stool, idly fingering the wooden handles of some cutlery set out to dry. Jack's bed seemed always unmade but he kept tidy control on his kitchen.

"Usually wherever I think hard enough I want to go." He hit the counter with the flat end of a fist. Charlie and the cutlery jumped. "Damn! Why is this happening now? Now when I've got a book contract?"

"According to Paige, this isn't your first bad experience." Charlie began to wonder how deeply she wanted to go into this. How much of it, through the power of suggestion, would transfer to her own dreams which, what she could remember of them, seemed bad enough now.

"I used to panic thinking I couldn't get back and my body would die without me in it and I'd just float aimlessly forever or spin off into some void . . . but then when I gained some control it became a wondrous freedom, a soaring freedom, freedom from the half-substantiated myths of modern, soulless science. I explained all that in the chapter you read, didn't I?"

But last night had been different. He had not been alone. Jack had sensed others out there before. "Why wouldn't there be? This is an unusual skill I've discovered I have. But there are others, maybe lots more than I thought." He flopped down on his bed and leaned back against the wall. "But last night there was evil out there with me. Awful evil. And I don't believe in evil."

"How do you know it was evil? Did you see it? Did it talk to you or what?"

"It was so powerful. I don't know what else it could have been. Lately I've been going as far as an old shipwreck up the beach toward Chinook, using it as a marker on how far away from these old bones I dare go."

"The *Peter Iredale* . . ." Charlie felt the surge of panic bubbles start to course through her bloodstream again. She gritted her teeth against them, drew in a breath, and tried to grin her disturbing thoughts away all at the same time.

"You got a headache?"

"Oh, no. I'm fine. It's just I've been dreaming about the *Peter Iredale* until I think I'm . . . I'm freaking out."

The intense eyes forgot their hard misery and stared first at and then through her. "You know, Charlie, since you came I've been stopping off to see you on my way? You don't suppose I could be . . . nah, that's too . . . when do you usually have these dreams?"

"Sometimes when I go to sleep at night, but more often just about dawn. Why? And I don't suppose you could be what? Jack, I was having these dreams before I ever saw the *Peter Iredale*."

"You probably saw it on book jackets or record covers, calendars. It's likely to be in any New Age store you ever went in."

"I think this is the first one I've ever been in. Why is it on covers and calendars?"

"It's considered a center of power to a lot of people who are into that kind of thing. Not it, so much as its location. Have you ever heard of a vortex?"

"Oh, boy." This was getting too deep for closed little minds like Charlie's. She slipped off her stool and started back through the store. "Just promise me not to stop off at my cabin again unless you're in your body, okay?"

But her client was right behind her. "About last night, I need to talk to someone, please? Did you ever sense evil, Charlie, lurking in your room when you were a kid and your parents wouldn't take you seriously? And the fear felt like it was outside your body and ready to swallow you?"

"Like a body cast." Charlie was out on the porch before he could grab an arm and turn her to face him.

"That's it . . . a body cast. You think my OOBE's have something to do with your dreams? Opened up the way for you?"

"I don't know. I don't want to know. I want the dreams to end. You don't believe in evil. I don't believe in OOBE's." But

Charlie would sure feel better if she knew for a fact she'd seen a picture of the *Peter Iredale* before she came to the Oregon Coast.

When Charlie knocked on the back door of Gladys and Olie Bergkvist's home, even the dogs seemed subdued. Gladys opened the door looking old and saggy but not terminal, not infected from heavy burns. Charlie stepped inside. "I'm so relieved you're all right. You *are* all right?"

"Yeah, I'm better. Hung over more than anything. You were there last night, weren't you? I remember all you helping me. I appreciate it. You want some tea?"

"Nothing, thank you." Charlie had finally learned the proper response for Moot Point. But she sat at the kitchen table and watched in awe as Gladys shuffled about the room in bedroom slippers and a short-sleeved duster imprinted with posies and berries. Eenie, Meenie, Miney, Moe, and Joe crowded at her heels and narrowly missed tripping her up when she turned back to the table with a cup of tea and a plate of toast. The arm that should have had the skin falling off, or whatever severe burns do, looked much the same as the other arm and didn't appear swollen or that painful to use.

The kitchen and attached family room with TV and fireplace overlooked a sunken living room and the wall of windows displaying the village and the bay. Green leafy plants and decorative pillows replaced the art works Charlie would have expected here. The furniture was fussy and ruffled and in cranberry-colored prints with bold splashes of blue for contrast, walls and drapes white, carpets a light cream. What Libby and her friends couldn't do to that carpet in a half-hour snack-and-soda session. . . .

Gladys dunked buttered toast in her tea and slurped it. "Sorry, but when I don't feel good this calms my stomach."

Gladys was the only villager who had ever shown any sign of fear of Charlie. She wasn't showing any now. Neither were the poodles puddled at their feet watching Gladys, her tea, and her toast with concentrated longing. Had Gladys been the only one to fear Charlie because everyone else had known from the beginning that Charlie had not shot Georgette Glick? Because there was no motive or any sign of a connection between Charlie and the victim? Or because they all knew who did?

"You weren't as badly burned last night as I thought."

Gladys pushed her sleeve up to expose a portion of her shoulder. "Skin's a little tight and scaly feeling up here. Paige, bless her, got there in time or it would have been real bad." She took her dishes to the sink and hoisted up the lower half of the window over it to let in the air, as if to prove how little damage had been done to her arm. "But I suppose what you really came here to do is ask more questions about Michael."

Charlie was thinking of asking about Gladys's husband, Olie, instead, when a series of gunshots split the air and Charlie hit the floor in a sea of poodles.

The dogs darted at her, yapping. One even came up and nipped her chin.

"Here, Philomena, stop that. What's the matter with you?" Gladys grabbed up the offender with her burned arm. "Did she hurt you? Doesn't look like the skin is broken. Sorry, but my lovlies aren't used to someone falling to the floor that way. You have the need to vomit or something?"

"Didn't you hear the gunshots? Get down," Charlie ordered.

Another rang out but Gladys sat back in her chair, Philomena still in her arms, and laughed in sharp bursts. "That? That's a truck backfiring up on the highway. Happens all the time."

"How can you be sure?" But Charlie rose hesitantly and slipped into her chair, staying slouched down, though, to keep a low profile just in case.

"Because nobody shoots off a gun this close to people's houses." Gladys brought her mirth under control but a spreading stain flushed her face and neck at the effort. "Might kill somebody."

Charlie was about to point out Georgette Glick was shot

right here in the village when Paige Magill appeared at the window screen without her smile and dimples. "Gladys, has the sheriff been here yet? He was just over to my place asking about poisonous houseplants and I—"

"Paige, come on in and have some tea. Jack's agent's here and she thought those backfires up on one-oh-one were gun-shots. Can you believe it?" Gladys continued a steady flow of chatter until she had Paige safely shut up and sitting at the kitchen table.

Charlie refused to cooperate. "Somebody poisoned Michael with a houseplant?"

"Who said that?" Gladys's flush paled. "The sheriff?"

"Nobody said that." Paige shot them both an unfathomable look before the almond-shaped eyes regained their placid assur-edness. "Sheriff Bennett was just asking me about the aloe treat-ment I gave your burns last night. He threatened to report me to somebody or other for practicing medicine without a license. That's not fair. He wouldn't have said that if I'd smeared some over-the-counter salve on you."

"He's full of bluster, Wes Bennett. Don't let him get to you." But Gladys had grown as somber as Paige.

Charlie agreed with Gladys about Wes and knew the two women were waiting for her to leave so they could talk. She would get nothing more out of Gladys. But she gave Paige a parting shot. "Have you talked to Jack? He had a ba-ad OOBE last night. And I did too."

Outside, Charlie stood looking up at Michael's loft. Had he been poisoned by a houseplant? Paige would certainly know all about them. But why would she poison Michael? Obviously be-cause of something Charlie didn't know.

Everyone had insinuated to death that Michael had killed himself driving off the cliff, drunk. Or, because he was a cre-ative artist type and moody, had committed suicide just driving off the cliff. But Charlie worked with arty people and they were often embarrassingly normal and rarely so silly as to drive off a cliff to commit suicide—the chances of ending up a human vegetable rather than dead being so obvious. Better and surer ways to achieve that sort of end abounded, and creative people had been known to come up with dillies.

Besides, the only time Charlie saw Michael he was anything but suicidal.

Chapter 27

Charlie had just reached the corner in front of the Earth Spirit, when a car with California license plates backed from in front of Frank Glick's house into a blacktopped drive behind it and turned around to head up to 101. Charlie was headed in the same direction but stopped suddenly to stare at the street running alongside the Glick trailer home. What did the Glicks drive? Why did it matter? Then again, why not? Charlie had to do something.

So she parked and walked across the street to peer behind Frank's trailer. At the end of the short drive sat Clara Peterson's old Ford. This was *her* off-street parking. A narrow band of weed grass ran between it and the Glicks'. Charlie continued on up past Clara's where an elderly but spotless Buick rested on a similar parking area. It must belong to Mary and Norma. So where did the Glicks park?

On her way back, Charlie spied a shard of red plastic in the grass verge between Clara's parking space and Frank's trailer. It was the kind that had one smooth side and one nubby, the kind that often covers taillights. But those on Clara's Ford appeared to be intact. Charlie stuck the shard in her pocket.

"Find a clue?" Sheriff Wes said behind her.

Charlie whirled.

"Tell me," she asked, "how someone the size of a tank with size twenty sneakers can sneak up on people like that? You're incredible."

"That's your answer. I'm incredible." Wes Bennett held out his hand. "Hand it over."

"Don't you have better things to do than follow people around and demand to see what they pick up off the ground?" But she gave him the plastic shard.

"Charlie, I can't stop you from snooping. You're a free citizen. So far. But do you have to be so obvious about it? Think a minute. Two people, two seemingly innocent people, are dead. One for sure murdered, the other most likely so. Charlie, I don't want you to be number three."

"You think the murderer is here in the village, don't you?"

"Yeah. And if you're as obvious to me as you are to him, I'm going to worry." He glanced at the red plastic in his hand and then over at Clara's Ford.

And Charlie caught sight of the parted drape closing on the bird lady's picture window. "Are you sure it's a he?"

"Seems to me some female feminist from LA pointed out to me just the other day the odds of murder being done by a member of the male half of the species." The welts on his face looked like white streaks now.

"Do you happen to know where Frank Glick parks his car?"

"There you go again. I just begin to think I can communicate with you and you start off on some irrelevant, useless piece of— Charlie, who the shit cares where old Frank parks his car? I'm worrying about your luscious neck."

"I care," Charlie told him and stalked off to the Earth Spirit.

• • •

"They didn't have a car," Jack said. "Charlie, I don't think I can write this book."

"Of course you can write the damn book. What happened last night was a nightmare. Writers have those too. Everybody does. Even agents. I had the same dream you did, remember?"

"You think my OOBE's are just dreams, don't you? How can you be my agent if you don't believe?" His voice snapped and every one of the customers browsing among the weird merchandise looked over at them. One woman approached hesitantly and Jack put on his best retail manner. "Can I help you find something?"

He left the cash register to show her how to use the earphones to sample the audio tape of dolphins trying to communicate with humans, and Charlie slipped behind the curtain, through the bathroom, and out the back side door. There was a surfaced pad for Jack's absent and ailing pickup here. But the Glicks didn't even have an off-street parking area. When she returned the way she'd come Jack stood inside the curtain, legs spread, hands on hips.

"Two people don't have the same dream, Charlie."

"Okay, for the sake of argument, let's say we both had the same OOBE instead. So what?"

"So I can't go through many trips like the one last night but I need to to do research to write the book. That's what."

"Look, OOBE's were only a small part of the proposal. As far as I'm concerned the weakest. We don't know what Susan Talbot and Morton and Fish are going to want included for sure. Some of the things in the proposal they may want thrown out, others expanded—they may not even want to go into the OOBE thing. So there's no reason to get all excited about that now. It's no big deal."

"You mean they want to write my book for me?"

"No, Frank, they want you to write your book for them."

He stared at her unblinking, accusing like Charlie the cat. Finally he whispered, "I don't think I'll ever understand publishing, Charlie."

"Nobody does, that's why so many people make a living trying to explain it. The real question here is how did the Glicks get along without a car, clear out here in never-never land?"

"Georgette had some kind of vision problem and Frank—"

"A seventy-eight-year-old woman with vision problems rides a Schwinn without lights in dense fog at night? Give me a break."

"She didn't seem all that bothered by it, got around all right. But they'd taken her license away years ago. And I guess Frank never did drive but I don't know the story behind that. I don't see why you keep harping on the Glicks."

"Well, one of them is dead, you'll notice. As in murdered. How did they do their shopping?"

"I don't know . . . if you want to go into Chinook all day there's a bus. There's a van service into Portland, always someone going to the food markets Georgette could ride along with. They ate take-out from Rose's a lot. She offers a senior citizen discount plus a menu that's usually half vegetarian. Local fruit and vegetable growers come around and sell out of their trucks right at your door. I don't think they hurt that much not having a car."

A voice "ahemed" behind him and Jack turned. "Can I help you?" he said before he'd even fully parted the curtains.

"Yeah, can I buy this?" a pimply young man in a *My Consciousness has Risen* T-shirt asked, holding up a miniature Buddha with the same spaced-out smile as the one on the giant Buddha on the floor behind him.

"Of course, and I am sorry," Jack gestured magnanimously while shrugging apologetically, "but I'm a writer and I was just talking business with my agent."

"Really?" The young man looked enormously impressed, mostly with Charlie.

She waved bye to both of them and headed for the door, not yet sure if Jack Monroe was a writer, but confident he was a retailer. Which fact was reassuring. These days writing was not a long-lived career. How many times had she cautioned, "Don't give up your day job"?

Charlie's foot was reaching for the bottom step when a voice hissed in her ear, "I didn't kill her."

"Excuse me?" But Charlie missed the step and would have sprawled ignominiously at almost the spot where Georgette Glick and the Toyota'd had their fateful meeting, if the Mary and Norma sisters hadn't intervened, one on each arm, to gather her up like a sack of their roadside litter before she had time to hit the ground.

"I saw you and the sheriff talking. I saw you pick up something in the grass. And I think I know what it was." Clara the bird lady wrung her hands, literally, and so hard her fingertips were turning white. Her two birdlike neighbors fussed with the inevitable coffee pot and sliced nutty/fruity bread, nodding, clucking in support of their friend, drawing their curtains against witnesses.

"She didn't kill her," Mary said.

"Oh, my, no," Norma agreed.

Mary had a minor case of the trembles, and a long neck. She reminded Charlie of the blue herons along the estuary leading to the restaurant decorated in garlic and serving those sublime steamer clams.

"She didn't kill Georgie? I don't remember anyone saying she did."

"Oh, but the sheriff suspects she did, you see." Norma fluttered paper napkins and blinked at all the slices of bread as if realizing nobody might want them.

"That's why we came to you, of course." Mary craned her neck and reached for something above the cupboards.

"What's why you came to me?"

Clara's magnified eyes had filled with magnified tears behind her trifocals. "Because you found a piece of Georgie's bicycle, didn't you? I was so sure we'd picked it all up. But it was dark and the next day I couldn't bring myself to look."

Clara and Charlie sat at the little table in the kitchen while the sisters stood together behind Clara, nodding and trembling in sympathetic fervor. Six pairs of eyes pleaded with Charlie. Clara stretched her hands across the table, having to reach around the sides of the cutting board full of sliced nutty/fruity bread, and Charlie clutched them to comfort the poor woman. They were icy. "You ran over the Schwinn?"

"I didn't know it was there," Clara said, dissolving. "She always parked it in front before."

The sisters clutched the sobbing woman's shoulders.

"We figure she was hiding it from Frank because they'd had a strong disagreement and she wanted him to worry about her being out in the fog," Norma said and released one hand from her neighbor's shoulder to move the butter out of harm's way.

"And he," Mary said, disapproval sharpening her face, "he insisted poor Clara drive him into Chinook to a motel because he wanted to pay her back—Georgie that is. Those two could be so silly and disgusting."

"And you know I don't see well, driving in the dark. I backed off the pavement a bit. But it never mattered before because there was nothing there to run over."

Charlie looked from one to the next and waited.

All three looked back at Charlie expectantly.

"We did think you might understand, where the sheriff might not," Mary prompted and turned her face sideways to glare down at Charlie with one eye.

"Right," Charlie said in her best take-charge manner, feeling at a total loss. This was not the first time she'd had to combine the two. "But first," she said playing for time and reaching for the butter, "Norma, pour the coffee. Mary, pull up two more chairs."

The coffee was weak after Rose's fresh-ground but the bread was much tastier than it looked, more like cake. "All right now, let's see if I have this straight. You all think that Georgette and Frank Glick had a disagreement that night, and one serious enough to send Georgette off in the fog supposedly on her bike just to worry him, and to send him to a motel in Chinook to worry her. I have at least one problem with this. He didn't go anywhere that night. He was here." Charlie would not soon forget the distraught man in the swirling yellow slicker rushing into the Earth Spirit, nor the clutch of his elderly but strong hand on her left bun.

"That's because she was on the picnic table." Clara crushed her bread in her hand and dropped it back on the plate petulantly. "She was always doing unexpected things like that."

"When poor Clara realized she'd hit the bicycle in the dark, she rushed around to the front of the house," Norma explained. "Frank had planned to run around the house when he saw her back her car out to the street and hop in, but—"

"But he was just standing there," Clara said, smearing tears across her cheeks, "looking down at the picnic table with his little overnight bag in his band."

"Clara tried to tell him about the bicycle, but by that time Georgette had made that into something of a moot point," Norma said and stifled a giggle. Even poor Clara blinked at her in surprise. Charlie grinned—how was it the name fit this place so well?

Clara said, "I didn't know Georgie had been murdered, that she'd been shot with a gun and a bullet. I thought, and Frank did too, that it was just her time had come."

"On a picnic table?"

"At your age," Mary said down the length of a long nose, "you don't realize what little choice we all have in the matter."

"All I could think of was that I'd run over her bicycle," Clara continued, "and the sheriff and his people would think she was on it when I did . . . all I knew for sure at the time was that she was dead . . . there wasn't much time to make decisions and then—"

"And then out of the fog, I drove up?"

"Well, we had to do something," Clara said. "We had a mangled bike and a dead Georgie. And the fog was so thick no one could see what we were doing. It was a spur of the moment thing."

Charlie couldn't help but think it so unlikely a story it might be true, but also that part of it was missing, even aside from the gaping hole that it didn't explain who shot Georgette. "Both you and Frank will have to talk to the sheriff," she said. "There's no other way."

"Frank won't even talk to you. He's furious that I am."

"Of course we don't know," Mary spread butter on her bread, "that Frank Glick really found his wife on the picnic table like he said, do we?"

"But I saw her there."

"He might have shot her and put her there, Clara," Mary said, and the sisters nodded their suspicions in unison while Clara Peterson's eyes widened in a sort of soap opera shock, like you'd expect before a fade-out for a commercial.

Chapter 28

Charlie sat on the front step of Frank Glick's porch, staring at the picnic table and fighting with her conscience. Who was she to insist Frank and Clara tell all to the sheriff and trust to the law to see they got a fair and honest judgment? Charlie had done everything she could think of to independently search for information to clear herself of suspicion for the very same murder, because she didn't trust the law to do it for her.

And Charlie was a total stranger with no apparent motive. These two senior citizens were prime suspects—the spouse and the other woman. The county Bronco was gone and Charlie had debated using the nearest phone to call it back.

But, say Clara's story was true, the reason offered for the Glicks' disagreement didn't sound strong enough to cause such reactions. Would Georgette be that upset about Frank's clippings refuting her nutritional beliefs? Or had Frank parked the bike in back of the trailer knowing Clara might run over it after he shot Georgette but before he asked Clara to drive him into a motel in Chinook?

Charlie'd left the bird lady and her birdlike neighbors promising them to talk to Frank and get back to them again before she talked to Wes Bennett.

If Frank was home he wasn't answering her knock at his door. Past the picnic table which was really getting to Charlie—God, Georgette's daughters had sat crying on it just last night not knowing—Charlie could see over Jack's store to the sea. If Jack built on a second story to the Earth Spirit it would take out about half of Frank Glick's view.

The day was actually comfortably warm. A wood-and-lattice porch cover above Charlie protected five or six hanging baskets of a lush thick-leaved plant in full pink bloom, and a herd of bees grazed contentedly. Did Georgie get these plants from Paige Magill's greenhouse or had she raised them from slips or whatever housewives do to create such splendid house jungles?

"You're being sexist. Frank could be the green thumb in the family. Many men upon retirement specialize in such things." Charlie had read a whole article on the topic in an airline magazine not long ago.

"He could also be the murderer."

"You could also be putting yourself in deep shit by running around talking to Frank or anybody else before sharing with the sheriff the responsibility for the information you now have and he doesn't. Hey, there's a murderer loose in this peaceful little village and, since you don't know who it is, that person could be the next human you approach and speak to. That person has killed twice and is not out there wanting to be caught. You could be a real irritant, Charlie Greene." As her boss, Richard Morse, often said, "Some people you don't need to irritate."

Say Frank, and maybe even Clara, were responsible for Georgette's death, why would they shoot her with Michael's gun and then kill Michael? The whole thing sucked.

Charlie was about ready to go bang on the door again when a car coasted to a stop at the informal grass verge bordering the street and Frank and Randolph Glick stepped out. They were arguing. Charlie wanted to talk to Frank but not face his son too. She slid over the side of the steps, the two men so engrossed in their bickering they didn't see her.

Charlie, Georgette's cat, did however. It rose from a hidden place in the same bushes beside the steps, took a swipe at Charlie's nose, made a *"hissthwapt!"* sound, and catapulted over the flimsy stair railing to bounce off the trailer home's front and zoom off.

The Glicks looked up briefly when the feline flew over the street and then looked back to their feet, avoiding each other's eyes as they strode angrily up to the picnic table on the patio.

"But think what it'll do to the girls. Think how it will confuse the grandchildren," Randolph said, stopping to lean on the picnic table with one hand while he gestured with the other like an Italian. "After sixty years . . . I just can't believe what I'm hearing. It doesn't make sense. You must be in shock or something."

"Well, you're a great one to talk, aren't you?"

"My situation was totally different and you know it."

"Which one?"

"Both of them. Dad, that woman has obviously got some kind of hold on you and I want to know what it is."

"I forbid you to disturb her in any way." The two Glicks would have stood nose to nose if the son's nose hadn't been a half a head higher. But there could never be a question of Randolph's paternity. Even the patch of anger looked the same color on each face.

"She was my mother, the only mother I've ever known. I loved her and you can't treat her memory like this."

"Well, that's all she is now, a memory. The rest of us have to get on the best we can. Thought if there was anybody I could talk to, it'd be you—another man. But I can see I was wrong. Now that we have your mother decently buried, you can just go right on back to your own life. And tell your sisters and all the grandchildren to do likewise."

"Decently buried? Mother was murdered and there'll be no decency until her murderer is made to pay."

"Three months is what I told you and three months is what I meant. Now get out of here." Old Frank stomped up the stairs past Charlie and she heard the door slam.

The angry color left Randolph's complexion as he sat back on the picnic table where his sisters had mourned their mother, where that mother—if Clara Peterson were to be believed—had lain dead before being stuffed under Charlie's car. He wept silently, shoulders heaving, great tears welling and spilling over. Like a child left helpless and marooned, his world destroyed.

Charlie'd had no reason to like Georgette's son but the scary thing, the pathetic thing, was that he made no sound. She had one of those damned female urges to blow her cover and rush to comfort him. Female urges invariably led to disaster.

Randolph Glick was easily old enough to be her father, but his dad was a real bonafide shit. She hadn't understood the argument and didn't know what the three-month threat was all about, but it was never more apparent that if old Frank was in mourning, it was only for the lack of someone to make his Cream of Wheat and select his jockeys.

Fortunately, before Charlie was moved to move on her female urge, Randolph straightened and pulled a cloth handkerchief from his hip pocket. He cleaned up his nose and his face and straightened his body and his tie. He glared at the trailer above Charlie and nodded to himself as if coming to a decision. Charlie knew Libby could turn strong emotion on and off that quickly, but she didn't know a man could. She was glad she hadn't left the bushy plants that hid her when she saw how hard was the look that transformed his eyes under lashes still glistening with tear fragments.

Randolph Glick stood, licked his lips, and pressed them tightly. If he'd been heading for one of the morning staff meetings at Congdon and Morse Representation, Inc., Charlie would have headed for the restroom instead of the conference room. He stepped off purposefully, not back to his car, but around the side of his father's house.

Charlie was about to rise from her squat to relieve aching ankles and feet when Randolph's father thundered across the porch and down the stairs next to her head. "I told you to leave that woman alone, didn't I? You're just out to make trouble where there's none to be made, damn you."

Charlie figured it was now or never and tried to push off to a standing position, but one leg had gone to sleep to the hip and she stumbled. She put one hand on the stairs next to her face and the other one missed. It came down on the ground just below the edge of the open redwood steps and onto the feel of warm cloth.

She nearly screamed, thinking she'd found another body. But the cloth lay on bare earth. Charlie could see by the sunlight filtering through the space between steps a garment with buttons and pockets, shaped into a shallow circle like a nest. It was covered with short hairs.

Cat hairs, Charlie would have bet. She stood and brought the garment up with her. It was a safari shirt with buttons and flaps and pockets. And most of the hair clung to the rusty stains on its front. Bloodstains, Charlie would have bet.

She fought off another female urge, this one to rush to the local animal clinic and plead with Doc Withers to take in Georgette's pet permanently. Charlie the cat might come home to sleep in the solace of its owner's blood smell, but Charlie the agent doubted it still ate here.

"Hey, animals are adaptable and that shirt is evidence," Charlie's rationality warned. But the other Charlie returned the safari shirt to as close to its original position as she could remember and stepped out of the bushes.

It sounded like all hell was breaking loose on the other side of the trailer house. Those could be old paint stains on that shirt, but Charlie squared her shoulders and walked into Frank's house to call the sheriff of Moot County. She was clearly out of her league again and she knew it.

· · ·

"Told Clara not to talk to you, damn it," Frank said.

"Both you and Clara are going to have to talk to the sheriff about this, Frank, before things get any worse. There's no other way." Charlie eyed the telephone. What if the dispatcher had decided hers was a crank call? What if Wes was nowhere near his pager or car radio? Or so far away from Moot Point it would take him too long to get here?

She sat in the same recliner she had the night of Georgette's murder. But now she knew how Georgette and her Schwinn had come to be under the Toyota.

Randolph had stormed in first, furious at not finding Clara at home and finding Charlie had invaded his father's home instead. With a calmness she didn't feel, Charlie informed them both she had called the sheriff and would wait for his arrival. That she'd talked to Clara and there was new information on Georgette's death.

"Well, that's all fine and good because I have some new information on my mother's death too. I know now that the Peterson woman shot my mother in order to get her nasty claws into my poor old father."

Charlie relaxed back into the recliner. She'd had it with these guys. "Your poor old father's a lech, Randy. How many women and children did *you* have to trash to prove how wonderful you are?"

"Two marriages, two divorces, lost track of the assorted offspring long ago, and the mistresses," Frank said gleefully. "And he wants to make trouble for me, man married to the same woman for over sixty years."

"She was my mother," Randolph said, "and our situations are as different as night and day. And *no one* calls me Randy."

"Probably don't seem so different to your assorted offspring," Charlie said, knowing she was talking to the wallboard. It would take bypass surgery or a near-death experience to cut through his self-centered coating. "I promised Clara I'd talk to you, Frank, before I called the sheriff, but I've had to break that promise. She and . . . the people she's with know I'm here and why. It's up to you if you want Randolph to stay or not."

"Just who the hell are you to talk to us this way? You're involved in my mother's murder too, probably in league with that woman next door."

"Shut up, Randy," Frank said.

"Now just a goddamn minute here."

"Get out," Frank said.

Both Charlie and Frank's son stared at the old man, startled by the energy and authority in his tone and expression. Randolph headed for the door. "I'm going to tell the rest of the family. They should know about you."

"I can't stop you," Frank admitted. "But you can't stop me from marrying Clara in three months time, either."

"We'll see about that," Randolph said and added with a sneer, "Dad. You both conspired with the Peterson woman to kill Mom. I don't know why yet, but it'll come out when this thing goes to trial." Randy slammed the door behind him.

Frank lay out on the couch, his authority deflated. "Just like his mother—bulldogs, both of them. We had one boy, three girls—every one of them turned out like her. Don't make sense. Hoped he might understand because he was a man like me, but you see what come of it."

"Want to talk to me before Wes Bennett gets here?"

"Me and Georgette was married over sixty years. Hadn't got along the last fifty-eight, but we stuck together. That's what our generation did. Only way to raise kids and have 'em turn out decent, as you can see by what's become of the world since the new generations decided to do it their way." He sat up again and Charlie could hear joints popping. He looked directly into her eyes and Charlie wondered if there was a confession coming. "But I never wanted kids—just wanted to fuck. Children happen and there you are. I'd look at another woman and old Georgie'd throw a hissy-fit. But Randolph, he shit Chanel Number Five, far as his mother was concerned, and still bounced around beds like his balls belonged to a Ping-Pong parlor. Clara

208

and me, we get along fine and she's not dead set to deprive me of every last thing I fancy just for my own good. We're comfortable together. That means a lot at any age. Now, nosy Miss Agent, have I answered all your damn questions?"

Even as he rose to his feet, even as Charlie's rational self reminded her that she was alone with the new chief suspect in a murder case, even as she remembered the stains on that shirt, curiosity got the better of her. "All but one. Did you kill your wife, Frank?"

Chapter 29

"Things was going just fine till you come along," Frank said, advancing as Charlie backed.

"You needed me to drive my car up to stuff her body under," she reminded him.

"That was Clara's idea. We was both so befuddled."

"Clara ran over the bike and—"

"And then she come running around the house crying up a storm. And me standing there looking down at old Georgette in the fog. And old Georgette had no plans to move on her own, let me tell you. But would you move, please?"

"Excuse me?"

"All this heavy breathing and shouting's inspired my bladder." He grinned, knowing she'd thought he was threatening her. "And you're blocking the door to the pisser."

Charlie shrugged and stalked out onto the porch. She sat on the steps and waited. Randolph's car hadn't moved. He still sat in it, staring straight out to sea. Frank was a lech and a shit, as self-involved as his son. Poor Clara Peterson must need the money badly or perhaps just needed someone who needed her to bake lemon meringue pies—the creamy kind instead of the Jell-O-y. Still, Charlie couldn't see Frank as a murderer.

Frank Glick joined her on the top porch step to watch, over Jack Monroe's roof, the Pacific roll in in picture postcard perfection, ignoring the car at the curb and the man in it.

"Is it true you don't drive? Never have?" Charlie asked.

"Some people never swim, others can never look down from great heights without fainting dead away. Some can't bring themselves to drive cars. But I never killed my wife. She was just laying out there on the picnic table, dead. Like she was meant to go then and did."

"What did you do before you retired that you didn't have to drive a car?"

"Moved into Georgette's old man's grocery business when I married her and took it over when he died. What driving had to be done, Georgette did. Lived all our lives, till we come here, in Sebastopol, California. Knew her in high school and in the Biblical way." Frank's long stringy eyebrow hairs rose for emphasis. "Her old man hadn't come after me, Randolph would have been born the bastard he's proven himself."

"You are everything I despise," Charlie told him.

"I live long enough to see you get old and ugly, I'll feel the same about you. But right now I love you, darling, can't help it." He moved closer and Charlie stood up.

Why couldn't she say the obvious, that he was already old and ugly? Why couldn't she be more like a man? "Like you love Clara Peterson?"

"Oh well, she's more of a comfort than a . . . she's the kind who makes a good—"

"Servant? Cook? Maid? Housekeeper? Nurse?"

"Yeah, housewife. Someone to comfort a man in his old age instead of torment him."

"Plus drive him around. But Frank, what can you offer Clara Peterson?"

"Hell, I'm offering to marry the woman, ain't I?"

"How many safari shirts do you own?"

He shrugged, "Three or four. Kids all went to that Banana Republic store to do their Christmas shopping one year. Can't think for themselves, you know. Had to call up their mother and ask her what to buy. Thought your last question was going to be did I kill my wife or not."

Charlie stood on the little paving stones at the bottom of the steps and faced him, trying not to look at the corner of the safari shirt showing between the stairs under his right boot. "You lied to me that day on the beach, didn't you? About your argument with your wife the night she died, it wasn't about clippings on how wrong her nutritional beliefs were."

"Certainly was. I had proof. Boy, I had her good."

"But that's not why she went off in the fog pretending to take her bike, maybe hoping to worry you."

"We didn't do much but argue, you understand." He sat quietly, staring around her to the sea, as if deep in thought, or, Charlie worried, hoping the sheriff would get here to stop all this unofficial investigating. "But I guess the very last thing we had words over was she wanted me to go with her to the Bergkvists and make Mrs. Bergkvist admit Georgette was not either a crazy old woman for thinking she saw Olie in town this summer. Hell, Olie's a rich man, he can have any woman he wants. Why'd he want to come home to that old wart if he had something better going? Told her to mind her own business for once. That woman had the longest nose on earth. But there was no talking to Georgie. So, she said she'd go herself. And I said fine. And that's the last I saw her alive."

"But you wanted Clara to take you to a motel in Chinook. I don't see the connection."

"Woman like Georgette'll eat you alive if you don't watch out," he explained patiently. "She was always going off to that institute and leaving me alone if I didn't do exactly what she wanted, see? Or the garden club, or this bunch of old biddies that played bridge. Every time the institute finished up a class there was a beach picnic. I never wanted to go to them because the people talked and acted stupid and it almost always rained and I was too tall to get under the tarps they'd prop up over the food. But all she could think to do was gripe that I was 'antisocial.' Older she got, worse it got. I never had no place to go except next door to Clara's. Daytime, if the weather wasn't too bad I'd walk into Chinook and buy stuff Georgie wouldn't let me have. But she was always going off on her bike, see. So that night I got fed up and decided two can play that game. Let her worry for once, the old fool. I didn't plan to come home till the six o'clock bus the next day either."

"She was shot in the head, Frank. There would have been blood. Clara said you both thought she'd died a natural death."

"The fog was gray, her skin was gray, her hair was gray—you couldn't see that well. So you decide what it is you think you're seeing. I didn't know about the blood till later."

"That's why you wore the yellow slicker over your clothes when you rushed into the Earth Spirit to accuse me of running over your wife."

"Already changed my shirt, give it to Clara to dispose of, but we weren't positive there weren't stains someplace we wouldn't see until it was too late. I need my reading glasses to see things close up and things got so jumbled I couldn't find 'em in time and Clara was too nervous about then to trust completely. Had to hurry in case you was going to leave soon or old Jack wouldn't let you in. So I slipped on my slicker. Changed clothes again when I got home before the sheriff brought you and Jack over here to question. You can't be too careful these days."

Charlie drove slowly into Chinook and tried to enjoy the drive and the outlandish scenery along the way. But her head was back in Moot Point.

Sheriff Wes had arrived to hear her story, gather Clara, Frank, and Randolph together in the Glick trailer, praise Charlie on a "nice job, Detective Greene," and essentially tell her to get lost. Charlie had been about to tell him of the bloodstained shirt under the steps, but his attitude pissed her off.

So she didn't. No doubt about it, a sheriff with an attitude misses things.

Charlie ended up at The Witch's Tit across from the Moot County Courthouse for a frozen yogurt lunch. So mad still at that particular county's sheriff, she splurged for chocolate sprinkles and cashews even.

She was crunching up the cashews with venom when Deputy Linda Tortle walked in, did a double take at the sight of Charlie, ordered a butterscotch sundae, and came to sit across from Charlie with her pickup ticket.

"Attacked any innocent men lately? You're the talk of the department, you know. First woman to ever beat up on Wes Bennett and get away with it."

Charlie crunched her cashews harder.

Linda allowed the professional drag on her long face to lift into a teasing and toothy smile. "Told you he was a bastard . . . didn't I? Thought I had."

The deputy went off with her claim ticket at an order barked from the PA system and returned with her caramel-colored lunch.

"Why do you work for him?"

"He's a good sheriff . . . hell, he makes a damn good bastard if that's all you aspire to. Charlie, he's not the first man to make big or muscle look sexy. Why do I have the feeling you already know that?"

"Why do I have the feeling some election year, he's going to read all about it in the local newspaper? And a woman named Tortle, not Tuttle, will be running against him?"

"And why is our sheriff been called off to the point by the California woman on an important development and low and behold we find the California woman right here in Chinook?"

Charlie told Linda about the spot Frank Glick and Clara Peterson were in at the moment.

Linda licked sticky butterscotch off her tongue onto her

teeth. "What reason would Frank have to kill Michael Cermack? I can see him and Clara being panicked enough to dump all the grisly under your car in an emergency maybe, but a planned and cold-blooded attack—no way."

"Hey, you can afford to say that. You're not an unofficial investigator, as in nonprofessional, who doesn't know the least thing about almost everything."

Linda sucked on her plastic spoon a minute and studied Charlie. "And our Wes ticked you off. And you didn't tell him everything because he was being a big shit, right?"

Charlie shrugged noncommittally and got up to leave.

"You know, there's a great coffee bean place about three doors down," the deputy said, getting up, too. "Could I treat you to some fresh-ground, roasted-on-the-spot, real caffeinated dessert, Ms. Greene?"

They soon strolled down the sidewalk toward the waterfront, like old friends, nursing thick paper cups of serious coffee.

"So what's it going to cost me to get this information you're withholding from Wes Bennett because he was being an asshole?" Deputy Tortle asked, breathing in the aromatic steam rising from her cup.

The cargo ship Charlie had seen while sitting on the wharf with the sheriff was gone. But a huge Hyundai ship like the one she'd seen approach from her cabin windows was loading sawn lumber from a barge out in the harbor. "I'll trade you for information that I want."

"How do I know your information's worth anything?"

"You don't."

"You tell me first and I'll decide." Linda put on her tough act.

"No deal."

"Listen, withholding information in a murder case can get you in deep waters fast, my friend. My advice to you is—"

"What information? Who said anything about information?" They stood in mild sunshine, but on the horizon behind the big ship and the barge of lumber the sky looked bruised and faintly dirty. A sea gull flew over them, shitting a three-foot-long string of white.

"What is it you think you need to know?" Deputy Tortle asked finally.

"The current status of the investigation into the whereabouts of Olie Bergkvist. I assume someone is looking into it. It should be easy to trace him if he flew into Portland, by checking computerized airline passenger lists."

"Mr. Bergkvist left Buenos Aires about a month and a half ago to attend some art doings in New Orleans. He was seen there and told friends he planned further travel before coming home. So far none of those computerized passenger lists list him as coming into Portland International. And we have been able to make no contact with him, but then he probably doesn't know we're looking for him."

"Is that all? Georgette Glick swore she saw him in town."

"That's all so far. We're still investigating."

"Could he have come by ship or train or rental car? Or to some other airport, maybe by small chartered flight?"

"Sure, and we're checking that out too. But if so it would be the first time. His pattern was to fly into Portland International and call his wife to come pick him up."

"Don't you think it's odd that Gladys doesn't know where he is right now? That he spends most of the year away from her?"

"Might be odd, but it's not illegal." They turned back to walk up the street toward the courthouse. Linda said, "Why are you so fascinated with Olie Bergkvist?"

"Two other people asked questions about him, too, and they're both dead. Georgette insisted she'd seen him and Michael was curious as to why he was so late coming home this summer."

They'd reached the Toyota and the deputy leaned pointedly against the door on the driver's side and folded her arms. "Now it's your turn."

"There's a bloodstained man's safari shirt under the front

steps of Frank Glick's house. Georgie's cat made a nest out of it and it's full of hair."

Linda Tortle stood absolutely still but took long blinks, reminding Charlie absurdly of a computer booting up. "When you withhold information," she said finally, "you don't fool around, do you?"

Chapter 30

On the way back to Moot Point, Charlie turned off at a forest service sign and drove up to a scenic overlook high atop a "mountain." Soaring walls of thick forest dwarfed the road and the Toyota. And Charlie.

Leafy vines crawled up tree trunks and weighed down bushes. Green moss spread along everything not covered by vine. Shorter trees, drooping under the burden of bright red berries, formed part of the undergrowth, and below them flowering bushes and below them clots of wildflowers fought for the sun at the edge of the road, like colored Christmas decorations against the forest green.

It was impressive yet depressing and Charlie was glad when, after a couple of miles of switchbacks and climb, her world opened out to the open sky above the open sea. A middle-aged couple sat outside their Ford pickup camper in webbed lawn chairs eating sandwiches. They nodded distantly as she stepped out of the Toyota.

She wandered over to the other end of the parking lot. A

waist-high battlement, two feet thick, made out of rocks and concrete kept her from falling off the edge. And she tested her acrophobia by peering over it in a safe, sideways stance with her balance still on the mountain side of the overlook.

Great. Charlie had come here to get away and think and there were all her problems spread out below. She drew back when the sweaty sickness came over her, but could still see in remembered sight the tiny ribbon of Highway 101 broken only by curves in the landscape and juts of the mountain forest . . . leading back home to Libby and to Congdon and Morse Representation, Inc., where she was sorely needed if not always appreciated.

There was the white lighthouse with its picturesque red roof looking tiny and pristine in its jade setting . . . where Michael Cermack had driven his equally red Ferrari off the point to his death on the beach below.

There was Moot Point in its half-oval nesting place around the bay, a series of dot roofs and flowering trees, of pencil streets, idyllic in its gorgeous setting . . . where Georgette Glick was shot, her body left sprawled on her own picnic table, and then stuffed under Charlie's car in the fog.

There were the massive rock rookeries off the point where pinpoints of birds hustled over and about their own nesting places. There was the *Peter Iredale* nearly invisible from clear up here, except for the whitewash of foam breaking around it at odd angles to the beach. And the beach, a line from horizon to horizon unbroken except for jagged headlands, the multilines of breakers fading into sea mist at the far reaches of vision.

. . . and there was something out of order down there. Charlie dared her sickness to peer over again. Bright yellow and blue tents had been set up on the beach below the village of Moot Point. Or maybe huge beach umbrellas . . . something.

Charlie leaned back to the safe side of the battlement and stared out to sea. The horizon now looked grubbier and meaner than it had in Chinook—even though sun glorified the scene below and warmed Charlie's shoulders up here.

The couple folded their aluminum and plastic-web chairs, hung them on the back of the pickup camper, climbed into the cab, and drove off leaving Charlie all alone with nature and her thoughts. She'd come up here to be alone and expected to feel relieved. Instead she felt uneasy.

She began to pace along the rock and concrete battlement, trying to ignore the strange forest sounds and birdcalls, trying to focus on what needed thinking about.

Did Frank and Clara Peterson kill Georgette to get her out of the way? How would they get Michael's gun to shoot her with and then get Charlie's fingerprints on it? And was either of them dumb enough to think if they shot Georgette and stuffed her under Charlie's car the local law would decide she'd died from being run over and not find the bullet in her brain? Clara, at least, read enough mysteries (not that mystery stories weren't full of holes) to know that would be highly unlikely.

And why Michael's gun? According to Doc Withers, firearms were not that hard to come by in Moot Point. And how and why would Frank and Clara kill Michael? Bloody shirt or no, Clara's confessing to running over the Schwinn and aiding and abetting Georgette's trip under Charlie's car or no, Charlie didn't see either of them committing either of the murders. Cover-up, yes. Murder, no.

The couple in the Ford pickup camper had carried out their sandwich wrappers but left scattered cherry pits and stems and the stain of leaking oil to mark their scent for the next visitors.

Did Rose poison Michael's lunch with a ground-up houseplant? Charlie had not seen Rose's living quarters, but her restaurant didn't boast houseplants. It wouldn't have to be ground up—maybe she'd used a whole leaf of something as a garnish on a sandwich. Why would she want to kill Michael? His paintings were important to her half sister's business, the gallery across the street. Gladys's house, on the other hand, was filled with houseplants.

Then again, Paige Magill was the authority on houseplants. Could two of the women have conspired to see Michael dead?

All three? Again, why? And why shoot Georgette? "In real estate it's location, location, location. In murder it's motive, motive, motive." (Charlie had heard that line on a network cop show one of her writers had finally made the staff of.)

And did either murder have anything to do with the sudden affluence that appeared to be sprouting up in the village? Charlie realized she was pacing so hard she was getting winded. Her stomach hurt.

Had she incriminated Frank Glick needlessly by revealing the stained shirt under his stairs? She had broken a promise to Clara Peterson, broken faith with someone who'd reached out to her for help. Then again, it was Clara's idea to stuff Georgie under Charlie's car.

Charlie was disappointed to find that Olie probably wasn't germane to the reason two people died, that he probably wasn't missing after all, and that Georgette hadn't seen him as she'd thought. Jack did say she had vision problems. Charlie wished now she'd asked Linda about what kind of poison killed Michael instead of wasting her one question on the Olie investigation.

There were so many birds making such a din in the forest around the lot she wished they'd all shut up and let her think. But the thinking and the exercising weren't helping. Charlie was even more tense and frustrated than before she'd come up here. She climbed back into the Toyota and closed the door on the birds. She leaned forward on the steering wheel to stare out the windshield. The grit on the horizon was moving closer. It reminded her of the desert. But you don't have dust storms on the Pacific.

Poison can make people sick and it can kill them. But can it make somebody drive off a cliff?

Charlie needed to talk to Rose about the lunch that may have killed Michael. "Oh, by the way, Rose, did you poison Michael's ham-and-cheese or his apple?"

She needed to talk to Gladys about the night of Georgette's murder. "Hey, Gladys, not that it's important, but did you happen to shoot Georgette Glick in the head when she came over to insist that she'd seen Olie? Then drag her across town under the cover of fog and dump her on her picnic table on your way to putting my fingerprints on the gun, putting it in a Baggie, and throwing it in the ditch?"

What Charlie really needed to do was to go home before she did any more damage to the investigation and any more harm to innocent suspects. She needed to take what talents she had back to where they could be useful. She started the Toyota and shifted into reverse, backed halfway into the center of the empty parking lot, and killed it a quarter of the way into a U-turn. Now she was staring out the windshield at solid forest green. Her stomach wanted some milk. There was more than one motive for the two murders, there had to be. And probably more than one murderer. One person couldn't or needn't do all the dastardly deeds done in Moot Point since Charlie's arrival. Would have no reason to. Multiple motives and murderers would answer every question but two. How did Charlie's fingerprints get on Michael's gun? And why did Charlie keep having dreams about the *Peter Iredale?*

The car had heated up in the sun and she rolled down the window, not so disturbed by the birds now. The wind had picked up. She could smell rain but there wasn't a cloud in the sky, just the dirty haze out to sea.

Well, okay, answer every question but three. The third being who were the murderers?

Charlie restarted the engine and finished the turn. She headed back down through the solid, towering forest, the Toyota silent when coasting, the dense foliage swallowing any sound of bird or wind.

Okay, every question but four. She still didn't know why. Her brief excitement deflated. The road was so bright, the forest borders so dark. By the time Charlie reached 101 she didn't feel much better than when she'd left it.

Just past the turnoff a pickup had pulled over to the side and set up an awning and a sign. *Fresh-picked fruit, ripe, never refrig-*

erated, organically grown. Charlie pulled the Toyota over too. The dude leaning against the pickup chewed on a toothpick and tried to look suave while she inspected the produce. He wore faded denims and a western-cut shirt, cowboy boots, and a ten-gallon pulled low over his forehead.

In Colorado, the only cherries Charlie could remember sold at roadside stands were sour pie cherries. In California she rarely had time to shop for fresh fruit—Libby wouldn't eat it anyway. But here there seemed to be a great variety of cherry types. She selected some safe old Bings and some plums, paid off the suave dude who nearly swallowed his toothpick when she gave him her thirty-five-millimeter smile, and took her purchases back to the Toyota.

She had just signaled a turn back out onto 101 when a siren sounded very close behind her and startled her into killing the engine again. Her poor Toyota must have decided she was losing it.

The rearview mirrors showed her the Moot County Official Black-and-White-and-Blue Bronco, with its light bar strobing dire warning at her rear window. Charlie's head began to hurt worse than her stomach. She was out of the Toyota before the giant Bronco's giant driver could do more than open his door.

"Listen, creep, I haven't left Moot County and I couldn't have been speeding. I hadn't even pulled out yet," she yelled at the man she'd scratched up and loved too well only that morning. "You have no right to treat people like this just because you're—"

Now Charlie was gesturing like an Italian and Wes Bennett caught her by the wrist. "The shirt, the goddamned shirt! You could have told me, Charlie."

"I had fully planned to, but you insisted on being such an asshole"—she struggled until he had both her wrists in one hand, the other holding her away as she danced around trying to kick his shins—"that there was no way to get a word in because the great big, big-deal sheriff sent me on my way before I could open my mouth to tell him anything because he felt threatened at the thought that I might know something he didn't. Which I did."

"My size intimidate you that much, Charlie?"

"Mine intimidate you?" she asked his shirt front.

"Yeah," he admitted after a long deflating sigh, "a lot."

It was about then that the suave cowboy fruit seller decided to wade in and even the odds.

"You find stress an aphrodisiac or what?" Wes asked.

"You're going to pay for hitting that man," Charlie told him. "You, your future, your career. What are you, crazy?"

"Hell, I didn't even know he existed, and there he was with his fist in my face. Charlie, he attacked an officer of the law."

"So did I." She dropped a Bing into his mouth. "He was only trying to protect a female in jeopardy."

"Jeopardy, Jesus." Wes raised up on one elbow to spit out a cherry pit in the paper bag beside them and pulled her back down on top of him. "I'm the one in jeopardy."

While he proved that point at least, the paper log flared in the fireplace of cabin three at the Hide-a-bye Motel, the quilt bedspread covered the floor in front of it, the sun still glamorized the balcony, the grit line still moved the horizon closer toward Moot Point over the vast Pacific.

"That piece of red plastic I picked up by Clara's driveway came from Georgette's Schwinn, didn't it?"

"Yeah, reflector," he said. "Are we having fun yet?"

"What kind of houseplant did you say it was that poisoned Michael Cermack?" she asked.

"Wasn't a houseplant after all, unofficial investigator. Oh God, don't do that. Okay, do that."

Chapter 31

Just below the wooden stairs leading to the beach from the Hide-a-bye Motel, Charlie Greene turned to grin up at cabin three. She had left Wes snoring on the quilt bedspread in front of the stone fireplace, had showered and dressed, and kissed his sleeping forehead. So much for the legendary hero who came awake instantly dangerous, rolling over gun in hand at the least disturbance. She could have run off with his pager, his gun, and the keys to the Bronco.

There wasn't much in the way of smog here. Dusk, twilight, and night took forever to arrive in late June. But the dusty mess on the horizon had not paused for pleasure as had Charlie. It had shortened the horizon and view to within a few hundred feet of the bird rookeries on the end of the point and blocked out the sun.

Perversely, just when her anger at Wes Bennett had reached its zenith she'd had sex with him again. *Was* stress an aphrodisiac for her? Before this morning, Charlie hadn't made love in a year. Maybe things had just built up so she was taking it out on him. Both her head and stomach felt better.

Perversely, now that she had her car back she'd decided to walk to the village. Walking casually down the beach she could check out the bright colored tents she'd seen from the overlook. She suspected they were for an end-of-seminar beach picnic thrown by the institute and that most of the people she wanted to see would be there. Her resolve to mind her own business seemed to have gone the way of the sunlight.

Wes hadn't arrested Frank or Clara, upon discovery of the shirt, but he had warned them not to leave the village. Wes considered their story ridiculous and probably untrue. Charlie thought it was so ridiculous it probably was true.

She rounded the point without getting her feet wet and strolled along picking up shells and disturbing shore birds until she came to the yellow and blue tents below the village. They were really plastic tarpaulin roofs on aluminum poles, sheltering tables and charcoal cookers sitting on the sand. Charlie wondered what vegetarians cooked over charcoal.

Rose's van was backed up to one of the tarps. The young man with the stiff mousse job unloaded containers of ketchup, pickles, and mustard. The girl helping him struggled with a giant coffee urn.

Doc Withers was engaged in trying to light coals in various cookers and then trying to dampen the flames to keep them from reaching the tarp roofs. The sea air thickened with the odor of fluid charcoal starter.

He wore a sweatshirt over Bermuda-length cutoffs, sagging knee socks, and massive hiking boots. His movements were even more awkward than his looks. He raised a box of wooden matches in the air to salute her, and then dropped them to grab a tent stake that flew loose on the end of its line as sea wind lifted a corner of the tarp.

Charlie dropped her shells and grabbed the line opposite when it decided to follow suit. The stakes had been set and then rocks rolled over them. This time Doc Withers tied the lines around the rocks. She helped him pick up wooden matches. "Looks like it's going to rain."

"It has to. Always rains for beach picnics. It's the law in

Oregon. Hey," he turned to yell at the girl helping to unload the van, "keep those fruit bowls covered or they'll have sand in them." Just as he turned back to Charlie the playful wind picked up another tarp corner.

Charlie made herself so useful she ended up staying on to help. And by the time the searchers arrived, every one of the people in the village that Charlie knew was already there helping too. Everyone except Clara Peterson and Frank Glick. Even Jack Monroe was there, still looking troubled and subdued, minding the coffee urns and soft drink dispensers. Even the Mary and Norma sisters had been pressed into service heaping beans and coleslaw and potato salad on paper plates. Gladys Bergkvist cut slabs of carrot cake with cream cheese frosting. Paige Magill handed out paper cups of ice cream and collected dirty plates. Doc Withers dispensed wine again. Rose Kortinemi saw to it that everything was getting done and all the helpers were kept supplied from reserves in the van. Brother Dennis played host and moved among the searchers showering attention on all who requested it.

Even the babushka lady, Irene Olafson, dashed from charcoal grill to charcoal grill, as did Charlie, flipping things over before they burned, ladling them onto plates, and rushing them to the serving table before they grew cold.

"Don't know how they eat this stuff, do you?" Irene asked Charlie once when they met dodging searchers while hurrying between grills, spatulas in hand.

It was odd, they were all very busy, but it seemed that whenever Charlie glanced over at any of these people—except for Irene—they seemed to be watching her. As if they knew she suspected a couple of them to be guilty of murder. Jack could just be thinking about his OOBE's and her dreams and his book. Mary and Norma glared their disgust at her betrayal of their friend and refused to speak to Charlie. Brother Dennis should have been paying so much attention to his paying guests that he didn't notice her. But he did.

So did Jack, Mary, Norma, Paige, Doc Withers, Gladys, and Rose. None of them seemed to be enjoying themselves much.

Charlie turned from one grill to go to another and literally ran into Deputy Linda Tortle. "You happen to know where our sheriff is by any chance? He's not answering his car radio."

"He was at the Hide-a-bye about an hour ago." Rose caught Charlie's eye and pointed out a corner cooker and Charlie was on her way.

"The Hide-a-bye?" Linda followed her. "Talking to one of Frank's family?"

Charlie shrugged and pointed a tongs at the black box attached to Linda's belt. "Can't you get ahold of him on that?"

"Well, yeah, if he's that close." She turned away from the noise of the crowd and brought the box to her mouth. There was quite a bit of intermediate chatter before she reached her boss and turned back to give Charlie a questioning look. "Yes, sir, she's right here." There were staticy barking sounds like a seal crossing a downed live wire. "Cooking tofu dogs, sir." More barking. "Tofu dogs and eggplant burgers." More barking. "Yes, sir. He says for you to—"

"I know, stay put. How can you understand a word he says on that thing?"

But Deputy Tortle was walking off down the beach still talking to the barking box.

The wind had died almost completely now and the tofu dogs and eggplant burgers didn't smell especially good. But the rain Charlie thought she'd been smelling half the afternoon didn't come. The dirty fog rolled up onto the beach instead and settled over the picnic. Jack, Brother Dennis, and Doc Withers lit replicas of old ship lanterns from the van and hung them on tent poles at the corners of the tarps or set them on tables. And the beach party went on.

As the call for charbroiled meat substitute dwindled, Charlie and Irene began dousing coals and scraping grills. Paige came up to Charlie and took the spatula from her hand.

"Get yourself some dinner while there's food left. I'll take care of this." The big smile must have drowned in the shadowed dimples because it got lost before it reached the almond eyes.

After a bad night and an incredibly eventful day, Charlie was more tired than she was hungry. But she decided to show Jack Monroe her mind was not completely closed and tried a tofu dog on a bun with ketchup, mustard, and pickles. It tasted like ketchup, mustard, and pickles on a bun.

"I suppose you're only going to eat half of that," he said, and popped open a diet Coke for her. She stood right in front of his table and ate the whole thing. His sardonic smile at least reached his eyes. "Good girl."

Irene had been relieved, too, and she passed Charlie with a plate of beans, potato salad, and carrot cake. "Not even any mayonnaise in the potato salad," she said and curled her lip, "just mustard and dill."

Charlie nursed the Coke and wandered through the crowd, shaking her head when Doc offered her wine. She'd had too many mood swings today to trust herself with alcohol in the midst of murderers

Funny, they had all seemed so innocent and predictable, if odd, yesterday. Tonight they all seemed suspicious and danger-ous. Even Jack, her client and Keegan's father. Keegan Monroe was simply one of Charlie's favorite human beings.

The fog didn't help. Neither did the foghorn which she was uncomfortably aware of again. It reminded her of her first night in Moot Point and Georgette's eyeglasses dangling from one bent bow and her bent Schwinn crossing headlights trailing fog.

How long did it take the sheriff to put his pants on and get over here? How long was she supposed to stay put? Why hadn't she come in the Toyota?

The progression from dusk to twilight to night was harder to determine in fog than it was in smog. But the fog seemed very dark outside the limited glow of the lanterns now and it seemed to haze up the people and happenings and even colors under the tarps like old film gone blurry.

Maybe Charlie's contacts needed a few drops of rewetting solution, but with this kind of moisture that didn't seem likely. Maybe she was too tired to judge. Maybe she'd had too much sex with too much sheriff . . . maybe—she waved off yet another wine pass by the holistic veterinarian and then changed her mind suddenly, as it seemed she'd been doing all day, and waved him back.

There was one plastic glass of red on a tray filled with white. She reached for the red automatically but noticed the look in his eyes and hesitated. Then she took the one red and watched him. This man might sleep with ducks but he was no professional when it came to hiding relief.

"I'm very worried about Charlie the cat, Doc. I don't think Frank's caring for it."

Maybe it *was* sticky contact lenses, night fog, and funny lantern light, or maybe it was Charlie the agent's growing paranoia —but Chuck Withers, DVM, appeared to be stunned. "Gladys said you didn't love animals."

"Excuse me?"

"Gladys said, and even Paige, that you—"

"Doc, I know Georgette's kitty goes home looking for her, but are you seeing to its survival? Because we both know old Frank cares only for old Frank."

The tray tipped as his thoughts moved elsewhere and Charlie reached out to help balance it. "Charlie the cat is right now in my house warm, safe, and fed. Probably snuggling up with Mortimer. There are no strays in Moot Point. If I can't find homes for them, they find one with me."

"That's marvelous," Charlie gushed. "And how is Eddie doing after surgery for his dewclaw?"

"You worry about Eddie too?" Doc's astonishment was growing.

"But not the same way I do about Charlie," Charlie admitted. "What I don't understand about Eddie is how Brother Dennis can keep him as a pet at the institute with so many strangers coming and going. Let's face it, Eddie is a very protective German shepherd." Eddie was one hell of a liability for someone running a place wooing the public, is what Eddie was.

"It's like Dobermans and mountain lions and sharks," Doc

said, one index finger and a wrinkling nose pushing his glasses, with the bow wired on, back up where they belonged. "They have a bad press. Some animals, in the concept of people, are bad. Like you could have the most loving, the sweetest Doberman in the world racing toward you, and if you didn't know the dog personally, if you had a gun in your hand, you'd shoot it, right? In self-defense. Not because it's a dog, but because it's a Doberman, therefore life-threatening. Eddie's one of the sweetest, gentlest animals you'll ever meet. He's got bad press because he's a German shepherd, that's all. He's also Brother Dennis's closest friend."

Charlie smiled a smile she knew to be as shallow as Paige Magill's and moved on with her wine and her diet Coke, checking out the other known suspects at the foggy beach party. It was like the video of an old Humphrey Bogart film where everyone was smoking cigarettes and the cameras shot through a haze. Charlie was seeing them through fog instead, but knew without a doubt they were watching her too.

Every last one of them.

She took a sip of the wine, a sip so tiny she could do no more than taste it and could barely work it up into a convincing swallow.

It had a bitter, almost puckery taste that seemed to suck the moisture out of her tongue. Was it the "structure" of home-grown Oregon wine? Or was it the same flavor Michael Cermack had tasted just before he died?

Chapter 32

This time Charlie Greene had planned to stay put. She really wanted to. But this time the sheriff of Moot County didn't show.

She'd helped pack things in the van and the tables, tarps, and grills in a pickup that arrived from somewhere down the beach, after Brother Dennis and Paige led the searchers back to the institute, a line of laughter and bobbing lanterns disappearing into the fog. She could hear the one long after the second had disappeared leaving Charlie with three choices. She could ride in the crowded van with Rose and Gladys or walk up to the village with Jack and Doc and the last lantern. Norma and Mary and Irene had already left with the next to the last. Or she could sit alone in the dark, in the fog, and wait for the sheriff to find her.

Charlie decided to walk with the men, wishing again she'd brought the Toyota. Maybe Linda or Wes would give her a lift back to the Hide-a-bye. Doc held the lantern as they ascended the steps and went ahead. Jack followed Charlie.

"Didn't you like the wine?" the veterinarian asked her at the top of the stairs.

"I guess I wasn't in the mood. And it had a sort of bitter taste." How do you know I didn't drink it? Did you watch me pour it into the diet Coke can? Or is it because I'm not dead yet?

"Taste?" Jack snorted. "What do you mean taste? White wine tastes like soda pop without the fizz—flat and *blech.*"

"But mine was red."

"Brother Dennis only serves white wine at institute functions," Jack told her. "Cheap jug white. I usually take my own."

Before Charlie could ask him if he had tonight, Jack announced he was in fact going home to get a bottle right now and take it up to the institute and join the celebration. The last thing he wanted after last night was to sleep. The word "sleep" floated back behind him on the fog and he was gone.

"How can he see to go anywhere?" Charlie asked. "I can't see a thing." Well, she could see a weepy streetlight not far away, but that was it.

"He knows the way." Doc raised the lantern. "If he keeps walking straight he'll walk right into the Earth Spirit. Some people can see better than others in this stuff."

"Did you get my wine from Jack's bottle?"

"He wasn't drinking on the beach, but there was a jug of red in the van for anybody who asked for it. People generally don't. Gladys and Rose drink red when they drink wine at all. But old Jack can get quite opinionated and superior for a man of awareness."

"Did Jack tell you I liked red?"

" 'My agent is too sophisticated to drink that white vinegar of yours,' is how he put it. So Paige went and got the red."

Between the fog and the angle at which he held the lantern, Charlie could see his face, but his expression seemed to waver indistinctly as it might under water. "Was it Paige who told you I didn't like animals, or Gladys?"

Fog sat like hoar frost on the tips of his raw-cut hair, streaked his glasses. "Why are you still suspicious of everyone? Haven't you heard Frank murdered his wife? You don't have to be so defensive anymore, so . . . California."

"I don't know he killed anyone, just that he and Clara put Georgette under my car to make it look like I did it. Just like someone put her on her picnic table to make it look like *he* did it. Frank's from California too, isn't he? Doc?"

Charlie had finally gone too far with one of these patient, gentle, nice, New Age murder suspects. She'd picked a hell of a time to do it. "Doc, don't leave me—I can't see."

"Stay by the lamppost. I'll be back." His voice arrived after he was gone, his lantern light bobbing upwards on the slanting mountainside. Then it was gone too.

"I don't believe this," Charlie told the lamppost and moved closer to it. "Doc!"

When you can't see much, you hear a lot. A door slammed somewhere, a rhythmic clicking sound approached her. A car horn and the screech of brakes up on 101 were closely followed by the nightmare crunch of impacting metal. The Pacific ploughed into the continent sounding lazy, as if its power were leashed by the fog. "Doc, come back, please?"

The rhythmic clicking had stopped. A low growl bristled hairs on Charlie's neck. The foghorn *oo-gaahed* dispassionately. Charlie had spent half her hours in Moot County trying to avoid the law. Here she was under the only light in sight and now there was no sheriff, no deputies, nobody but . . . Eddie.

The clicking began again, came closer . . . Eddie's toenails against the street. Eddie's toothsome grin entered the fog soaked circle of light, his eyes briefly refracting red from inside a lamp shade. It made his tiresome, monotone growl sound amplified and hollow. Bowzer, the schnauzer, had worn one like it to keep him from chewing on himself when he had an allergy.

"I understand you have a bad press, Eddie. Like sharks and Dobermans. But that you're really sweet and gentle. Hell, your own doctor told me so. And he told me you're Brother Dennis's closest friend. Hey puppy, nice puppy, I said *Brother Dennis*."

Eddie, who hadn't been a puppy for a dog's age, snarled unspeakable things in his own language. Up on 101 sirens screamed in orderly and official panic toward the flesh-and-metal emergency she'd heard scarce minutes before.

"Hey, who says aloe is faster in emergencies?" she asked Eddie.

Which was a mistake, because he took it as an insult and soared off the road toward her as he had the first time Charlie met him. The lower end of one of his front legs was wrapped in white. The lamp shade struck her in the mouth, his front paws struck her chest. But the sharp pain where the back of her head hit the ground was the most impressive.

Charlie's stomach hurt again. Her mouth tasted strongly of mustard. Her head ached in a tight constricting band encircling everything from her eyebrows up. The foghorn sounded nauseated too. She was waiting to figure out what was happening when someone said, ". . . wine?"

"Not this late. Maybe it was a hit-and-run car in the fog."

"It was a dog wearing a lamp shade," Charlie said, finally figuring out she wasn't seeing anything because her eyes were closed. Nausea swamped her when she opened them.

"Charlie, are you all right?" Paige wavered into Charlie's wavy vision under fog-smeared lamplight. Was it Charlie's imagination or did the village florist and dream keeper sound disappointed?

"No," Charlie reassured her. "I'm going to lose my tofu dog." And she rolled over in time to do just that. While she gagged in misery, gasped, sputtered, and coughed, the conversation above her continued as dispassionately as the foghorn.

"I think we should all go up to the institute and explain things on a reasonable basis."

"She doesn't look like she's in any shape to be reasonable."

"Could she be hurt bad? There's ambulances up on the highway."

"Rose!"

"Well, she's not going to believe in anything you could do for her so it wouldn't help."

"Especially after what you already tried to do to her."

"Gladys!"

"Let's just go ahead as we'd planned but take her with us."

"Can't very well leave her here."

"He's going to have to do something about Eddie. This is too much."

"Anybody know who it was up on the highway?"

"We've got our own problems right now. Here, help me get her in the van."

Charlie was still reeling from her sickness when she was picked up by the armpits and deposited on the floor of a vehicle smelling of damp soil and hothouse flowers.

She was too dizzy at the moment to control her own life, but when they stopped and got her out of the van she intended to bolt off into the woods. In the dark . . . in the fog . . . old Eddie running loose in his lamp shade . . . oh, great. Was the massive sheriff off sticking needles under Frank Glick's fingernails to get a confession? Maybe he was trying to clear up the mess of an accident on 101. He sure wasn't here.

Charlie began to sweat. She floated over the *Peter Iredale* in the fog, touching the ship's vanished structure with her senses. Seeing nothing but vague shapes, obscured in murk, that refused to materialize once she reached them. She was too dizzy to be frightened now, too sick to care about the evil that might be there, too tired to be curious.

"One step at a time, Charlie, you can do it," Paige said in her ear. Paige had a sweet little-girl voice. "You'll feel better when we get there."

"Get where?"

"Up the stairs. Here, can you guys carry her? I don't think she can make it."

"I was going to go back for her. I just wanted to find out what to do first, what to say." That was Doc Withers. "What happened?"

"Eddie knocked her over. She hit her head."

The air hung heavy with incense. Charlie knew it was incense because Libby burned a lot of the stuff in her room. That too was probably driving Edwina up the wall. Charlie usually just checked the funny smoke out for funny cigarettes and felt so relieved at finding none, incense made sense.

At this moment, however, it didn't. Charlie cracked an eyelid and winced, cracked the other more slowly. The people with her didn't notice. They sat in the smoke fog with their eyes closed, their legs lotused. Paige and Rose on one side of Charlie, Brother Dennis at her feet, Doc Withers and Gladys on her other side.

They weren't making mantra sounds. They merely sat uncomfortably around Charlie, as if she was the table at a séance, heads bowed. She could almost hear the effort of concentration over the repetitive mechanized music playing monotonous and soft off a tape somewhere close, not quite masking the party chatter wisping up through the floor below. Charlie was tone-deaf and machine-made music was particularly grating. But that didn't explain what she thought she was hearing now.

Gladys and Rose were definitely having trouble with their knees, which wasn't surprising—neither was a tiny, springy Oriental. Charlie could damn near hear the pain of joints demanding to stand and crack and pop. Brother Dennis was having problems with a dry swallow—too much wine and salted chips this evening. Doc was growing increasingly worried, disoriented, vague, uncomfortable, unsure. Paige on the other hand clasped her lips and her eyelids tighter and nodded. She might well have the answer.

Every last one of them was hoping the others were

doing what they had all agreed to do, while individually none of them could keep from being distracted by their own worries. How could Charlie know any of this? No one was talking. Answer to what, Paige? What, Doc, are you so worried about?

Paige was the first to notice Charlie awake. Doc Withers the second. They both looked from her to their leader, Brother Dennis, and he too awoke. He blinked at each of them and noticed Charlie—oh yes, the problem at hand.

"Charlie Greene," he intoned like a television Baptist, "all of us here have been doing our best to explain matters to you, each in our own way and telepathically. We are all of us good and honest people and we hoped that you could feel that come through in our inner voices. We wanted you to hear our story on the most intimate level possible because we've found ourselves in a terrible dilemma and need your understanding. Have you heard us?"

Rose and Gladys unfolded their legs. Charlie sat up and waited for the red circles behind her eyes and the pinging in her ears to subside. Her table and their chairs were made of cushions, as if someone had removed the wooden parts of a dining room set.

"Oh yes, I've heard you, Brother Dennis. I've heard you hoping like hell that Jack Monroe can run the show downstairs until you get back. I've heard Doc here worry about lovable Eddie running loose in his lamp shade. I've heard Gladys worry about her poodles, which she had not had time to let out to puddle before she came here. And Rose should be worried. It was her box lunch Michael ate before dying of poisoning. Gladys's knees are killing her. What is Paige worried about? Olie Bergkvist?" Where was this stuff coming from?

From Charlie's imagination of course. Incense and funny music and a knock on the head will do wonders for the imagination. There was nothing she had said she couldn't have deduced from what she already knew.

But it was right about here that it became clear, even to an injured and foggy head, that each of them felt nearly paralyzed by guilt. It didn't take telepathy to know it either. It was plain to read on their faces.

"You didn't *all* murder Georgette and Michael?" Charlie said, too stunned to think before she spoke. "You couldn't have."

Chapter 33

Edwina Greene would have said, "If you can make a sorry mess sorrier, Charlie, you're sure to do it."

Libby would have said, "Brilliant, Mom, seriously brilliant."

Deputy Tortle would have said, "Jesus, when you play it stupid, you really go for it."

Richard Morse of Congdon and Morse Representation, Inc. would have said, "Comes the day, Charlie, when you got to actually bite the bullet and place your brain on the chair and make the goddamned effort to think."

Sheriff Bennett would likely have said, "I can't believe you did that. Even you—a female-woman-human-being person."

There was fear in the room and that much fear concentrated from that many people, whether or not they were all good and all honest, was dangerous. You needn't be telepathic, sensitive, intelligent, or even sane to figure that out. A corpse on a gurney in a morgue could have figured that out.

Charlie had the urge to lie back down and pretend to be sick again to gain time to make better plans, but decided it was a little late for that. She could end up on Georgette's old gurney right alongside Michael if she didn't stay alert. She could even if she did stay alert.

So she sat there and watched them all think, while the party continued downstairs and the remorseless synthesized sounds pretended to be music. The room was circular, with windows nearly all around revealing nothing but black outside. The incense smoke thinned as the sticks burned to their ends. Charlie was gradually feeling better, stronger. The sheriff knew the crowd she was with last and knew where they were all likely to be. So if she was a good girl and stayed out of any more trouble and waited, she might have some help getting out of this.

If Jack was downstairs it could mean he was not involved in this dilemma Brother Dennis mentioned. If Charlie could get down to the party they could hardly harm her in front of witnesses.

This must be Brother Dennis's living quarters. By its size she guessed it to be the head of the octopus while the arms shaped the first floor of the institute. That left one more small story above—the hat atop it all. On the cabinet next to the sink nozzle sat a fancy Krups coffee maker, and next to that the passageway to the stairwell and a wall space void of window that could make room for the stairs leading to the floor above from a common landing. Odd building this.

And the people on this floor were getting odder by the minute. They all stared at Charlie but spoke to each other.

"No help for it now," Paige said. "If only she hadn't come here. Everything would have worked out."

"This can't go on." Doc Withers looked prepared to choke. "Something's got to stop it."

"He's right, it's really going to look ridiculous," Gladys said. "Small place like this."

"We're all in this together, don't forget," Rose warned. "That includes you, Doc."

"Why couldn't you have seen reason?" Brother Dennis finally addressed Charlie. "You're not looking at five murderers, but five human beings."

Charlie was looking at five human beings changing before her eyes. Paige Magill looked her age now and then some, the once-plump rosy cheeks etched and saggy, her mouth drooping and resentful. Doctor Chuck Withers's boyish awkwardness had degenerated to twitching white-faced dread. Rose Kortinemi's swarthy face and sardonic expression had become suffused and puffy with a dark resolve. Brother Dennis Thornton's bony sallowness had taken on a yellow tinge and his eyes a resigned sadness. The skin on Gladys Bergkvist's face hung in lumps and sacks, tiny blood vessels mapping the ridges like rivers. But anger burned in her eyes.

Above the scratchy, tinny music up here and the chatter and laughter from below, the howling of a dog rose into the night in keening lament. Probably amplified by being funneled through a lamp shade.

"You realize," Gladys said, "that if it hadn't been for that goddamned dog, none of this would have happened?"

The spell had broken and Charlie's captors looked away from her to each other. Charlie was on her feet and running for the stairwell. She'd have made it, too, if it hadn't been for the cushions. They poufed and slid and when her Ked slipped between two of them she went down.

How was it Charlie came up out of stupid nightmares screaming, but never thought to do it before they had her mouth taped? It had simply not occurred to her. Now she lay upstairs in the cupola-hat room, wrists and ankles trussed with tape as well, and called herself unspeakable things.

This was Brother Dennis's recording studio and office. They'd left a desk light on, which wasn't very smart. They were amateurs in deep trouble, five loose cannons. Very dangerous. Hindsight told her she should have made an effort to divide and conquer. Hell, it wasn't possible for five people to pull one trigger.

Charlie didn't know if they were down on the cushions planning strategy or out trying to quiet Eddie right now. She did know adhesive tape was one marvelous binder—the more she struggled against it the tighter it got. Why had anybody ever bothered with rope? Her head ached again, but what worried Charlie most were the twinges of nausea. If she vomited now, with her mouth so tightly taped she'd choke on her own puke and save the deadly five the trouble.

Great. This was not the kind of thing that was supposed to happen to people in Charlie's line of work. This happened to performers on TV or in film who staged getting killed and then got up and went home to bed. Charlie tried to imagine Edwina raising Libby through the teenage years and broke out in a sweat with the effort to keep from gagging.

Sheriff Wes Bennett was probably even now at the gates in his good old Bronco steed. He'd come charging up the stairs any minute.

Bullshit.

Charlie spent a few moments talking with her stomach, her gag reflex, her cop out fantasy world, her headache, and her adrenaline flow, and then began looking seriously around Brother Dennis's office. Had her captors been pros they would have taped her eyes shut too. Which made them no less dangerous. Charlie hadn't a clue as to what weird idea they'd come up with next. All the writers she worked with had to use fairly formula criminals and perpetrators because entertainment is highly formulaic. That kind of dangerous person had some predictable parameters. Charlie's amateurs did not.

The desk light was above her and didn't illuminate much on the floor, but after rolling over once she found a loosened hinge on a cabinet door, rubbed her cheek against it, and decided it wasn't sharp enough to cut tape.

A line of tape ran from her ankles to her wrists behind her back. If she could cut that she could stick her feet through the circle of her bound arms and bring her hands up her front to tear the tape off her mouth and then dislodge it from her ankles. Sounded great in theory.

Charlie rolled over again and found herself sitting up, her back against the wall, the line of tape connecting ankles with wrists stuck to the rear of her pants. But she *was* sitting up, staring at Brother Dennis's desk across her knees. His desk had a cutout section in the center and the legs of a chair sat in it. And Charlie was sitting up, so she could conceivably, even trussed by tape, sit in a chair. Desks often had drawers with things like scissors and letter openers in them.

Charlie tried to be quiet as she rolled herself over and over until she was on the other side of the desk.

The damn chair had wheels. Charlie'd worked in offices long enough to know they generally do, but she had hoped. Getting into the chair in her trussed condition without moving it around was not going to be easy.

Eddie's spine-prickling howl rose again. It was awesome. Why would none of this have happened if it hadn't been for Eddie? Eddie hadn't shot Georgie and he hadn't poisoned Michael. Did they discover something Eddie had done and had to die for it? But you don't kill people to protect a dog.

Charlie flopped her chest across the seat of the chair, caught the edge of the seat with her chin to keep it from rolling out from under her, and was just barely balanced on the ends of her bent knees, her trussed ankles pulled up to where the tape stuck to her rear.

Charlie was totally helpless, is what Charlie was. How she'd ever expected to get herself seated from this angle she hadn't a clue.

Maybe if she flopped forward one more time and landed on her stomach she could turn over on her back, then hoist her way up to a sitting position from there. Charlie's rational mind told her flat out that wouldn't work even as she tried it.

Charlie's rational mind was right. The chair took off on its four wheels and its ball bearings across the wooden floor. No cushions to trip it up here. Just electrical sockets in the floor and wires and big rubber plug-ins. No telling which the chair hit when it came to a halt, dumped her, and then fell over on top of her.

It was a desk chair with a small oblong back made for assis-tants-once-known-as-secretaries who had to sit straight at a keyboard all day, not the boss kind where you can lean back with full back support and put your feet on the desk. So Charlie could see Doc Withers's expression when he hit the top of the stairs, running, from the floor below. His fear had transmogrified into terror.

Why had they sent their weakest link? Or was he the only one down there, the others off on more important duties?

Doc Withers pulled the chair off Charlie. For a moment she thought the hand he jabbed toward her was reaching fingers to feel her nose to see if it was dry or wet. His fingers went for the pulse in her neck instead. What, did he think she might be dead? She was still blinking wasn't she?

The more she thought about it, the terror plus the doctor in this guy had possibilities.

Charlie moaned behind the tape and rolled her eyes—bulging them until she almost popped her contacts. How did you make you suggest nausea? She talked to her gag reflex and it solved the problem.

"My God, don't vomit now—you'll choke to death," Doc said, and it felt like he ripped half of Charlie's face off when he tore the tape from her mouth.

He rolled her over and she made a pretense at retching, the real thing not all that remote a possibility.

"What do you care if I choke to death! You're going to kill me anyway," Charlie whined.

"I never killed anybody in my life." His hand on her back prevented her from rolling over but he jerked for some reason and his wired-together eyeglasses fell to the floor next to her face.

Charlie wished like hell they'd broken. "I was sure of it," she said now, triumphantly. "The rest have some kind of hold over you and are making you go along with them. You know how I knew?"

"You don't know anything," he said defensively.

"I know because anybody who can write like you can can't be a murderer."

"Thought you didn't like my book."

"You thought I didn't like animals, too. I'll have you know I have a pet kitty named Tuxedo. He's still a kitten. He's black and white and—"

"Thought you wanted to vomit, all you want to do is talk. I'm going to put this tape back on." He rolled her over.

"Holistic Medicine for Pets would be a perfect candidate for Morton and Fish's new line of New Age nonfiction. I was going to show your proposal to Jack's editor there. But now I won't be able to, will I? Because I'll be dead. Nobody will because you'll be charged with murdering three peop—"

He slapped the tape back over her mouth before she could finish. But the tape was no longer as tight or as sticky.

And his expression wasn't as dangerous. "There're a lot of people out there looking hard at alternatives to the mess the establishment has gotten personal lives into. They are educated, thinking people, and most of them relate to animals we call pets. These are caring people," he said earnestly. "They'd buy a book like that."

Charlie nodded agreement and tried to make her eyes look earnest too. She began to feel a surge of hope.

Until Paige Magill's face appeared suddenly over his shoulder. "Doc, what are you doing up here? What's going on? We need help with Eddie."

"She overturned a chair and I heard the noise, came up to see what was happening."

"I thought I heard you talking about a book. She hasn't gotten to you, has she? You know what has to be done."

"I was just telling her off about her low opinion of my proposal is all. How often do you get to tell one of these kind of people off?" But he winked quickly at Charlie before he stood. "Where's Eddie? And why can't Brother Dennis handle him?"

"Brother Dennis is having to handle things at the party right now." Paige gave Charlie a suspicious look, rolled the desk chair back to the desk, and switched off the light. "You're the only other one who can handle Eddie. He's out at the grave."

Chapter 34

Charlie lay in darkness, no better off than before, maybe worse, listening to Eddie howl out at some grave. She'd be willing to bet it was Olie Bergkvist's, but what difference did it make? Maybe Eddie was just digging hers. Tears burned her eyes and without thinking she opened her mouth to moan an expletive.

The tape came loose from her face on one side. She listened to see if it might be a good time to start screaming. But now she couldn't even hear Eddie. Could the partiers hear her over their noise on the first floor? Could there still be somebody on the second?

Charlie did have an excellent idea where the desk was located. She sidewinded her way in that direction. Shoulders first, then rear with its taped appendages, then shoulders again. She'd come up against the back wheels of the chair. One hand could feel the shape of one little metal wheel. Great. Now what?

Well, she could go back to the screaming idea. Her mouth was about all she had going for her. . . . Still, she wouldn't have to try to sit in the chair now to get to that long thin

drawer most desks had above the knee space, where sharp office
supplies were kept. If she could nudge the chair out of the way
she could open the drawer with her teeth.

"*You get a scissors, manage to position it so you can use it, and
then you're going to use your teeth to make the scissors scissor and
cut the tape strung around behind your back? Give me a break,*" her
rational mind pleaded.

"*I can't just give up. I have to do something.*"

"*You can lie still and wait for the sheriff. You can lie still and wait
for the good animal doctor to figure you and he might find a way out
of this. He did look as if you'd persuaded him to turn on his buddies.
What you can't do is bring somebody back up here by making another stupid mistake—as in noise. Somebody who'll be a lot smarter
than Doc Withers.*"

What Charlie couldn't do was lay still and wait for someone
to come up here and kill her. She nudged the chair and it rolled
away to hit something in the dark. No alarm sounded below.
She used one shoulder to leverage her way up a layer of desk
drawers until she was balanced, but again just barely, on the
ends of her knees, her chin resting on the desk top. Charlie
wished Paige had not turned off the light.

The tape pulled away from the seat of her pants just then,
and Charlie discovered why the pros used things you could knot
instead. Her Keds hit the floor with the sudden release and her
chin left the desk. She fell back onto her heels and when she
rose off them, trying to pull away the excess line of tape running
from wrist to ankle so it wouldn't stick again, she found she'd
grabbed a trailing of loose tape. She gave it a tug and felt the
pressure on her wrists lighten as she heard the sucking sound of
tape separating. Working it with her fingers, rotating her wrists
painfully, Charlie unwrapped the tape that bound her hands
behind her back.

When she sat down this time it was with her knees and feet
in front of her. But she couldn't find an end to unwind in all
the stickiness to unwrap the binding on her ankles. So, balancing against the desk, she stood and felt around until she found
the lamp and the lamp's toggle switch. She left the light on

only long enough to find a pair of scissors. She found them not in the drawer as she'd expected—a drawer she'd never have opened with her teeth because it had no knob or handle—but right on top.

Lowering herself quietly to the floor, Charlie proceeded to scissor and saw at the sticky tape.

Charlie Greene stood outside the back door of the Moot Point Consciousness Training Institute, disoriented. There had been no one to stop her on the cushioned second floor and no one to save her on the first. All human sound had disappeared, and all light. Everyone couldn't have gone to bed that quickly.

After two flights of stairs, Charlie had ended up at the back door and decided in the total silence of the dark she'd rather be outside. Outside was dark too, so dark she couldn't see the fog, but she could feel its damp fingers brushing her face. She heard a car pass on 101 above her but saw no lights, either because of night fog or the obstruction of trees.

She waited for her rational mind to offer up a sensible solution, but even it was silent. So Charlie began to feel her way around the building. She'd traversed the ground outside two tentacles before she realized that could take all week. But none of the windows she'd come to had shown any light, as if the fog had cut off the electrical power to the institute.

Even up here, this high on the mountain, the fog smelled fishy. And so did the sudden absence of human life.

What could have happened to them all while Charlie struggled with the tape and the desk?

Charlie saw a tree, and then another. Not complete trees, just pieces in the fog. Eddie's lament rose in mournful tempo from the direction of those trees and Charlie turned around to skirt the house in the opposite direction, figuring that her captors would be off at the grave trying to control the dog. She was halfway back the way she'd come before the fog choked off all sight again and she couldn't see where to step next.

Charlie recognized her own shadow suddenly silhouetted by

the limited circumference of flashlight on the night fog in front of her. Unfortunately she noticed it a fraction of a second before someone gathered her elbows together behind her back in an iron grip.

Rose had gone to get Brother Dennis at the Earth Spirit, where he and Jack had moved the party to listen to some spooky tapes on channeling—a sort of New Age version of late-night ghost stories. The talk at the party had apparently turned to the recent murders in Moot Point and it seemed to fit into the party atmosphere. It was also a way to get the searchers away from the institute for a while. Charlie learned all this from the conversation between the two as they forced her to walk ahead of them.

Eddie had not responded to Doc's attempts to quiet and calm him and had instead insisted upon clawing the earth and howling, even with Paige and Gladys trying to drive him off with shovels. But he came immediately to heel when Brother Dennis walked into the circle of light, Rose Kortinemi pushing Charlie along behind him.

"Look who got herself free and was hanging around outside?" Rose said. "Lucky we moved the party."

"He's torn the dressing off his foot." Doc knelt to examine Eddie, who sat next to his master's left knee, trembling. "I can't understand his passion for digging here."

"Me neither," Gladys said. "He hated Olie. Maybe that's it." And then to her half sister, "Should you have brought her here?"

"Doesn't matter anymore. We have two things to do and quick, before the party comes back."

Doc Withers looked up from his patient and his glasses slid down his nose as his eyebrows shot up. "Where did you get that?"

Charlie turned to see Rose holding a long-barreled handgun. She'd stopped in at Irene Olafson's on the way to get Brother Dennis. The gun had belonged to Irene's husband. The widow, when washing windows at the restaurant, had told Rose that she had checked it over and loaded it when she heard there was a murderer loose in Moot Point. "Even told me where it was."

"You didn't kill Irene for it?" Doc rose slowly from his crouch, his face pasty even in the oscillating lantern glow.

"She was sleeping like a ton of bricks after I sent what was left of the jug wine home with her tonight. When we're done with the gun, we put it back and she'll never know."

"You planned this even at the picnic?" Brother Dennis said.

"Somebody had to plan ahead. What were you guys going to do, beat her over the head with shovels?"

"I take it this is Gladys's missing husband, Olie, buried here," Charlie said. "Don't you think a fourth murder is going to be hard to get away with, Rose?"

"Olie wasn't murdered." Gladys Bergkvist sank heavily to the ground next to the tortured earth, oblivious to the stench rising from it. Charlie thought she could see clothing, and a grayish substance that could have been flesh, but she didn't particularly want to study it. "She's right, Rose. It'll look too funny. And the sheriff's got the hots for her. He won't let it rest."

"He may not be much of a danger for a while. Maybe never." Rose and the weapon moved up beside Charlie. "That accident up on the highway? That was him. And Clara and Frank Glick."

"Wes was *in* the accident?" Charlie said. "Are you sure?"

"That's right, sweet cheeks. Your knight won't be charging up to save your little tush, if that's what you were counting on. Mary and Norma were clucking themselves into strokes about it when I was down at the Earth Spirit just now. They seemed to think it was all your fault."

"Frank apparently panicked and forced Clara to drive him out of town," Brother Dennis added uncomfortably. "She got rattled and pulled out in front of the sheriff."

"The word is there are three badly injured people in the hospital in Chinook right now," Rose said. "And my powers are telling me now is the time to do what has to be done."

Charlie watched them thinking again, their eyes darting from Rose's to the long-barreled gun to the grave to Charlie. Eddie whined and Brother Dennis patted his lamp shade absently. Paige had been uncharacteristically quiet through all this, but she stepped into the center of the lighted circle now and turned completely around to study each face but Charlie's.

"We all know about Rose's powers," she said softly. "We've relied on them before. And if it hadn't been for Charlie here—"

"Or Eddie," Gladys said desolately.

"Charlie and Eddie," Paige amended. "With the sheriff out of commission, the party not back yet, the fog still holding—Rose is right. There's no time to lose."

"Eddie hasn't killed anybody. Olie was already dead when he mauled the body," Brother Dennis said. "Eddie wouldn't harm a soul."

"Yeah, but if he hadn't kept digging him up like that, Georgette wouldn't have had to die. I suppose Michael would still have come across Olie's luggage in the garage though," Gladys conceded.

"I didn't kill anybody either." Doc Withers was talking to Charlie. "All I did, or Brother Dennis too, was to bury Olie and carry Georgette to the picnic table. All Paige did was to get your fingerprints on Michael's gun. We had nothing to do with Michael, and Olie really did die of a heart attack. It just might have been hard to prove after Eddie got through with the body. And poor Gladys didn't—"

"Yeah, but he had the heart attack because he was on his way up to the institute to confront you about sleeping with his wife," Rose said.

"Well, he didn't love her. He never stayed home." Doc turned again to Charlie. "Do you know his will bequeathed almost all his money to an artists' colony in New Mexico in the names of his first wife and their son? Left Gladys nearly nothing. Made her sign an agreement when she married him."

So if Olie merely stayed missing instead of dead, Gladys could siphon off the money and invest it in certain businesses in Moot

Point, among other things. And everybody involved would have a financial stake in keeping quiet about his death. "But Eddie kept digging him up and Georgette wandered across the grave that night in the fog and had to die," Charlie said. "Which one of you shot her?"

"I did," Rose answered calmly, "in case you're thinking I won't have the nerve to use this thing."

"We offered her money too, but she got hysterical and locked herself in my bathroom," Gladys said. "Rose went up to get Michael's gun—he was eating at the restaurant—and when she came down the stairs Georgie was climbing out the window. Her psychic powers told her Georgie would never listen to reason."

"Just like you," Rose said. "It's a foggy night now, too."

"There's no more time for talk, Rose," Paige warned.

"You men get away from that dog," Rose ordered, but a little breathlessly. "And you, California girl, go stand next to him."

"If Rose killed Georgette and Michael, why do the rest of you have to pay for it?" Charlie tried to keep fear out of her voice but her tongue made funny clicking sounds because her mouth was so dry. "I mean friendship's a wonderful thing but—"

"She didn't kill Michael, I did." Tears streamed down Gladys Bergkvist's lumpy cheeks. "I had to. He found Olie's luggage in the garage. Said he wanted half of Olie's money to keep quiet."

"Jesus, you buried your husband," Charlie said, "why didn't you get rid of his luggage?"

"Well, first there was Georgie snooping around and then the police and then you. Didn't seem like there was time. It's not like it wasn't hidden. Michael really had to—"

"Shut up, Gladys. We're all in this together," Paige said, "because we're all accomplices. We all knew what was going down. We have to stick together. Do as Rose says and get away from that dog. We can't let one dog stop us now."

"I didn't know you poisoned Michael." Doc Withers looked at his lover as if in a new light, but sidled away from his doomed patient. "I thought Rose poisoned his box lunch."

"I put ground-up cherry leaves and twigs in his wine. He always took a bottle along when he painted. Paige once told me not to let my puppies chew on cherry twigs because they release cyanide when you eat them. I didn't know he'd drive off the point. Don't know what I thought he'd do."

Rose prodded Charlie over to Eddie with Irene's gun. Brother Dennis stood his ground next to his faithful canine friend. But Eddie bolted and flew through the air.

And Charlie finally managed to scream.

Chapter 35

"Police! Freeze," Deputy Olsen yelled. "Holy shit!"

Shots rang out. Charlie went down. Eddie sailed past her.

"Eddie, no!" Brother Dennis commanded. There was a definite melee occurring with grunts, shouts, growls, and screaming.

The screaming was Charlie. "Stop it, damn it. Am I hurt? I don't think so." For once nobody was paying any attention to Charlie. Not even Eddie.

He was trying to maul Deputy Olsen but the lamp shade kept getting in his way. Olsen was on the ground under the dog, both Doc and Brother Dennis trying to pull him off. Gladys Bergkvist was curled up like a slug under attack. Her half sister, Rose, stood mumbling down at her own foot, Irene's deceased husband's long-barreled gun dangling from her hand. Paige Magill was on her knees struggling to get Rose's shoe off.

But over it all, somehow, a quiet, relaxed voice of reason managed to prevail. It drawled, "That dog has got one second to live unless you get it under control before then, dudes. And you ladies freeze for serious, because I don't plan to miss."

The tall lean shadow of Deputy Linda Tortle squatted in the classic television stance with gun held balanced and aimed in both hands out in front of her.

That voice moved the dudes to heroics and Eddie was saved. He went to the animal shelter in Chinook. What was left of Olie Bergkvist joined Michael in the morgue. The others went to the jail in the Moot County Courthouse. Except for Rose and Charlie. They went to the hospital.

Somehow, in the chaos of the leaping dog and people scurrying every which way, Rose had shot herself in the foot. She got nowhere insisting her doctor of choice was Paige Magill.

After making Charlie perform various eye and balancing exercises, another doctor decided her head injury was not serious.

"How bad is he?" Charlie asked Linda Tortle when they finally leaned against the two-toned wall (hospital puce and mortuary gray) outside Wes's room, waiting for the nurse to complete her ministrations and give them permission to enter.

Linda peered down her long nose at Charlie and smiled a lazy, triumphant smile. "Bruised, scratched, dislocated shoulder, lumps, aches and pains. Miracle it wasn't worse. He was really tooling."

"But Rose made it sound like all three were near death."

"That's because she got her information from two highly excited sisters. Frank and Clara are a little worse off, but not much. Lucky they were wearing seat belts and driving big, heavy, rusty, old Detroit steel though. Makes me think I'll keep my Pontiac yet a while after all."

"If you can afford to feed it," Charlie parried, vastly relieved they weren't about to die. "So, uh, while he's sitting in the hospital getting his cuts and scrapes cleaned up, a female detective overhears the confessions and saves the life of another intended victim. Good work, Deputy Tortle, but the bumbling Olsen will probably get the credit for it."

"I can't discuss the case of course, but I expect there's a

certain intended victim witness who'll be called back for the trial to tell it like it really was."

"I think it's bargain time again, don't you?" Charlie asked nonchalantly.

"Jesus, you're cold-blooded. Okay, one question."

"Two."

Linda groaned behind clenched teeth, raising her palms toward the ceiling in a pleading gesture. "Okay, two. But that's it. You are something else, you know that?"

"It's what I *don't* know. I don't know why you lied to me about Olie's airline schedule. Or didn't he come by plane?"

"Right on schedule. So Georgette Glick probably did see Gladys Bergkvist driving him into town from the airport. All I didn't tell you was that there was a computer shutdown on Delta's files for that time and when I talked to you, Delta was the one airline we hadn't been able to check out. I walked back in the courthouse after our lunch today and they'd retrieved damaged files and there his name was."

"Was Wes rushing to the village to tell me that when he had his accident?"

"You know what the real mystery is here? Why didn't anybody hear Rose shoot Georgette in such a small, quiet place as Moot Point? The shot was fired outside, it wasn't that late at night, and sound carries on fog. I doubt there was a silencer for that revolver."

"Backfires," Charlie assured her. "Was he rushing to save me when he had the accident then?"

"What do you mean backfires? Oh, trucks on 101. People probably hear them all the time. Good work, Agent Greene. Hell, I should have thought of that."

"Well, why *was* he rushing to Moot Point?"

"Don't ask me. So, you tell it exactly like it happened when the first one of them goes to trial. Deal?"

"I haven't asked my second question yet."

"You sure as hell have. Why was the sheriff rushing to Moot Point? And why didn't I tell you all I knew about Olie's flight schedule? And I did. I just didn't know it all when I talked to you this noon. So, we got a deal?"

"No, this is what we've got. Olie Bergkvist comes home and learns of Gladys's affair with the local veterinarian and stalks off to the institute to confront him. Why not to the holistic animal clinic?"

It was Tuesday night, Linda explained, and when there were no outsiders in for seminars the privileged few met for the heavy stuff with Brother Dennis at the institute on Tuesday nights. Channeling and telepathy, tarot and even séances. "So Doc would have been at the institute. Probably Gladys too if Olie hadn't come home."

"How do you know all this?"

Linda shrugged. "Common knowledge. And I did have some contact with Doc and the institute once, remember. I heard they were seriously looking into Rose's psychic powers too. Gladys told me on the way to the courthouse that she was running along behind Olie trying to reason with him when he went down. She left him there in the woods to get help at the institute. When they all got back, Olie was not only dead but being mangled by good old Eddie, who 'would never harm a soul.'"

"And so they talked it all out to their mutual advantage."

"And decided a missing Olie was more profitable than a dead one, so Gladys could liquidate the assets. Paige said as long as he was dead anyway, they weren't hurting Olie. But Eddie kept digging him up and Georgette Glick snooped it out and Brother Dennis discovered her at the grave and convinced her to go down to Gladys's with him where all would be explained and they could con her into joining into the conspiracy for a price. Georgette wouldn't con. She locked herself in the bathroom and tried to crawl out the window, whereupon Rose shot her."

"Do you really think Rose's psychic powers told her to run up and find Michael's gun so, just as she was coming down the stairs from his studio, Georgette was climbing out the window?"

"Who cares? She confessed. You're a witness and Olsen and

me. And the rest are going to fall apart and spill all to make it easier on themselves anyway. Meanwhile, a suspicious artist named Michael Cermack comes across Olie's luggage in the garage his Ferrari shares with the Bergkvists' cars and demands more quiet money than Olie's widow is prepared to pay, and she doses his wine with cherry debris. He probably convulses, and having started the car stomps down on the accelerator and runs the Ferrari off the point. It's all there."

"Jack wasn't part of it? He was closely connected with the institute," Charlie said.

Jack Monroe and Brother Dennis had grown apart recently and Jack was no longer of the inner circle. Deputies Turtle and Olsen had come into town looking for Charlie and stopped at the Earth Spirit where the party was in full swing. Jack had told them he hadn't seen Charlie since the picnic but he had an uneasy feeling something weird was going down up at the institute because Brother Dennis had insisted on crowding the party into the Earth Spirit. "Jack said it would have been easier for him to nip down to get the tapes and take them back up to the institute which has a lot better sound system. Then Brother Dennis orders him to keep the searchers there and runs off with Rose. How many questions is this, anyway?"

"How did Paige Magill get my fingerprints on Michael's gun?"

Deputy Tortle couldn't answer that one. Neither could Wes Bennett. He manufactured his own release, prematurely Charlie thought and so did the hospital staff, by the sheer force of his size, his office, and his bullheadedness. Charlie rode back to the courthouse with him and he spent the entire trip gloating over the fact that both confessed killers were women. "Have to see about building more female holding cells."

Paige wouldn't see her but she did see Jack Monroe, who was busily rounding up legal counsel for his friends, and what comforts were allowed them. "I'm sorry I got you involved in all this, Charlie," he said as they both stood wearily on the courthouse steps and watched a glimmer of dawn lighten the foggy night. He mussed her hair in a fatherly gesture. "I just can't fathom five intelligent people getting themselves into such a mess. It's heartbreaking. Nor why I was so dense I didn't suspect anything until it was nearly too late for you."

"Did you ask Paige about my fingerprints on the gun? It's driving me crazy."

He nodded. "She said she took it to your cabin to hide it in your car to further connect you to Georgette's murder, but the sheriff had taken your car. Then she found your door unlocked and slipped in, thinking to hide it inside. But you slept so soundly she was able to get your prints on it without waking you. So she put the gun in a Baggie and threw it in the ditch, knowing Mary and Norma would find it if the sheriff's department didn't."

He started down the long flight of concrete steps lit by a milky globe on a pole every five feet or so. He stopped under the first one and turned to look up at her, those strange electric eyes glinting in the globe's light. "Charlie, I know you don't believe in it, but Paige swears you weren't really asleep when she got your fingerprints on Michael Cermack's revolver. She's seen my body when I've been having an OOBE and she swears that's what you were doing too."

Charlie hated the cold finger of doubt playing up and down her vertebrae. "Try and make your deadline, and send me a copy of the manuscript when you send it to Morton and Fish. Plus copies of any correspondence. And Jack, if you ever OOBE again? Don't take me with you, okay?"

"I know I can't leave it alone. But I tell you what, Charlie Greene, if I ever see you on my bodiless travels I'll give you a sign. I'll do this." He walked back up to her and mussed her hair again. Then he disappeared down the courthouse steps and into the fog.

Dawn was adding vague highlights to the fog but the sun hadn't breached the Coast Range yet when a weary Charlie and a wearier sheriff struggled out of a Moot County Sheriff's Department sedan and lowered themselves onto a driftwood log on the beach that had become the grave of the *Peter Iredale*.

"Why did you bring me here, Wes, you know what that wreck does to me."

He chuckled short, like it hurt to even do that much. "Some ghosts need to be put to rest."

"And why won't you tell me why you were rushing to the village so fast you mashed into Clara's old Ford? I don't care if the reason had nothing to do with me."

He chuckled again and groaned for it. "Oh, Charlie Greene, you do have you an ego, don't you?"

"So?"

"So first things first." The sheriff of Moot County pulled a chicken breast (original recipe) from the Kentucky Fried bag on his lap. "Us poor little injured men need strength."

"Damn it, Wes—"

He stuffed a salty drumstick between her teeth. "I was rushing into Moot Point to tell you about a phone call I got at your cabin from your boss—Morse? After he read me the riot act and my rights, he ordered me to tell you he'd talked to your mother and learned about your problem with this wreck here and wanted you to know that, yes, you had seen it, a picture of it— sketch, he said—in the lobby of the bank building your office is in."

Charlie tried to visualize the lobby. The whole building was in the process of being redecorated, and the lobby had been done first. There were all kinds of strange artwork on the walls. She looked out at the shadowy shape of the wreck emerging from the fog into the morning. "And that's one of them. It's just as you come out of the elevator on the ground floor." She hugged the huge lawman and he gasped. "Oh, I'm sorry, but I feel so much better."

"So you don't have to worry about nightmares and flying around in the night sky without your body."

Charlie kissed his swollen, bruised nose gently. "Right, Sheriff. There're no such things as OOBE's."

"Or things that go bump in the night. All that's now a—"

"Don't say it."

"Moot point." His eyes crinkled but his voice turned husky. "You sure you have to go home this morning?"

"Yes, but not right away maybe. I mean I do have a life and two jobs that need me. Then again, you did injure yourself trying to help me out of my superstitious—" Charlie jumped to her feet and the half-eaten drumstick fell to the sand.

"What's wrong? A bird crap on you?"

Charlie ran her fingers through the hair on top of her head. "Did you just see my hair move, Wes?"

"Probably just the wind."

"There is no wind."

After All

By the time Charlie and her buttery-smooth Toyota headed south, she and the sheriff had managed to rationalize away, as a vestige of an old nightmare, what had seemed to her an invisible hand mussing her hair.

She loved zooming along 101, and the gorgeous now sunny Pacific on her way to work she could handle. She was tired, glad to be heading home, pleased that the big sheriff had pleaded with her not to.

Mostly she was relieved to have avoided the lures of the alternative world she'd come uncomfortably close to in the last week. She'd take the rational any day.

The radio played sounds her tone-deaf ears couldn't appreciate but her spirit could celebrate. The windows were open to the sea air on one side of her and the forest on the other and she was in charge of her little world for a brief enjoyable moment.

"Back to Kansas, Toto." Charlie Greene laughed and patted the dashboard. But she made one stop on her way out of Oregon. And that one was almost furtive. Charlie pulled in at a roadside greenhouse and bought a young potted aloe plant.